WOULD YOU BELIEVE . . .

—Paul Newman's hockey movie *Slap Shot*, re-titled to appeal to Japanese audiences, was released in Tokyo as *The Cursing Roughhouse Rascal Who Plays Dirty*.

—A New York man saddened by a breakup with his girlfriend decided to end it all by dropping a VCR in his bathwater. His attempt failed, fortunately, because he forgot to plug in the machine beforehand.

—A Rhode Island high school tried to improve students' grades by limiting their trips to the toilet. "The need to use the lavatory," the principal said, "is not related to biological urges, but to the urge to get out of class."

One thing is certain. This wildly outrageous book is non-stop laughter!

MAN SUFFOCATED BY POTATOES

MAN SUFFOCATED BY POTATOES

Intelligence Reports from Planet Earth

Collected, Revised, Amended, Digested,
Regurgitated and Proffered
—for Your Edification and Dismay—
by

William A. Marsano

A SIGNET BOOK

NEW AMERICAN LIBRARY

NAL BOOKS ARE AVAILABLE AT QUANTITY DISCOUNTS WHEN USED TO PROMOTE PRODUCTS OR SERVICES. FOR INFORMATION PLEASE WRITE TO PREMIUM MARKETING DIVISION, NEW AMERICAN LIBRARY, 1633 BROADWAY, NEW YORK, NEW YORK 10019.

SIGNET TRADEMARK REG. U.S. PAT. OFF. AND FOREIGN COUNTRIES
REGISTERED TRADEMARK—MARCA REGISTRADA
HECHO EN CHICAGO, U.S.A.

SIGNET, SIGNET CLASSIC, MENTOR, ONYX, PLUME, MERIDIAN and NAL BOOKS are published by NAL PENGUIN INC., 1633 Broadway, New York, New York 10019

First Printing, September, 1987

1 2 3 4 5 6 7 8 9

PRINTED IN THE UNITED STATES OF AMERICA

To LILLIAN
—who did not type the manuscript—
and for other reasons

Contents

ACKNOWLEDGMENTS

Thanks are due to writers and editors everywhere; their ceaseless reporting of events (and occasional direct involvement) provided the sea of foibles from which this volume is taken.

There are others whose contributions were direct—fellow conservators of the bizarre who gave generously of their own clippings or who merely kept an eye peeled for likely items once they felt certain that my activities were not utterly immoral. Thanks, then, to Richard Charteris; Dr. Geraldo Koren of the Bulbul Society; my brother, James; my son, Julian; Andy Mills; and others whose names have slipped my mind. A special vote of gratitude is due Alan Kaufman, for coming to the rescue not once but twice when he easily could have refused.

What Passes for an Introduction

Why?

Why this collection of perversities and stupidities? What good is it? Who needs it? How much is it?

Well, Gentle Reader, we all make mistakes, don't we? Some of us go beyond that. Your correspondent celebrates and collects them. Most of these tiny tales are footstools and footnotes to what journalists consider "real news." They are to be found at the bottoms of newspaper columns, filling the space between the bottom of the page and the place where the latest recital of, say, Middle Eastern butchery simply ran dry.

Reading about the Middle East palls after a while. Names and places change slightly over the years, but the essential fact remains the same: In that quarter of the world people murder one another for any reason they can think or for no reason at all. It's not much different with news of economics or international tensions: The news shifts, but it never really changes. It is unedifying, oppressive and, after several repetitions, not really news at all. You could make a fair case for every newspaper running the same headline every day:

OUTLOOK STILL GLOOMY.

And under that headline would be the same story every day, with the same lead sentence:

Things remain tough all over.

Not so with the footstools of the news. As you are shortly to discover, people are endlessly inventive in the smaller things of life. When not involved in the conquest of helpless nations, the manufacture of dangerous or useless products, the conduct of holy wars and such, they engage in doings that are bizarre, absurd, preposterous and frequently hilarious.

The clerk of a small Midwestern town is fired when it is discovered that she has ordered too many ballpoint pens. So many, in fact, that closets, storerooms, desk drawers, shelves and cabinets were found to contain enough pens to provide several gross for every man, woman, and child in town. Further investigation showed that the clerk had fallen under the romantic influence of a persuasive salesman for a stationery supplies company.

Somewhere in California, a young woman decided to fit herself out with a sexy pair of skintight jeans. Having bought the tightest pair she could find, she went further, using the traditional technique of immersing herself in a tub of water and allowing the jeans to dry and shrink on her body. The jeans shrank tight enough to bring her blood circulation to a total stop.

In Mexico, a small village goes into religious fervor over a teenage girl who is about to experience a virgin birth. The fervor gets out of hand and results in knife fights between members of the girl's family and the men they suspect got her pregnant.

And so on and so forth goes the human comedy.

No educational result, moral uplift or redeeming social value is claimed for this book. A few pages a night will send you off amused or perhaps relieved to know that others are worse off, more bizarrely miserable, more dangerously stupid. The reader may also see some of these items as cautionary tales; if so, he may learn something or achieve the occasional insight. But the object is bemused pleasure.

Anyone looking to draw a moral from such happy lunacies will do better to investigate Professor Laurence Peter, author and codifier of *The Peter Principle*. Peter, a Canadian (which is to say, the living definition of a prophet without honor in his own land) looked over the same field and came up with the greatest law since Parkinson's. The Peter Principle says that in any hierarchy, an individual tends to rise to his level of incompetence.

Peter's book is well worth reading and should be required for businessmen, politicians, bureaucrats and a good many others, especially those at the bottom who wonder why the guy at the top, as Lyndon B. Johnson once put it, "can't find his ass with both hands." The book was a great and deserved success, which suggests that it has been read by quite a few of those who could most benefit from it. The world is still a mess, but that doesn't invalidate the Peter Principle. It simply suggests that many organization men read books the way many fat people read fad diet books: They think their problem is solved by the reading.

This book, unlike Peter's, attempts to solve no problems, relieve no strains, provide no fast, fast, fast relief. It is the product of black humor and a twenty-year habit of clipping recorded lunacies from newspapers, magazines, books and pamphlets, and stuffing the clippings into envelopes and drawers with no thought in mind but that the material was too good simply to throw away. During a recent move from one home to another, all of my little caches of clippings began to surface at more or less the same time. What a lot of them there seemed to be; what to do with them?

A light dawned, a publisher concurred, and a terrible beauty was born.

Whither the future? We know it lies ahead, but then what? We make no claim to have provided a definitive volume and admit that a second or even more may be necessary. Would-be contributions may send their own clips to the author in care of New American Library, 1633 Broadway, New York, N.Y. 10019. Dates and sources are desirable but not absolutely necessary, and all clips used will be acknowledged in print. On the other hand, names will be withheld on request of those who fear their cover will be blown or who simply don't wish to be identified with unwholesome activities.

MAN
SUFFOCATED
BY POTATOES

I.

HOME SWEET HOME

"Home Sweet Home" is one of many expressions conveying regard for one's own roof, and we hear them repeated so often that we can be excused for believing home ownership is a bed of petunias. But the flower beds are full of manure more often than blossoms, and there are other pitfalls to ownership. It puts you in close contact with bankers, for example, plus lawyers and real-estate agents. No wonder the trend today is toward the cities, where folks can associate with muggers and drug dealers.

Home is out there in the suburbs, where cultural life centers on the supermarket parking lot. They are isolated people, these suburbanites far from the city centers. Think of them as the Bridgeport (Conn.) *Telegram* did when it wrote, "So far the death toll is officially estimated at 5,000, but is expected to rise as help reaches outlying towns."

Minimalist Complex for Rent

Some Houston residents felt they were getting skinned by the new owners of their apartment complex.

The Philadelphia *Daily News* reported that the new owners had elected to turn the place into what they called a "clothing-optional community."

Sort of optional, anyway. The new rules required that no clothes be worn in the complex's public areas—including the sauna, pool, and hot-tub rooms, and the grounds. Clothes would be permitted inside the individual apartments.

The Truck, Though, Was Absolutely Spotless

An Arkansas couple had a fire in their $150,000 house, and they confidently expected that the volunteer firemen would put it out. But when the firemen arrived, they said the residents had not paid their $20 annual dues. The department charges $250 to put out fires, but only for people who have paid their dues.

So they let the house burn to the ground.

"I thought I paid it," said the husband. "They said I didn't." Neighbors offered to fork over the $20 on the spot, but the offers were rejected. "We've had a policy," said a fire-station spokesman. "If you're not a member, we don't fight the fire."

The firemen arrived in three trucks and remained nearby, while the house burned, to make certain the flames did not spread. A neighbor said, "The fire department was just standing around. As a matter of fact, they were out hosing down their new fire truck in the street to keep it clean."

The Maytag Man Would Have Done Anything to Help

A Louisiana man wasn't satisfied with the work on his refrigerator, so he complained to his repairman. The repairman went out and came back with a rifle. Then he shot the refrigerator. The upset owner made a grab at the rifle, and he was shot too.

Nothing Says Lovin' Like Somethin' From the Oven

A Washington housewife cooked herself to death in a freak accident that occurred while she attempted to clean her oven. A coroner said that she was killed by a combination of heat and the fumes from a commercial oven cleaner.

The woman, who was five feet tall and weighed only 103 pounds, was on her knees and reaching inside the oven with the can of oven cleaner. She had already set the heat at far too high a level, and then she was overcome by the fumes. That caused her to collapse onto the oven door, and her weight on the door caused the stove to topple over on top of her, trapping her inside.

Tests made by deputies later suggested that only a small amount of pressure on the door was sufficient to cause the oven, a floor model, to topple over. It also appeared that the unfortunate woman had not followed the instructions on the oven cleaner's label. "You might say she was well done," said Pierce County Sheriff Alan Marrot.

Nuke 'Em!

No. 1

A woman escaped serious injury from an accidental detonation in her home, but the same cannot be said for her house. The woman had apparently had it up to here with bugs, and she decided on all-out warfare. She closed the windows and then emptied the contents of fifteen cans of insecticide spray on her crawling little enemies. A stray spark ignited the fumes, causing an explosion that blew the roof off and blew out every window in the house.

No. 2

An English home owner was at his wits' end in his long and unsuccessful war against the mole that had been burrowing unsightly tunnels throughout his property. Enough with traps and poisons—he planned to go *mano à mano* with the mole. Moles are nocturnal animals, so he drove his Jaguar onto the lawn to hunt the mole down with the aid of its headlights. The car stalled, and when he got it started again, it lurched into gear and out of control. Onward it rolled, the driver trapped inside, until it crashed into his house. The car's fuel tank ruptured and burst into flames, which quickly reached the house and burned it to the ground.

He couldn't even phone for help—the telephone cable was burned through before he could call the fire department. "I was lucky to get out alive," he said. "I still want to see that mole dead."

Bridge Over Baffled Waters

Ordinary home owners merely keep up with the Joneses in such items as lawn decor, strewing the greensward with such atrocities as plaster duckies, cast-iron stags, elf families, etc. But the developers of Lake Havasu City, Ariz., saw an opportunity to go beyond all that while giving their housing development a touch of Old World charm.

They had learned that the city of London found it necessary to replace London Bridge, no longer adequate to the demands of modern traffic, and intended to tear it down. The developers made a deal to buy the bridge and have the parts shipped to Arizona, where they would be reassembled at one end of the community's lake. All this was done, and the result was an enormous disappointment.

London Bridge was all right as far as it went—it stood up, all right, and it undeniably crossed the lake—but it didn't go far enough. The developers belatedly realized that they had bought the wrong bridge. London Bridge is an ordinary stone-arch bridge of no particular distinction. What the developers thought they were buying was the Tower Bridge, which, when last seen, was still in London.

Over the River and Through the Woods to Grandmother's House of Doom We Go!

Children's Hospital in Boston published a study showing that 42% of all accidental poisonings that occur out of the home occur when children go to visit their grandparents.

Do-In-Yourself

The number of home owners who injure themselves while saving money on do-it-yourself home-improvement projects—falling off roofs, slicing off fingers with power saws, dropping heavy objects on their (or others') feet—is astronomical. A Massachusetts man went all the way.

His house was supported on jacks for renovation, and he was underneath doing some repair work when it fell on him.

II.
TRAVEL NOTES

Travel for pleasure ranks as one of man's greatest inventions. Travel is broadening, according to Anonymous, that great phrasemaker without whom thick volumes of *Bartlett's Quotations* would be mere pamphlets, and the sentiment has often been echoed. But for many, travel is narrowing. What of those who fling themselves aboard package tours of Europe that promise fifteen countries in fourteen days? (The fifteenth country is always Liechtenstein—a lunch stop—after which the tour bus hurtles onward.) The provincials take such tours to justify their belief that they are better off at home. If they must travel, they prefer the good old U.S.A., where Holiday Inns promise them "no surprises"—identical rooms in every inn they stay in, no matter how far they roam.

Today's exemplar of the smug provincial is a couple who signed themselves the Wilburs when sending the following bulletin to Dear Abby:

Recently my wife and I toured England, Scotland, Wales, and Ireland, and we noticed a strange habit in all these countries that puzzled and disturbed us. While eating [people in those countries] held their forks upside down as compared to the way we Americans hold ours.

"I tried to explain to them that the fork is curved so as to facilitate the lifting of the food to the mouth. They "rake" their food onto the fork with their knife. (And you should see how they eat their peas!)

Also, after cutting meat, they do not set the knife down and change the fork from the left hand to the right; they eat left-handed, which looks rather awkward.

Abby, please inform us as to where they acquired these strange eating habits."—The Wilburs.

The Ugly American obviously still lives.

Why Some Trips Abroad Just Don't Work Out

"This study program is designed, not only as a technical smorgasbord of visual arts ingredients, but also like a catalytic palette of concept stimulus and reverberations of other fundamental determinants to the artists of societies."
—Letter from the coordinator of an American Travel Association seminar.

Grab Your Hat and Get Going!

A 22-year-old Peruvian woman drapes herself in a pair of boa constrictors in public places. The snakes writhe about her, and she occasionally puts their heads in her mouth. Her purpose, she says, is to encourage tourism.

We'll Get You for This, Orville and Wilbur!

Executive Travel is a magazine that has made a modest collection of airline horror stories for the edification and dismay of its readership. And air travelers in general collect and swap stories, often as a way of reassuring themselves that others have had it worse. Inevitably a little embroidery creeps into some of the more florid adventures, but all in all, the tales are founded on truth.

One passenger reported being on a plane that appeared to be ready for takeoff when there was a loud and persistent banging on the aircraft door. Finally the crew checked, and found that the banging was being caused by the anguished captain, who had somehow been locked out of the plane.

On your Third World airlines, passengers are likely to carry living baggage in their laps. Chickens are common; one passenger reported sitting next to a man who reached into a wicker basket and fetched out a rattlesnake, which he calmly proceeded to feed. In some areas the passengers routinely include peasants and mountaineers who have to be restrained from starting open fires in the aisles to cook their meals.

In Quebec, a local airline that still uses DC-3s had occasional embarrassments at Dorval Airport in Montreal. One flight was aborted twice because as the plane went down the runway its passenger door flapped open. No one, with the possible exception of the passengers, got very excited about this—the pilot just taxied back and the crew tried to shut the door each time. When it appeared that the door lock simply refused to cooperate, one of the crew asked a passenger to lean over and hold the door shut for the takeoff. The passenger refused, and it seemed as if that flight would never get off the ground—until the crewman hit upon a temporary solution. Grabbing a seat belt, he looped one end around the door handle and then fastened the other end to one leg of a passenger's chair.

To settle an overbooking problem on a flight in Nigeria, officials made all the passengers run laps around the plane—the fastest ones got the seats.

On one flight a passenger was asked to sit in the john for takeoff. The crew explained that they'd like to have his seat for one of their own because it was close to an emergency exit.

Commercial airliners sometimes bomb civilians. Occasionally a passing plane drops a large green glob of God knows what onto the landscape. Inevitably chemical analysis proves the glob to be leakage from a plane's chemical toilet. When leakage occurs at altitude, the stuff freezes onto the outside of the plane. It keeps getting bigger and bigger until it finally breaks off. "It's not supposed to happen," said an official of the Federal Aviation Administration, "but it does. We've had them crash into people's kitchens."

A Pan Am senior pilot had a similar problem early in the 1950s. The automatic pilot in certain aircraft would go on the fritz after takeoff. Then, just as mysteriously, it would begin to function as the pilot made his descent.

The senior pilot spent most of his time poring over blueprints of the plane, because only one type of aircraft suffered this fault. Eventually he noticed that the autopilot air-pressure tube (which sensed external air pressure as a way of maintaining altitude) was right next to the outlet of one of the plane's toilets. He concluded that discharge from the toilet froze at high altitudes, eventually blocking the nearby air-pressure tube, but thawed during descent, allowing the autopilot to function once again. He planned to test his theory by flushing the toilet numerous times in flight to blow the lines clear.

On the next available flight, after handing the controls to the copilot, he went aft to test his theory. He was in the john and flushing away—raising and lowering the seat repeatedly to operate the old-time flush mechanism—when a passenger stepped into the john. She was startled to find it occupied but not nearly as startled as she was when the pilot looked up from his flushing and said, "Pardon me, ma'am. I'm just working on the automatic pilot."

In the early days of aviation pilots delivered such surprises deliberately. Sometimes they would board their aircraft wearing parachutes. Another trick was to litter the cockpit floor with rubble from the maintenance shop and then leave the cockpit door open. As the plane rumbled down the runway a slow avalanche of piston rings, nuts, bolts, springs, valves and other junk would slide down the aisle.

Places to Go, People to See

"Fang, Thailand—There is considerably more to Fang than meets the eye."—The complete text of a travel article printed in the Oklahoma City *Oklahoman*.

Friendliest Skies

An Air New Zealand stewardess was given the ax for acts not included in her training manual. According to press reports, the airline's lawyer argued that her firing was justified because she stripped in the first-class cabin, made love in the john to an employee of a competing airline, and "engaged in other acts which cannot be discussed in a family newspaper." All on a single flight.

The stewardess said her actions were not unusual and that outlandish behavior by cabin crew members was the rule, not the exception.

All Aboard! All Aboard! All Aboard Amtrak!

Amtrak's Silver Meteor had a run of bad luck on a run from Miami to New York some years back. It hit and killed a woman in Georgia, demolished a pickup truck in South Carolina, and went off the rails after smashing a tractor-trailer in North Carolina. Trains, of course, make round trips, and this edition of the Silver Meteor was no different. On its way back to Miami it wiped out a driver who tried to race it to a crossing in North Carolina.

Well, What About Going to Bed?

On a recent presidential trip the White House Press Secretary Larry Speakes filled reporters in on the president's schedule for his visit to Des Moines, Iowa, detailing his activities for morning, afternoon, and early evening and noting that "there are no nighttime activities for the president. In fact, there are no nighttime activities in Des Moines at any time."

Bring Your Bathing Suit, Suntan Lotion, and Pack Mule

Seven-day Caribbean cruise on Holland America's S.S. *Veendam*. Sailing from Tampa March third. Port stops: Cozumel, Montego Bay, Grand Canyon.—Advertisement in the Brunswick, Maine, *Times Record*.

Safety First

Airlines, naturally wary of hidden bombs, keep careful track of the number of passengers and their pieces of luggage. When they have an item they can't account for, some airlines express their concern for safety in an unusual manner. They pull the plane out of the flight line, unload the baggage and ask the passengers to claim their luggage. Any piece not picked up is subjected to a thorough examination.

But suppose the unclaimed item really is a bomb? Suppose it goes off?

Unfriendliest Skies

Air Canada is unpleasant enough to be known by some Canadians as Air Ugly, and when Allegheny Airlines changed into U.S. Air, some of its victims said it was because Allegheny was "the airline that dare not speak its name." Nevertheless, the world champion user-hostile airline is Russia's Aeroflot.

On most airlines, passengers are treated as a necessary inconvenience; on Aeroflot, survivors say, they are treated like baggage. In-flight refreshment is not unknown, but it often consists of little more than a basket of cellophane-wrapped sour balls passed from hand to hand. Steward-esses, usually ill-humored women filled with lead shot, are famous for their brusque and unhelpful manner. Planes arrive early or late as often as on time, and there is never an explanation for anything. Whatever inconvenience is caused to the passengers is deemed to be their own fault.

On some short routes in the boondocks, Aeroflot still uses DC-3s; during cold weather they are heated by small charcoal stoves.

Some years ago an Aeroflot plane touched down at a tiny but busy fuel stop in Siberia only to find that the base itself was almost out of fuel. There wasn't enough for the next leg of the flight, so captain, crew, passengers and plane sat down to wait.

For reasons never discovered, getting more fuel to the base turned out to be something of a problem. So did altering routes to bypass the base. Planes kept landing but not leaving, one after another. By the time the fuel situation was resolved, more than a week had passed. The population of the tiny base had grown to nearly 2,000 cold, hungry passengers and a great many airplanes.

III.
THE CULTURAL CLIMATE

Several variations of the remark exist, but essentially what Hermann Goering said was, "When I hear anyone talk of culture, I reach for my revolver." It would be incorrect to say that there began the downward slide of modern civilization, but it's fair to say that the Nazi Luftwaffe chief spoke for many at the time and speaks for many now, though today many others would say instead, "I reach for my cash register." Culture is flogged through the mails, exploited on television, hawked in shops, and otherwise commercially abused. "Dese," as Jimmy Durante used to say, "are de conditions dat prevail." And now, as he also said, "with further ado . . ."

Sit on It!

Sold at auction for $50, a worn painted plank with three holes in it was shortly afterward hailed as a work of art. The object, according to Elaine de Kooning, had been painted thirty years before by her husband, artist William de Kooning, whose works have sold for as much as $2 million.

The plank was identified as the seat from an outhouse.

More Pepperoni Would Be Nice Too

Paul Martin as a young warlock handled his part competently. But there's a wish that he and director Johnson have given it more pizza, more of that flair mentioned earlier. —Review in the Eugene (Ore.) *Register-Guard*.

Soon to Be a Valuable,
if Unattractive, Collector's Item

Rock star Michael Jackson has been honored not only with gold and platinum records but with something much rarer— his own postage stamps.

Both the British Virgin Islands and the island of St. Vincent put Jackson on stamps—the BVI stamps, issued in pairs, have a face value of $1.50, and the St. Vincent stamp is marked $2.

The stamps were printed and shipped to dealers before someone at the Commonwealth Office in London saw the BVI issue and advised the island's government of the rules for Commonwealth stamps: No one may be pictured on a stamp unless he is (a) a member of the British Royal Family, or (b) dead.

The British Virgin Islands immediately recalled the stamps from general circulation, but dealers who stocked up to cater to stamp collectors were not interested in giving any of theirs back. As examples of stamps never legally issued, they are a philatelic rarity—and a possible gold mine.

As a clerk at Marlen Stamps and Coins of Great Neck, Long Island, put it, "We have them—and they're now selling at $200 per pair."

As for the St. Vincent stamps, tough luck. St. Vincent is not part of the British Commonwealth, and it did not have to recall the issue. But since they are perfectly legal, they are also perfectly ordinary and will continue to sell for the regular paltry price.

Lost in Translation

American movies are often rather strangely retitled before they are unleashed on Oriental moviegoers. Burt Reynolds's *Smokey and the Bandit* was retitled *Racing Cars in Unorderly Fashion*, Paul Newman's hockey movie, *Slapshot*, was released as *The Cursing Roughhouse Rascal Who Plays Dirty*, and *Demon Seed* came out as *Sperm of the Devil*.

TV series take their lumps as well. Viewers in Thailand have been treated to *Laverne and Shirley*, despite the fact that independent, unmarried young women living apart from their families go against the Thai cultural grain. For that reason, the government television network preceded each episode with a slide informing the public that the series was about two women who had escaped from a lunatic asylum.

Can't You Just Imagine What They'll Do with AIDS, Darling?

Two of the nation's best-known retailers, Bloomingdale's and Tiffany's, caught the flavor of the times and expressed it in retail terms.

Bloomingdale's offered a line of high-priced "street couture"—ripped and tattered designer-label clothes and rags inspired by the Now look of poverty-stricken people who must get their personal fashion statements out of other people's garbage cans. Tiffany's, which has been preaching about good taste for decades, permitted its window dressers to display jewelry of gold and diamonds in dioramas decorated with figurines of homeless street people.

It's Pledge Week Again—Why not Add a Little Zip?

Nova, the PBS science series, waxed quite unbuttoned over an episode entitled "Locusts: War Without End." The press release described it as "much more than a tale of battles against insect pests. It explores the amazing private life of the locust, much of it never before revealed on film. The screen is filled with dramatic close-ups of locusts shedding their skins, copulating and digging holes deep in the ground to lay their eggs."

The real drabness of the PBS soul comes through more often, as in this TV listing for an insufferably earnest holiday offering:

(12) A BERKELEY CHRISTMAS—DRAMA SPECIAL. A drama about a university student whose plans for Christmas vacation are upset by a pregnant hitchhiker. The 1972 story is followed by a film essay dealing with coastal pollution.

More Shows You Won't Want to Miss

(6) MOVIE—"The Agony and the Ecstasy" (1956). Stan Laurel and Oliver Hardy.—*Los Angeles Times*.

(9) "Love and Death" (1974). Woody Allen's most literate film; a spoof of "War and Peace," which he wrote, starred in, and directed.—Toronto *Globe and Mail*.

(4) PERRY COMO'S CHRISTMAS SPECIAL. The members of a Greek family are murdered systematically in a bizarre fashion—Toronto *Sun*.

Loyal Fans

No. 1

Pepper, a resident of Boulder, Colorado, prefers John Wayne movies, football games, cartoons and soap operas —a wide range of the junk TV has to offer. Pepper is a dog.

"This dog has become obsessed with TV," says her owner, Doug Osborne. "I'm trying to break her of the habit." Osborne said Pepper got hooked over a holiday, when he was out of town. His roommate was watching Johnny Carson, and Pepper, who had previously ignored television, perked up when Carson introduced a singing dog act.

Now Pepper watches anything, and she hunkers down a mere six inches from the screen, which has Osborne worried about her eyesight. She whines when she wants the set turned on and moans when she wants the channel changed. She trots around in circles when Osborne reaches for the remote-control tuner. And she really will watch anything. She will stare contentedly at a blank screen.

No. 2

Firemen in England raced to the burning home of a 65-year-old man and were surprised to find him calmly waiting for them at the front door. They were even more surprised to find that his wife and daughter had insisted on remaining inside to continue watching television.

No. 3

In Toronto, an elderly spinster sat watching television with her sister for much longer than was good for either of them. Prompted by a suspicious neighbor's call, police forced their way into the sisters home. Both were seated before the set when the cops arrived, the only thing unusual in the scene being the older sister, who had been dead for two months.

No. 4

Continental Cablevision of Madison Heights, Michigan, had a little trouble with some of its electronic switching equipment, resulting in X-rated programming being fed into the homes of many subscribers who hadn't ordered it. The alarm was sounded by a scandalized customer who called a local radio station to say, "It was really awful—we saw it for four hours."

Just 39 Shy of Top 40

A deejay in Iowa found the Christmas blues getting him down, and he sought relief in a song called "Grandma Got Run Over by a Reindeer." It seemed to help, so in the next three and a half hours he played it a total of twenty-seven times.

This program director told him to stop, but the disc jockey kept on playing it, which led to his suspension. He was reinstated, however, after hundreds of listeners phoned to support him—some from England and Ireland—and after he promised to behave himself.

The Old Switcheroo

Concerts—July 7: Montpelier Philharmonic Orchestra, Cyril Diederich/Mstislav Rostropovich conductor, Leonard Bernstein cello (Tchaikovsky).—*International Herald Tribune.*

Packed House

The second concert will be held on Nov. 14 and will feature the New Christy Minstrels, who through recording success and television exposures that demanded personal appearances have performed before an estimated total of 45 million fans who applaud loudly at each performance. —Halifax, (Nova Scotia) *Mail-Star.*

Da-Do-Ron-Ron-Ron,
Da-Do-Ron-Ron, Mao Baby

Under Mao Tse-Tung, revolutionary principles and thoughts were supposed to be an intimate part of every facet of Chinese life, and thus Shanghai, the Tin Pan Alley of Communist China, turned out such twist-and-shout numbers as:

"Mother Joins the Ranks";

"Last Night I Dreamed of Chairman Mao";

"Mother, I want to Go to the Mountainside and Harden Myself With Physical Labor"; and the ever-popular

"We Will Not Allow the United States Imperialists to Ride Roughshod Over the People."

IV.
EDUCATION AND WHATNOT

Education has been something of a problem in this country for a long time. Since about the beginning, in fact. Americans have long regarded "book learning" with wariness and even contempt; our enduring national myth is that the nation was created by men of action, not words; men of muscle, not mental prowess.

That is true only up to a point. Much as we like to recall the Minutemen and the Green Mountain Boys and the suffering stoics of Valley Forge, we like to forget that though they indeed did most of the fighting, and the cause for which they fought is the eternal desire for freedom, it was intelligent, educated men who expressed and codified the principles that led to the founding of a democratic republic ruled by law rather than by a collection of independent colonies under the sway of anarchy.

This light regard for education has been met with a tendency to mystify and glorify through jargon. All professions try to enhance themselves in this way, and the more insecure professions simply do it more. Strong is the urge to impress upon the layman that there is much he does not know! In addition, there continue to be battles between educational traditionalists and zealous reformers, with mixed results. What began as an effort to lift schooling out of the mire of rote memorization in Dickensian settings, and to make it a pleasure to be sought rather than drudgery to be avoided, eventually got out of hand and became, in some cases, the undisciplined teaching of inconsequentials.

At one high school a program devoted to "living skills" included courses in balancing checkbooks and how to order by mail from catalogues. Elsewhere, college courses were offered in which no grades were given. The "new math" was widely hailed until even its advocates realized that students who mastered it were still unable to make change from a dollar. The subject once known as English became Language Arts, and many of those who passed it with high grades proved later to be unable to express themselves literately in their mother tongue. Things went downhill fast. At one point several states passed laws requiring teachers to prove themselves competent in the subjects they taught, and in English as well; teachers' organizations objected mightily. College SAT scores continued to fall; those who worried about it were told not to worry—college enrollment was on the increase nevertheless. The less optimistic observed that one reason might be the institution of "open admission" policies (under which some schools dropped all entrance requirements). It all seemed to make no more sense than *U.S. News & World Report*'s insight: "The main reason for this growth in college enrollment is that a larger percentage of young Americans now go on to college than in the past."

Colleges have proved themselves as capable as high schools when it comes to teaching rubbish. They have been found to offer courses in UFO Spotting and in Prostitution. For credit.

The latest development in education is a trend toward imported teachers, sometimes with unfortunate results. Recently nine University of Pittsburgh students (as well as others elsewhere) demanded and received tuition refunds because some of their courses were taught by foreign-born instructors whose English was unintelligible.

Following are further symptoms of educational malaise.

Write This Down—You'll Be Quizzed on It

Analysis of variance, Statistics: A procedure for resolving the total variance of a set of varieties into component variances, which are associated with various factors affecting the variates.—Definition in *The American College Dictionary*.

New Frontiers in Idealism

Professor Slive's academic field is in seventeenth-century Dutch art. Professor Slive has taught at Harvard since

1954 and chaired the Fine Arts Department from 1968 to 1970. His thorough knowledge of the Fogg Museum along with his realization of its many responsibilities suggest a broad-minded but careful administration. Slive sees one duty of the Fogg as making students "virtually literate."
—*The Harvard Independent.*

Not to Worry

According to J. Mitchell Morse, a professor of English at Temple University, juniors and seniors majoring in English at fully accredited four-year colleges and universities throughout the United States express themselves in the following manner:

"The modren day literature had it's good merit's as well as it's bad one's but I don't think so."

"Joyce was living symotanious to Kafka all though the did not aide each other in utilyzing the same standart of excellent like stream of conscience."

"George Orwell makes me feel like I was desserted on some destitute island in Politics and the English Language. He points out the destruction of the language, is caused by people, attempting to deceive the writing and using bad speech practices."

"The victims screams for helping herself was effident thru all the allies around 100 Murch Avenue as if the thick smoke billowing from a factorys exhaust pipe."

"The revolutionerys can not ignore the reactionary forces that threaten to undue his work and propel his achievements into preexisting revolutionery conditions."

"The blind and the death suffer unjustly because of there handicaped which are considered as being dim witness and are felt to be in a class for the retarded even when there not."

Teachers who are upset by such mutilations need not worry, according to the Council on College Composition and Communication. In a policy statement entitled "Students' Right to Their Own Language," the CCCC says that grammar, spelling, punctuation and vocabulary are "surface features" that have no effect on the "deep structure," "meaning" or "content" of a sentence; therefore instructors should not demand accuracy in such matters. To do so risks inhibiting the students' "creativity and individuality."

"Simply because 'Johnny can't read' doesn't mean 'Johnny is immature' or 'Johnny can't think.' He may be bored," the CCCC says. "If we can convince students that spelling, punctuation and usage are less important than content, we have removed a major obstacle in their developing the ability to write."

The Return to Fundamentals in the Nation's Schools

The above headline appeared in The New York Times.

Community Support Helps

Several residents appeared at Monday night's meeting of the Board of Education and applauded loudly when Board Member Joseph Hammond, speaking of the Lakewood Council, said, "I wouldn't trust them with a ten-foot pole."—Paramount (California) *Journal*.

Could You Repeat That, Please?

The use of computers in facility management is the topic of a program entitled "Computer-Aided Facility Management," to be held Dec. 7 to 11 at the Facility Management Institute in Ann Arbor. The program will focus on understanding the uses for computers in the management of facilities.—Ann Arbor (Michigan) *News*.

Eureka! I've Found It—Again!

A group of Colorado archaeologists announced their expedition to a "lost city" in the Peruvian Andes, claiming that the pre-Incan site may rival Machu Picchu. One of the expedition's leaders said, "The site has been the subject of rumors and unsuccessful expeditions since the beginning of this century, if not from the time of the Spanish conquest" in the 1500s.

He did not claim to have discovered the site, crediting

that to "a Peruvian expedition" of the 1960s, but the *Washington Post* said the press release issued by the university "suggested that the site had faded into obscurity" after the Peruvian expedition had made only "a brief visit." In fact, the *Post* continued, the "lost city" has been reported on "in dozens of books as well as magazine and newspaper articles and in a 1970 CBS News documentary."

Now at Bookstores Everywhere

"Samuel Beckett: Humanistic Perspectives." Edited by Morris Beja, S. E. Gontarski and Pierre Astier. Original critical essays that approach this particularly multicultural writer from a variety of disciplines and that come close to being the measure of a man and an artist found particularly congenial to the modern sensibility as one in whose work the illusions and deceptions of the outer world resist each system that attempts a faithful, comprehensive and coherent account, and that, in the end, must inevitably collapse under too great a weight of enigma and error. Ills. $20.00—Advertisement by the University of Ohio Press.

Raising the Standards

No. 1

A high school in Rhode Island will try to improve students' grades by limiting trips to the toilet. Students' visits are now restricted to two a day. The principal is convinced there is a link between poor grades and frequent trips to the bathroom. "To a certain extent," he says, "the need to use a lavatory is not related to biological urges but an urge to get out of class."

No. 2

Philadelphia public schools will no longer give an A for effort to any student. Henceforth, the student who is ignorant but hardworking will flunk just as surely as the one who is ignorant and lazy; only academic achievement will count.

A fourth-grade teacher recently said none of her students had earned a grade higher than D, and that her best pupil was working on second-grade readers. "It's something that had to happen sooner or later," she said. "It's ridiculous to have kids in high school who can't read or write."

Relaxing the Standards

Were some University of Georgia students excused from meeting academic requirements because they happened to be athletes? So it would seem. The university's vice-president for academic affairs said she granted academic exceptions to some athletes because "I would rather err on the side of making a mistake."

It turned out to be a hell of a mistake—a long series of mistakes. The question arose because the university fired a teacher, Jan Kemp, who protested the practice of turning flat-out flunking grades into passing marks. Mrs. Kemp cited as an example the grades of nine football players whose grades were altered so they could play in the 1982 Cotton Bowl.

Mrs. Kemp sued in federal court, charging the university with violating her constitutional right of free speech. Her anger stemmed from the university's unjust treatment and from its cynical exploitation of student athletes, most of whom, however weak they were academically, expected to graduate with a degree and get a contract in professional sports. Almost none got either.

Faking the grades in the remedial studies program, in which Mrs. Kemp taught, virtually guaranteed that the students would leave the college as dumb as they were when they entered.

The university's defense was somewhat weak. The judge did not accept the excuse that "other colleges do it too." One witness for the university suggested establishment of a "pre-literacy" program for scholarship athletes unable to read or write. The university's president said athletes had "utilitarian value" as revenue-producers through ticket sales. He said the university would not raise its academic standards unless other schools did likewise—that would be tantamount to having Georgia's athletic programs "disarm unilaterally."

The defense seemed to sum up the university's attitude when it said, of a hypothetical athlete, "We may not be able to make a university student out of him, but if we can teach him to read and write, maybe he can work at the post office rather than as a garbage man when he gets through with his athletic career."

Leroy Ervin, in charge of the program from which Mrs. Kemp was fired, went so far as to accuse her of being a "bigot." (Mrs. Kemp is white, and many of the remedial students were black.) But Mrs. Kemp was able to produce black witnesses, including a former athlete, who defended her.

After hearing six weeks of testimony in Atlanta, the jury decided for Kemp, awarding her a judgment of $2.5 million.

Mrs. Trotter, the second-most powerful official at the university, said she was "surprised" and "disappointed."

Just One Example of What the Fuss Was All About

NBA star Elvin "Big E" Hayes got into professional basketball after attending the University of Houston. The word is used advisedly; he attended but did not graduate.

Recently he returned to study at the university to get the thirty credits he needed to get a degree. He observed that there was a difference between going to school then and going to school now.

"All of a sudden, I'm trying to read books, write papers, take finals," he said. "It was the hardest thing I've ever done. When I was in school here, I could say, 'Get that paper written for me' or 'Get that done for me.' Everybody did things for me."

In those days, of course, Hayes had utilitarian value for Houston's basketball program.

On the Other Hand, He Could Have an Allergy

Resembling the "stereotype" bespeckled professor, Finlayson's professional career is as unique as his outside interests—Shands, the house organ of Shands Hospital at the University of Florida.

Return to Sender

Dear Education Program Member:

The pace thickens!
—Letter from the Education Program of Barnard College.

Best Science Project

A Georgia 10-year-old needed an idea for his school project—and got one when a convicted murderer was sent to the electric chair in Alabama. The student, who supports capital punishment, decided to build his own electric chair. His completed project, though nonlethal, does light up. He used an old belt for the leg and arm cuffs, and made the headpiece out of a baseball cap. His model won him an award for the most creative project.

Best Project in Agriculture, Home Ec, and Dentistry

A California high-school boy seeking to better his D average in agriculture class used his teeth to castrate a sheep in class, raising his grade 100 points. His teacher, who had performed an oral castration in class earlier, promised the boy extra credit if he would do it too. The teacher noted that oral castration is still used by shepherds in some parts of the world.

As Today's Graduates Take their Places in the World . . .

No. 1

"It's like Odysseus [the Greek mythical figure] going through Scylla on Charidis," said the 28-year-old who recently graduated from law school.—The Bergen County (N.J.) *Record*.

No. 2

As an MBA student and a future business person, I take personal exception to Ray Conlogue's article . . . in which he says, "In this country, businessmen can get an MBA without reading a play." That statement implies that business people as a group are cultural philistines. . . .

Furthermore, the choice of an MBA's reading material is a matter of time and taste. The reason why some of us have not yet got around to reading "Anna Karenina" may simply be because we don't like Dickens.—Letter to the Editor, the Toronto *Globe and Mail*.

... The Outlook Continues Gloomy

No. 1

[The college] is sitting on a launching pad, ready to really flex its muscles and be a dynamo.—Dr. Billy Greer, as quoted in the Brevard (N.C.) *Transylvania Times*.

No. 2

This chapter was written as well as authored by Albert Z. Guttenberg.—Footnote from a college textbook.

V.

HOBBIES, RECREATIONS, AND DIVERSIONS

Hobbies are both a big business and no business at all. The cost of plastic airplane models for American youths for one year no doubt equals or exceeds the gross national product of several Third World nations; on the other hand, it probably doesn't come close to the drug payoffs collected by single banana-republic dictator.

Malcolm Forbes has some of the more attractive and most expensive hobbies. He rode through China on a motorcycle—no outrageous expense in itself—but he also had a movie made about his jaunt. Forbes has a truly wonderful collection of tin toy boats, toy soldiers and a lot of other stuff, all displayed in a "museum" on the ground floor of the Forbes Magazine Building in Manhattan. It's open free to the public and is probably a tax deduction. Forbes also goes in for hot-air ballooning with all sorts of fancy people as his guests. He has a balloon in the shape of his chateau in France, and when he visited India, he wowed the locals with a balloon in the shape of a Mogul elephant.

Forbes's most expensive hobby is collecting Fabergé eggs—glittering, elegant, bejeweled Easter eggs made by Carl Fabergé for the czars (or tsars, if you will) of Russia. They are extremely rare—Fabergé didn't churn them out on an assembly line, after all, and not all have survived the years. Those extant turn up at auction only now and then, but they always fetch enormous prices. Forbes bids eagerly for them, and so do the Soviets, who denounce everything to do with their czarist past at the drop of a hat but become conveniently forgetful when it comes to such treasures.

Whether you root for capitalism over communism, or the little guy going up against a whole country, or just silly little competitions, it's easy to like Malcolm Forbes, if only because in his years of collecting he has managed to buy more Fabergé eggs than the Soviets have.

Other hobbies may have less international flavor to them but also cost less. Francis A. Johnson of Darwin, Minnesota, earned a niche in the *Guinness Book of World records* by amassing, over the course of twenty-eight years, the world's largest ball of string. It weighs 10 tons and is 40 feet in diameter.

Equally absorbed was the man whose hobby was painting. His painting was very simple—he just painted a piece of wood. No pictures, no designs, nothing but coats of paint on a piece of wood. And always the same piece of wood—a piece about a foot long, a couple of inches wide, a half-inch thick. He used to do one coat a day, no more, no less. He chose whatever color he happened to have handy and didn't change colors until he'd emptied the can he happened to be working on. When last seen, he had 4,000 coats of paint on his board, which—paint included—had grown to about six inches thick.

Perhaps you will find you own hobby among those below.

Art With a Social Conscience

The *Capital Times* is having a party on Saturday, from 11 A.M. until 2 P.M., at the Madison Civic Center-Montgomery Ward Building to honor the hundreds of endangered-animal coloring-contest winners and the thousands of contest entries.—The *Capital Times*, Madison, Wisconsin.

Shoot Anything That Moves

The moose-hunting season got off rather on the wrong foot on an island off Alaska; at the same time it got off to a perfectly traditional start. The apparent paradox is resolved once you consider American hunters' disconcerting tendency to shoot each other.

In this instance one hunter spotted a brownish object huddled in the bush and, convinced it was a moose, shot it. The nimrod's aim was true and deadly, and so much the worse for his target, which proved not to be a moose at all but another hunter who happened to be crouched on the ground with his back against a tree. He was, in fact, waiting for a moose of his own to shoot.

"His right hand was still in contact with his rifle," said the discoverer of the body, which was slumped against the tree.

For moose and hunters who wish to avoid being shot, this island is a good place not to be. It measures only 23 square miles, and 200 hunters are often on the loose.

Over the years hunters have shot numerous things under the impression that they were game animals. In most hunting areas every farmer worth his salt knows enough to paint the word *COW* in huge white letters on every member of his dairy herd. Over the years the many victims mistaken for deer or moose have included a clergyman riding a bicycle and a yellow school bus.

Stand by to Ram!

A Long Island powerboat dealer told police he fell asleep at the wheel. But even though the wheel was part of his thirty-nine-foot cabin cruiser, he nevertheless managed to involve himself in an automobile accident.

Police estimated that the boat, a $100,000 model, was roaring through Great South Bay at 35 m.p.h. on a balmy June evening, and an eyewitness saw the whole thing.

Enjoying the breeze on his patio, the witness saw the boat charging toward the south end of the canal near his home. As he looked on, the boat appeared to strike some kind of obstruction. Then, as in various James Bond movies or a Marineland stunt show, it sailed seventy feet through the air, blasted its way ashore, tore through a fence, crashed over some rocks, mowed down a few pine trees and eventually came to rest on top of the witness's Volkswagen.

No one was injured. Police, who said the captain of the boat appeared to be under the influence of intoxicants more potent than the smell of fresh salt air, found him strolling about belowdecks.

Amateur Carpentry and Electrical Wiring Award

"I've seen a lot of weird things in seventeen and a half years as a policeman, but this is about the weirdest. I can't understand why anyone would want to sit in a chair and get hurt."

This Ohio policeman was referring to the goings-on in the basement of a hobbyist whose interest was in strapping kids into the homemade electric chair in his basement and taking their pictures while he gave them nonlethal but stinging 140-volt electric shocks. Police recovered more than 200 photos of some three dozen kids who had been "given the chair." The hobby came to light after only one of the teenagers talked to the cops, saying he had agreed to be zapped.

Police were not able to explain why the man indulged in his hobby nor why the teenagers volunteered. After the teacher was arrested, several students appeared at police headquarters to defend him.

Separating Sheep From Goats

Said Mr. Metcalf, "This will be a very exacting type of expedition and one which will sort out the wheat from the chaff. It is not everybody's cup of tea. It teaches them to stand on their feet in an age when everything is handed to them on a plate."—The *Glasgow Evening Times*

Unusual New Gift Idea!

An Illinois man gets a coconut every Christmas. He doesn't know why, nor does he know who it comes from. But every Christmas, one way or another, he gets his coconut. It always comes with a note that reads, "To the Daddy from The Thing."

This has been going on since 1948, and he admits that it used to bug him, though he is now resigned to it. The delivery method is also unusual. The coconuts have been delivered by FBI men, the police, mayors, helicopters, horseback, parachute and a college basketball team.

For Rambos, Rambas, and Rambini

Marietta, Ga., is the home of The BulletStop, the gun club with a difference—it rents machine guns. And takes American Express.

Paul LaVista created the BulletStop to capitalize on fantasies generated by Rambo-style movies, films that encourage people to believe that relief—from frustration, stress and life's little annoyances—is just a short burst away.

For $3.50 customers get use of the firing range. For $10 they get 50 rounds of ammunition, which disappears out the muzzle in a second or so. For another sawbuck they get their choice of automatic weapon: the Heckler & Koch, a sophisticated West German assault weapon; the simple but deadly Uzi submachine gun from Israel; and the homegrown, all-American AR-15, blood brother to the Vietnam-era AR-16.

Some customers start off a bit cautiously with semiautomatic fire—one shot per pull of the trigger—but it usually isn't long before they decide to switch to full auto (as they put it in Nam, "flip your iron to rock and roll").

Lunchtimes are busy for LaVista—he gets a big business crowd. "Instead of martinis, they go for machine guns," he says. "You'd be surprised how many American Express Cards we take." But Saturday night is the noisiest night of the week. "It's packed," LaVista says. "Lots of husbands and wives and younger couples. Couples come in on dates. These ladies—that's an experience worth watching. They really get into it."

Lavista happily admits that "we've got some real machine-gun junkies," but points out that the appeal of heavy-duty firepower is broad. Farmers, housewives, secretaries, and lawyers like to squeeze off a few bursts, and not long ago a group of London doctors visiting hospitals in Atlanta stopped in to cut loose en masse.

It is all "good, clean fun," LaVista says. "And you won't get AIDS from machine guns."

Mr. Guillemin, Meet Paul LaVista

This New Jersey sculptor applied his arts and skills to construction of a handmade cannon—a bronze model twenty-six inches long. He tested it in a field, firing at a steel oil drum some distance away.

Two thousand feet away, the cannonball crashed through the bathroom of an 88-year-old woman, who was shaken up but not injured—she had been in the kitchen at the time.

According to a township spokesman, "The steel ball ended up in the first-floor bathroom, hit a rear wall, ricocheted into the toilet, shattered the bathroom mirror, then ricocheted into a wall and dropped to the ground."

The weapons enthusiast was charged with criminal mischief and released on his own recognizance but avoided more serious charges by convincing police that his cannon was not meant to be a weapon but a work of art.

It's Not Who You Know,
It's Who You Remember You Know

Lowell Davis, 83, of Savannah, Missouri, is writing down the name of every person he can remember meeting—however briefly—since he was three years old. So far he has 679 pages filled with nearly 3,500 names carefully recorded in a yellow binder. "I had them jotted everywhere," Davis says, "on old envelopes, scraps of wallpaper, shoebox lids"—but now he's gotten organized. He has the names grouped chronologically according to each town he has lived in, and Hazel, his wife for the past fifty-six years, helps him recall as many as he can. Whenever possible, Davis adds a brief descriptive note. Sample entry: Leonard McKnight—fond of chicken gravy.

Clarence and Sam, Meet Lowell and Hazel

Clarence and Sam Chapman of Tamaroa, Illinois, are friendly people who wave a greeting when someone passes by. In fact, they wave at every single person who passes their junkyard. They sit out by the side of the road, all day and every day, and wave, wave, wave. They know almost none of the people in the cars that pass, and most they will never see again. That doesn't faze them.

"It's kind of hard to believe," says Clarence, 63, "but some places people have just forgotten how to be friendly.

A lot of people look at us funny or turn around and stop just to say, 'You waved at us—do I know you?' " From time to time Clarence and his son, who is 36, sell or trade some junk, but when not commercially engaged, they wave. Sam took a master's degree in philosophy at Southern Illinois University in 1975 and then joined his father at the junkyard. "Let Socrates keep his mountain," he says. "I've got my junkyard."

Sticky Situation

Their neighbors in Vancouver knew little about Hans Dietman and his elderly mother except that she was a pensioner who spent her hours soaking stamps off envelopes for her son. Now they know at least that she was very good at it.

Otherwise, all that is known is that Dietman and his mother left Canada without notice. The only thing they left behind were their stamps—50 million of them.

"I've never seen anything like it, and I've been in the business ten years," said the manager of a local stamp store. Fifty million stamps certainly outweigh any other known collection, though the stamp expert said the collection is not necessarily the most valuable—but even at the minimum listing price of three cents each, the stamps would be worth a bundle.

Make Valuable Collectors' Items Out of Ordinary Items Others Simply Throw Away!

Marian Baker, Harris Center staff member, will demonstrate and help participants turn window- or road-killed wildlife into museum mounts.

The program begins at 9:30 A.M. Bring a lunch and, if possible, your own road kill, foam or cotton stuffing for the animal, sharp knife and scissors.—The Peterborough (N.H.) *Transcript.*

Turn Your Hobby Into Easy Profits!

Photographers

Only market in America paying top dollar on acceptance for violent death photos—disasters, gruesome car accidents, bizarre murders, unsolved crimes, senseless killings. Must be on-the-scene shots—A Chicago news-features syndicate.

VI.
GRAVE NEWS

"The grave's a fine and private place," wrote the poet Andrew Marvell, "but none, I think, do there embrace." You see how gracefully poets handle such a subject? Dramatists are more robust; for example, Shakespeare, in the graveyard scene in *Hamlet*.

Our present age has its own view, as suggested by this advertisement in a Toronto publication:

Computerized Death Predictions

Unfortunately, we are ALL going to die. The question is when? Our computerized method could give you the answer to when you are going to have your FINAL and ultimate date with destiny. Only $5.00 plus a self-addressed stamped envelope will provide you with your own personalized computer-ready application.

You get a lot of that sort of thing in Canada, Land of the Young at Heart.

King Tut Would Be Green With Envy

No. 1

A Rio de Janeiro man has designed coffins for those who wish to go in style. The coffins are loaded with $5,000 worth of microphones, headphones and other stereo equipment, plus alarm systems. The coffins are made of plastic, polished steel and mirrors.

No. 2

"Willie the Wimp," as Willie M. Stokes was known both to cops and persons engaged in commerce of an illegal nature, was found by Chicago Police as they rather expected to find him: dead of a gunshot wound. What was not expected was the Wimpmobile his family requested for him: a coffin gussied up to resemble a late-model Cadillac, complete with mag wheels, a pretty fair imitation of a Cadillac grille, and a hood ornament. Wimp himself, hat on head, was slid under the lid with his upper body exposed and propped up into something like a driving position.

Okay, Kids, Here Comes Momma

Florida undertakers and Deke Slayton, one of the original astronauts, are combining forces to send mortal remains into space for burial in orbit.

"Celestis is a post-cremation service," said John Cherry, who formed the consortium of funeral directors. "Once the funeral services are over, the 'cremains' will be sent to us. Then we further reduce and encapsulate them [the ashes of an average body can be compressed into a cylinder $3/8''$ in diameter and $1''$ long]; identify each by name, Social Security number and a religious symbol; and place them into the payloader."

The payloader, as it is called, is to be launched by Space Services of Houston, Texas, of which Slayton is president. Space Services will also launch remains for Starbound, a Tyler, Texas, company that is served on a "space-available" basis. Slayton says seven other morticians' groups have expressed interest.

The Department of Transportation has expressed no objections to the plan so far, and there is no reason to believe that it will. The State Department, NASA and the Defense Department have been invited to comment on the Space Services-Celestis contract. The Commercial Space Launch Act of 1984 authorizes the Department of Transportation to license all commercial space launchings. "The United States Government wants to encourage private-sector activities in space," said Jennifer L. Dorn, director of the Department of Transportation's Commercial Space Transportation Office. "We have received Space Service's request for mission approval and expect an expeditious review."

Mr. Cherry said the service would be advertised abroad—Canada, Britain and Japan being likely spots.

He said market research showed that cremation was used in about 12% of the annual deaths in the U.S., and that Celestis could be commercially successful if it could capture 3% to 4% of that amount.

In 1981, Space Services' first try at a launch ended when its rocket blew up on the launching pad, but in 1982 it became the first private company to launch its own booster rocket, a 36-footer called the *Conestoga*, into suborbital flight. The burial mission would be performed by an advanced model of the *Conestoga*, capable of hoisting 1,500 pounds of freight.

"We've put men on the moon," said Rusty Miller, president of Starbound, "so I think this is a way to keep pace with the times."

Celestis' fee for space burial is $3,900 per customer, or capsule. Eventually Celestis hopes to offer deep-space burials, in which the capsules will be ejected into the cosmos from the nose cone of a rocket, but orbital burial is the first step. For the first launching the payloader will give a reflective coating that will help relatives of the departed spot the space mausoleum as it passes overhead.

Get a Piece of the Rock

1. Dying Too Soon. 2. Living Too Long. 3. Becoming Disabled . . . need not interrupt your future plans.—Ad for an insurance-planning firm in 1975 directory, Colorado University Medical Center.

Why Don't We Just Put it in the Garage and Throw a Tarp Over it?

A "domestic rampage" in a California town had already cost an unfortunate woman her daughter and two granddaughters, so she was in no condition for what occurred during her daughter's burial. First it was discovered that the grave was not large enough for the coffin. Then the attendants tried to get the coffin into the grave by lowering it on its side, but the mourners protested. Then the grave diggers tried to make the coffin fit by breaking the handles off; this, too, raised protests. Then the attendants jumped up and down on top of the coffin in an attempt to pound it into the grave. Finally the funeral was postponed. Another try was held six days later, and at that time cemetery workers brought the coffin to the site on the back of a pickup truck also loaded with tools and dirt.

The woman planned to sue the cemetery for half a million dollars.

Bite Your Tongue!

"We were disturbed by the ridicule," said a spokesman for a national funeral director's association, "because death, especially to the person who has just experienced it, is not funny."

VII.

KIDS! WHAT'S THE MATTER WITH KIDS TODAY?

Our title here comes from the Broadway musical *Bye-Bye Birdie,* whose author in turn got it from the wails of generations of parents going back to about the time the cave men learned to do more than grunt.

The complaint is always the same in meaning, but its form changes slightly from time to time. It is usually uttered by a parent who sees his kids doing exactly what he did as a youth, and the precise words he uses are those he learned by rote, having heard his own parents mutter, mumble or scream at them several thousand times.

Actually it is fair to suggest that what's the matter with kids today, or at least some kids today, is their parents. Kids have it pretty tough these days, now that, in some quarters of our society, they have moved into the realm of fashionable appliances, rather like espresso machines and Cuisinarts.

Among the yuppies, the habit is to lead a career-oriented and self-indulgent life for as long as possible as a reward or vacation following the enormous effort involved in getting through college. (Such a hassle!) Then, the condo and the summer place having been bought, the designer furniture having been distributed through the rooms and the kitchen enlarged to accommodate a restaurant range, the BMW or two having been thoroughly shown off, the practice is to "get into" parenthood. Children afford additional ways to express wealth, as through strollers that cost several hundred dollars, designer-label toddlers' outfits and private schooling at all levels.

Single parenthood is often unavoidable for victims of

divorce, but it has become fashionable for the unmarried. Some career women in need of a fresh crisis decide they must have a child—the last, the final accomplishment—to prove to themselves and the world that they are complete women. And what happens to the child? Like the children of couples who insist on two careers and two incomes, even when they don't need them, the child is sent off to a day-care center run by strangers.

It is a little easier for the child if his parent (or parents) has real money—he is then turned over to the care of his personal nanny. It isn't easy for the parents, though. Recently *The New York Times* reported feelingly on the trials of career women on the city's Upper East Side: they were often deeply hurt, on retrieving their children from the nannies, to learn that they had taken their first steps or said their first words in the presence of strangers. The moneyed mothers told the reporter they felt cheated out of those special landmark moments. But it wasn't as if they regretted having dumped the kid and gone to work. No—what they wanted was for the nannies not to tell them.

Homosexual and lesbian parenthood has also become something of a rage. Somewhere in California recently, a lesbian couple had a child by artificial insemination. Semen was procured from somewhere, and the operation was performed at home, the implanting device being a turkey baster.

So it isn't always a picnic being a kid, something you may want to keep in mind for the duration of this section.

My God! You Mean Half of the Next Generation Will Want to Join the Young Americans for Freedom?

According to a survey published by the Search Institute, American youth has other things on its mind besides world peace, famine in Africa and nuclear devastation.

Of 8,000 kids between the ages of 10 and 14, the survey said, 56% were seriously concerned about their grades, 53% about their looks and 48% about their personal popularity.

Only 38% worried about hunger in America, and 36%

were concerned about the level of violence in this country—
hardly much more than the percentage concerned with
drugs and alcohol. But still, a lot more than those (25%)
who spent much time worrying about nuclear war.

Add the Word *Desperate* and You've Got Title That Will Sell!

Haig Bagerdijan published a calendar entitled "The
Men of Harvard Law School," of which he was, in fact,
one. "We wanted to change the image of the Harvard
man," Bagerdijan said.

In any case, he was one of those who posed for the
calendar. He was pictured pouring a glass of wine while
wearing a dressing gown, gold jewelry and the sultriest
look he could pull together.

You Mean You Didn't Realize It Was a Symbolic Demand for World Peace and Nuclear Disarmament?

An Indiana university may reduce its enrollment by
about eighty students all at once.

The students were charged with participating in a "Nude
Olympics," in which they ran naked about the campus.
The students were charged with breaking the university's
rules against lewd, indecent or obscene conduct and im-
peding order and discipline.

How Could You Fail to Spot the Symbolic Reference to the Famine in Etthiopia?

Time was when, even in the Midwest, American students protested, demonstrated and marched for causes
important enough to remember the next day. Many were
expelled, some were arrested, and four at Kent State
University in Ohio, were murdered by the National Guard.

The tradition of protest continues in the Midwest. *The
Wall Street Journal* reported that Notre Dame was wracked
by a protest in its south dining hall. Protesters blocked
the cafeteria's serving aisle when they learned that their
favorite breakfast cereal, Cap'n Crunch, had disappeared

from the menu. Order was restored when university officials promised fresh supplies of Cap'n Crunch as soon as possible.

On the Other Hand, Cap'n Crunch Is Something Some People Can Live Without

Nikki Sixx, a member of the rock group Motley Crüe, was quoted in a press release as explaining the facts of life to the establishment: "We're the American youth. And youth is about sex, drugs, pizza and more sex."

Come on! At Least They're Not Smoking in the Johns!

In Arkansas, a survey of 125 kindergarteners showed that one quarter of them had at least tried chewing tobacco. A similar study in Ohio showed that 30% of rural children between fourth and twelfth grades had also tried chewing tobacco.

Dr. John Bonaguro of Ohio State University observed that children in those grades were not old enough to buy tobacco and concluded that they must be getting it from their families.

Just How Worried About Their Looks and Popularity Are They?

In Grosse Pointe, Michigan, a 15-year-old boy tried to get his braces removed with the help of a .45 automatic.

The boy selected a dentist's office at random and asked to see a dentist. He said he wanted his braces removed, and when the dentist refused to do so without parental permission, the boy pulled a gun. "Would this make you take my bands off?" he asked. "Yes, it would," the dentist replied.

The boy was put into a dental chair, and the dentist tried to stall for time. He noted that the boy was committing a crime, but the boy said he didn't care about going to jail "as long as I can have my bands off." The dentist managed to alert his staff and continued stalling, slowly removing some of the braces while the boy kept the pistol, loaded and cocked, in his lap.

When the police arrived, they had the dentist paged to get him out of danger, then rushed the room. The boy was bent over the spit sink when the cops rushed the room, but he reacted quickly, getting off two shots before he was overwhelmed.

Short Criminal Careers

No. 1

According to police, a 17-year-old boy, successful at robbing a house and a gas station, dreamed of greater things.

"Mom," he allegedly said, "I want to do a bank."

Authorities say his stepmother apparently approved of the boy's desire to get ahead in his career, and made sure that he had the necessary holdup note, helpfully cutting letters from newspaper headlines and gluing them into a legible demand for money.

Then, while mother waited at home, he drove the family car to the local savings and loan, showed a teller his note and gun, and made off with $1,500.

Nevertheless, police caught up with the thief and his mom a little while later, at which time they had questions about the burglary and gas station robbery too.

No. 2

Two 9-year-old boys in California decided to burglarize a home and both ended up in police custody, but not before one of them wound up stuck in the house's chimney.

Firemen spent three hours rescuing the boy, which required a jackhammer assault to break open the back wall of the chimney from outside the house. Hauled out of the chimney, the boy told his rescuers, "Don't tell my mother."

No. 3

Three teenage crooks failed to hold up a South Bronx pizzeria by being more dangerous to themselves than to their victim.

The three entered a pizzeria at 10111 Ogden Avenue shortly after noon one day and announced their intentions to the proprietor. One of the three waited outside, another held a gun in front of the counter, and the third went behind the counter to rifle the register.

The one who opened the register pulled out the cash drawer and handed it across the counter to his confederate, who then dropped his gun, which went off and shot him in the leg.

The gang then fled—two running, one limping—but paused while the gunman went back to the pizzeria to retrieve his gun, which he had understandably left behind. The trio resumed their escape, but were nailed by police three blocks away.

So Wet

A West Philadelphia teenager threw himself into the swirling black waters of Cobbs Creek in an attempt to determine whether the glue on his new pair of false sideburns was waterproof.

He drowned.

The youth's two friends, who accompanied him, tried to talk him out of his experiment, reminding him that he could not swim, but they failed. Then they tried to talk him into diving into a shallow portion of the creek but failed in that, too, and the boy then dived off a concrete wall into sixteen feet of water. The friends also tried to rescue him when he surfaced, floundering desperately, but they failed again.

Police recovered the body half an hour later. The left sideburn was missing.

Maybe It Was Revenge for
All Those Socks and Mittens

A neighborhood Santa Claus who arrived by helicopter at a shopping center was greeted by a howling mob of 600 kids who knocked him down and stole his bag of toys.

Lee Garen, of Fort Lauderdale, Florida, said la..., "I thought I was going to be killed." Garen, who had to be rescued by police, added "They broke the barriers and rushed me. I got knocked to the ground and couldn't even move."

Garen said that at least one of the kids "was about fourteen, and he should have known better. I did manage to kick him in the knee."

VIII.

THERE'S NO BUSINESS LIKE SHOW BUSINESS

"We had faces then!" was the anguished cry of the faded screen star in the movie *Sunset Boulevard*. And that was about thirty-five years ago. Hollywood used to love to make movies about how horrible Hollywood was. After a while, seeing all those movies about the awfulness of the place but noticing that no one ever cleared out of his own free will, one came to the conclusion that all those movies were being made to discourage others from discovering the secret.

But as the years passed, Hollywood truly did become awful—full of cocaine and big deals made by little people; marked by a complete disappearance of glamour and excitement, which are, after all, what we are paying for. If they remade *Sunset Boulevard* today, they would have to rewrite the line to say, "We had faces then—and the faces had brains behind them!" Also, occasionally, taste and charm, or at least smart studio people who would part with a buck to make it look that way.

Today we have Richard Gere getting arrested for pissing in the street.

A note to readers of tender organizational sensibilities: Some of you may be outraged at finding the likes of tabloids and TV newscasts in the show-business chapter. I agree that it's an uncomfortable fit, but surely you wouldn't have me put them under journalism?

A Penny for Your Thoughts, or You Get What You Pay For

In 1927, as now, acting instructors could be hard on young hopefuls with big ambitions, and an instructor at the John Murray Anderson Drama School didn't hold anything back when he said, "Try another profession. *Any* other profession" to a struggling young actress who happened to turn into Lucille Ball.

Gimme a Little Kiss, Will Ya, Huh?

One of the bigger stories of 1985 was Cathleen Crowell Webb's withdrawal of her rape accusation against Gary Dotson, who had been convicted on her evidence and had spent six years in jail.

Since married, moved elsewhere and born again, Mrs. Webb suffered from a guilty conscience and finally found the strength to admit that she had lied in court; that she had, in fact, framed Gary because she feared she was pregnant by her boyfriend at that time and needed a scapegoat.

The case fell like a bombshell into the already contentious area of rape, which is a crime that often involves a great deal of insensitivity and unkindness toward the victim by authorities, family and friends. More important, rape cases are often a matter of "my word against yours" when there are no witnesses, making prosecution difficult.

Interviewing Dotson and Webb on the *CBS Morning News,* cohost Phyllis George got past all that to focus on her real interest, reported the New York *Daily News.* As the interview ended, she suggested to Dotson and Mrs. Webb, "How about a hug!" Somewhat more aware than George that their lives were not a situation comedy, Dotson and Webb simply stared at her.

On Other Pulitzer Mornings . . .

Beaming up brightly from Rio de Janeiro, the *New York Post* reported, Jane Pauley perked up the *Today Show* audience one morning by talking with Fernando Gabeira, a former terrorist involved in the 1969 kidnapping of a U.S. ambassador.

Pauley explained that Gabeira had been granted amnesty by Brazil but that he was "unfortunately not yet welcome in the U.S."

She did not explain why it was unfortunate that he had not been officially excused for helping to abduct Ambassador C. Burke Elbrick, then 61, who was beaten and threatened with death for three days until Brazil traded his freedom for releasing fifteen political prisoners. Possibly she considered the explanation self-evident.

Pauley was equally sensitive in 1979, during the height of the hostage drama in Iran.

After a live "interview" with supposed "leaders" of the Iranians holding American citizens hostage had become nothing more enlightening that fifteen minutes of incoherent ravings and accusations, Pauley broke for a commercial with a winsome smile, saying, "Well! I wonder how you say, 'We'll be back in a moment' in Farsi."

And Starring, Not Necessarily in any Particular Order . . .

The following names have turned up in the credits of movies and television programs down through the years.

Arthur Space
Peanuts Brown
Paul Savior
Harold Oblong
Jon Cypher
Khigh Alx Dhiegh
Beverly Hills
Candy Barr
Thalmas Rasulala
Hersha Parady
Dodo Denny
Maggie Malooly
Gary Cashdollar
Carolyn Stellar
Noble Willingham
Rhodes Reason
Eric Christmas
Sierra Bandit
Thaao Penghlis
Alan Fudge
Catherine Bacon
Roger Pancake
Paul Pepper
Alice Lemon

Marcus J. Grapes
Christopher Wines
Christina Pickles
Whitman Mayo
Mary Fickett
Joanna Pang
Steven T. Blood
Ted Noose
Danny Butch
John Orchard
D'Mitch Davis
Marjorie Battles
Fuddle Bagley
Bob Random
Ninette Bravo
Gordon Jump
Audrey Totter
Wonderful Smith
Richard Bull
X Brands
Chu Chu Mulave
Dennis Fimple
Hilly Hicks
Kaz Garas

Bucklind Beery
Patience Cleveland
Stymie Beard
Joanne Nail
Joy Bang
Julie Licker
Dawn Biglay
Snag Werris
Ben Piazza
Electra Gailas Fair
Brenda Venus
Chuck Couch
East Carlo
Kaye "Ding" Dingle
Fred Smoot
Linda Sublette
Kathleen Gackle

William Wintersole
Than Wyenn
Duncan Gamble
Erica Petal
Suzanne LaCock
Leslie Aquavivi
Rusty Blitz
Pat Tidy
Bill Dearth
Claire Touchstone
Meeno Peluce
Astride Lance
Sandra Ego
John Yesno
Clare Nono
Eddie Donno

Enter Right Away!

Win a wondrous trip to Australia. Visit the sun-drenched continent across the globe, from Sydney to Surfers Paradise!—Promotional advertisement, the *New York Post*, March 4, 1985.

Shark Eats Woman

Adelaide, Australia—A twenty-foot Great White Shark attacked and killed a woman yesterday while her three children and other bathers watched in horror—News item, same paper, same date, same edition.

They Smile When They Are Low

According to theater lore, it is bad luck to wish a performer good luck. Therefore the friends of Cheryl Giannini, who was about to open at the American Place Theater in *I'm Not Rappaport*, dutifully wished her the traditional "Break a leg!"

And, in dance class, that is exactly what she did, putting herself out of the show for two months.

Film At 11!

Two cameramen for a TV station in Anniston, Alabama, warmed up their equipment and waited attentively but otherwise did nothing while a distraught unemployed man doused himself with lighter fluid and set himself on fire.

Don't We Have Jerry Falwell for That?

Admittedly, 1985 was a bad year, what with unceasing air disasters, unbridled terrorism, AIDS, a catastrophic earthquake in Mexico, and famine in Africa. *News 4 New York*, the local New York newscast of WNBC-TV tried to come to grips with it all in a special report entitled, "Is God Punishing Us?"

Taking It Off, Putting Us On

Some strippers have a little imagination and most don't. The more fondly remembered are the former, some of whose noms de peel include Candy Barr, Tempest Storm, Linda Hop (a former Playboy Bunny) and the stirringly named Helen Bedd.

A somewhat frayed joint in Philadelphia, the Troc, apparently had only one stripper, who was pushed out into the colored spotlights under a different name each week. The name was often made up to attract the celebrants of the various conventions that would blow into town, but as Philly tended to attract your B-list conventions, the Troc's stripper was often reduced to luring members of the Amalgamated Floor Layers Union under the name of Lynn Oleum.

She and the Troc did top themselves when a photoengravers' convention turned up. The Troc's ads beat the drums for "Rhoda Gravure—the Printer's Devil."

And a Fun Guy at Parties Too!

People, the magazine that whenever possible puts dead people on its cover, and that ran such stop-press cover blurbs as:

> Princess Michael: a Nazi
> skeleton in the closet

and
John Lennon: his
sister's exclusive story

outdid itself with its "special double issue" looking back on 1985.

Right there on the cover, ballyhooed as one of the Twenty-five Most Intriguing Celebrities of 1985 was—hey! —Josef Mengele!

For those inclined to disbelieve their eyes, the contents page continued: "Josef Mengele is bagged at last: His bones are wrapped in plastic and stored in a Brazilian safe."

The three-page story, which opened with a life-size photo of Mengele's skull, included a facsimile autograph and photos of Mengele, one in his Waffen SS uniform and another taken near the end of his life, in Brazil. In the latter he is seen giving the children of his protectors "a ride in a canoe he had built himself."

The story added such details as Mengele's devotion to gardening and the fact that because there are no fingerprints, X rays or dental records, "Israel, pointedly, has not yet closed its files on Josef Mengele," a deft hint at why, to *People*, at least, Auschwitz's Angel of Death remains "intriguing" after all these years.

IX.

LOOKIN' FOR LOVE IN ALL THE WRONG PLACES

So far we have been able to introduce each section of this book with the few paragraphs of insightful commentary or witty remarks. Seminal remarks would seem to be required in this particular chapter, but almost anything at all is going to be difficult to manage here. We are dealing with extremes that don't leave room for much further comment.

Below we describe the misadventures of some amorous fellows who came to grief at the hands of a legal system not noted for its sentiment. Whatever you think of their acts, consider that they were all for love, and that what they did, or were accused of doing, may well have been less objectionable than singles bars and surely no worse than placing, or responding to, personal ads.

My Kingdom, Or Something Like That, For A Horse

According to a local newspaper report, a man from Southern California was arrested and convicted of trespassing at a stable and of sexually assaulting a Shetland pony. The trial took two days, and the highlight of the proceedings came when the prosecution took the jury out into the courthouse parking lot to meet the equine victim.

According to a spokesman, the purpose of the visit was to allow the jurors to see the size of the pony, so they could decide for themselves whether the defendant could actually have engaged in a sexual act with it. A verdict of guilty was handed in soon afterward.

Soooooeeee, Pig, My Darling!

A student at a California technical college who allegedly raped a pig was arrested for sexual assault on an animal.

The assault, which took place at the university's Swine Unit, was witnessed by a group of students and an instructor who were present to prepare for a livestock show.

Charged with a misdemeanor, the student was released on his own recognizance after promising in writing to show up for arraignment. Prosecution of the student would be "really tough," said the teacher afterward. "In fact, the guy's back in class." Dodson added that his principal concern was that "I'd like the word to get out that it's bizarre behavior and we don't want it."

The Feathers Really Flew

According to a spokesman for a police department on Long Island, a 22-year-old man from a nearby town was arrested by police and charged with burglary and sexual misconduct.

The spokesman said the police had received a call reporting a break-in at a local duck farm and responded immediately. But by the time the cops arrived, the farm's owner had already captured the intruder, who had been found, with one or more ducks, in one of the farm offices.

The charge of sexual misconduct, described by police as unusual under the circumstances, was lodged after they heard a report from the farm's owner and made an inspection of the physical evidence. "It was him and the ducks," said the police. "Supposedly he was quite involved."

X.
FOODS THAT KILL

Oh, you probably think this is another hysterical outburst by some granola-crazed fanatic who reads *Prevention* magazine. (*Prevention* is the magazine that once published a letter saying people no longer have to cook their pork well done and also warned against eating clams and oysters because you can't tell whether they have defecated before they were harvested.)

No. None of that stuff. This is a warning about real foods that really kill. Nobody needs to be told anymore that too much fat is bad, that too much lean is bad, that too much, period, is bad. Rich foods lead to heart disease, obesity and gout. Too little leads to anorexia. Trying to have the former and the latter at the same time leads people to excuse themselves from their host's table and sneak off to the bathroom, where they shove their fingers down their throats and vomit into the toilet bowl (the Fonda girl, Queen Jane of Bulimia, confessed to same as a way of publicizing her commercial health programs, and made a bundle out of it).

It's food en masse and in general that needs to be watched. Maybe it's not safe to walk into an apple orchard when the trees are in full fruit. What if it fell on you—a lot of it, I mean? All those apples! Heavy. Suppose you went into a field where the corn was as high as an elephant's eye. You might never come out again. No one could see you in there. They wouldn't find your bones until after harvest. Didn't you ever get the feeling, while picking blackberries, that all those long, willowy canes with all those sharp thorns seemed to have a genius for stabbing you? That they had minds of their own, so to speak?

Yeah. Now you see what I'm driving at. The facts speak for themselves. . . .

Maritime Enterprises Been Berry, Berry Good to Me

In Bedford, Massachusetts, 47-year-old Joseph Frois was minding his own business at the plant of Maritime Enterprises, a packer of frozen cranberries. One of his jobs was to check the machinery (sort of a giant vacuum cleaner) that sucked frozen cranberries out of the freezer rooms for processing and packaging.

In November 1985, only two weeks before Thanksgiving, he climbed onto a ten-foot mountain of frozen cranberries to check the machinery—and disappeared.

"You can walk on the berries," said David Lizotte, a police spokesman, "but he must have hit a soft spot." Frois sank into the mound of berries over his head and suffocated. Fellow workers realized what had happened only after one of them spotted Frois's hand sticking out of the pile of frozen berries.

Plant workers trying to rescue Frois were soon aided by a fire department rescue team, but he had been buried for more than an hour, and by the time he was dug out, it was too late.

Wheat—The TNT of Plants

An explosion and fire at a grain elevator in a South Dakota town blew up a 100-foot grain elevator, killed three people and jeopardized the town's economic base. Four people were injured.

A spokesman said the elevator would have to be "restructured" (i.e., rebuilt; they are no slouches for jargon in the Dakotas) soon, lest the population face "a whole lot of hurt."

Investigators could not pinpoint the cause of the explosion, but there were dark hints about grain dust, which, when suspended in air, can explode.

Nowhere Is "Too Safe"

Ingrid Kerztin, 17, who may have been seeking to escape citrus menaces in her native West Germany, was killed while vacationing in Tarragona, Spain, drowned in an Indian River of oranges.

A spokesman for Spain's Civil Guard said Kerztin had been walking along a national highway, doubtless free of care, when the oranges caught up with her. A fruit truck driving along the highway swerved suddenly and violently to avoid a traffic accident with cars parked in the left-turn lane. Although the truck managed to avoid the cars, it went off the road. As it did so, it capsized, spilling sixteen tons of oranges onto young Ingrid. Police responded quickly, but when she was dug out an hour later, she was dead.

Vats—A Menacing Subspecies

No. 1

Perhaps it was a case of the masses rising up to slay those who exploit them. On the other hand, it might have been just another senseless death. In any case, Downingtown, Pennsylvania, was shocked when a worker at the local Pepperidge Farm plant was killed in a vat of chocolate.

Robert C. Hershey, 37, a native of nearby Coatesville, fell into the vat when he apparently removed its cover for obscure reasons. The local rescue squad had to cut their way through the vat's steel side to pull his heavily coated body out of its rich, dark tomb.

No. 2

Nazar Zia, 28, died in a vat of gravy in Warren, Michigan. Zia, who resided in nearby Royal Oak, was an employee of Elias Brothers, which operates a chain of restaurants in the Detroit area. The facility in which Zia worked was the company's commissary, which prepares bulk gravy for several Elias Brothers restaurants.

No. 3

A Country Pride Foods plant in El Dorado, Arkansas, was the scene of two deaths in a vat of chopped chicken.

Plant worker Jewell Thompson, 50, had donned a gas mask and climbed down into the vat to unclog a valve, but he started to climb back out when he apparently detected ammonia fumes, despite his mask. He had gotten to within a foot of the top, police said, when he fell back in. After calling for help, 56-year-old Willie Earl White went to Thompson's aid, only to be overcome by the fumes himself.

No. 4

In Toronto, a man was killed when he fell headfirst into a vat of pizza dough.

Beyond Food—The Vat Menace Spreads

In Deer Park, New York, Robert Stevens, 46, died at the plant of Germaine Monteil Cosmetics when a vat of molten lipstick fell over on him.

Man Suffocated By Potatoes

One man was killed and another injured in Wiggins, Colorado, when the support beams in a farm warehouse failed and unleashed an avalanche of potatoes on the two men.

According to Morgan County Coroner F. D. Joliffe, the two men were trying to shore up the beams when the accident occurred.

Scott Tidemann, 32, was rescued, but Henry Ruppel, Jr., 39, of Fort Morgan, was buried under five feet of spuds, and suffocated before he could be dug out.

XI.
FOODS THAT HARM

Some foods don't actually kill but merely assault, though actually we have no idea whether the attacks have more serious intent or are intended as warnings or expressions of annoyance or resentment of some obscure kind. In any case, don't let your guard down.

Likely Story

An Australian man thought he was safe enough—he was playing golf out in the open, where potential enemies would have little cover, and the golf course was several miles from the ocean.

Nevertheless, in the middle of his round he was slammed squarely over the head by a large fish.

The piscatorial assailant weighed one and a half pounds and was identified as a mullet. Bystanders speculated that the fish might have been accidentally dropped by an eagle or other large bird.

Just a Squeeze of Lime, Thanks

An 18-year-old woman who vacationed at a popular resort returned home with more than memories. She had a painful rash on her thighs, bad enough to require medical attention.

Her doctor examined the woman and reported that she had red rashes "with scalloped borders . . . present on the mid-medial thighs." Seeking the cause of the rash, Dr. White questioned the woman, who said that at the resort she had participated in a drinking game in which people rolled limes between their thighs. It was concluded that the rash may have been caused by the limes, which contain citric acid in their rinds.

Innocent Spaghetti—or Evil Punji Stick?

A Michigan housewife wound up in the hospital after trying to clean her kitchen sink.

She was stabbed by a shard of dried pasta.

The nasty noodle was one of the remnants of some soup her husband had left in the sink the day before. While lying in the sink the limp noodle dried out, regaining its dangerous sharpness and rigidity. Reaching into the sink, she struck the noodle at an unfortunate angle, and the pasta pierced her beneath her fingernail. The pain increased later as the noodle, absorbing blood, began to swell. By the next morning the pain was so great that she had to be taken to the hospital, where half her fingernail had to be cut off before the noodle could be removed.

In addition to the pain and expense, the woman suffered the indignity of "funny looks" from other patients when the admitting nurse called out, "Okay, who's the lady with the noodle in her finger?"

XII.

MILITARY AFFAIRS AND THE MILITARY MIND

When we are dealing with the military, we are dealing with war—past, present or future—and although it is always easy to laugh at the military (as in "Military justice is to justice as military music is to music"), it is unwise to take lightly a force that has shaped civilizations (and sometimes ended them) ever since man learned to turn undisciplined fits of temper into organized forces trained and armed for defense and conquest.

And we're also unfair, unless we recognize that even the military is not monolithic, all of a piece; we were plenty glad to have the military in World War II.

Georges Clemenceau's remark that "War is much too serious a matter to be entrusted to the military" is apt enough at times, but not all times. The military's masters—politicians—have made their own muddles. Allied political leaders gave away a good deal of what the military won in World War II. American politicians prevented victory in Korea and guaranteed failure in Vietnam. For these *hommages* to Clemenceau a high price was paid, and it was soldiers who paid it.

There were other occasions as well. In 1588, the Duke of Medina Sidonia tried to talk Philip II out of putting him in command of the Spanish Armada. "My health is bad, and from my experience of the water I know that I am always seasick," he wrote to his king. "The commander of such a vast, vitally important expedition ought to understand navigation and naval warfare; I know nothing of either. If you send me, depend upon it, I shall have a bad account to render of my trust."

Nevertheless, the military in general is the most minutely organized and thoroughly ossified of hierarchies, which businessmen unwittingly acknowledge when they ape its terminology, as when they refer to their sales forces as "shock troops" and their maintenance and re- pair services as "field support units."

Apologists sometimes like to talk of war as chess in flesh-and-blood form, because chess is abstract warfare played on a board. But after that the analogy falls to pieces. Chess is a contest of strategy brought to its con- clusion by a flash of insight. War is a series of blunders that turns on luck. A good example is the Battle of Midway, the greatest modern naval battle of this century, which was the beginning of the end for the Japanese military in the Pacific.

Between wars it is easy to see the military's flaws. A desk-bound soldier-functionary is wrongly passed a docu- ment he shouldn't see; he reads it, initials it, and passes it on. His commander spots the error and sends the docu- ment back, telling him to erase his initials and initial his erasure. Spotting such lunacy is easier still when prepar- ing for a war we know must not happen. The military seems to be involved mostly in keeping its job and look- ing busy by ordering weapons that need not work very well because no one believes they will be used. The idea seems to be to spend as much money as possible this year to establish a floor for next year's budget.

It may be a crude natural defense mechanism: When warfare becomes too dangerous, the military unwittingly finds itself incapable of fighting. In the face of an increas- ingly edgy nuclear defense system—one that twice put the nation on full alert in 1980 when a computer chip worth forty-six cents went on the fritz—that may not be enough.

My, How the Money Rolls Out

Congressman John R. Kasich, Sen. William Proxmire, and others have discovered that:

- An ordinary machine screw used in the Minuteman II missile cost $1.08 in 1982 and $36.77 a year later.
- A circuit-card assembly for the missile's guidance system cost $234.05 in 1982 but rose to $1,111.75 by 1984.

- An electrical plug for the FB-111 aircraft that cost $7.99 in 1982 cost $726.86 by 1983.
- The Navy paid $110 for electrical diodes that whole-sale for four cents apiece. Even at retail, the same diodes cost only 99 cents for a packet of ten at Radio Shack.
- A plastic knob used on the handle of the cockpit-release lever of the Navy's A-7 fighter-bomber cost $37.25. That was in 1979. By 1983, each knob cost $400.

And the list goes on. Sixty-seven-cent bolts cost the military $17.59; hexagonal nuts worth 13 cents at a hardware store cost $2,043; a circuit breaker available in stores at $3.64 cost the Pentagon $2,543; a ten-foot aluminum ladder worth maybe $100 cost $1,676; $100 piston rings fetched $1,130.

A sofa installed in the officers' wardroom of a Navy destroyer cost $18,000.

The Air Force was buying coffee makers for more than $7,000 each. When investigators protested, the Air Force said the price was justified because the coffee makers were built to such high standards that they would keep on working even after a crash so violent that all the crew members were killed.

Perhaps the most imaginative example of overpricing is the Air Force's stool-leg cap—a little nylon glider that goes on the end of the leg of a stool. These are, for ordinary purchasers, so cheap that hardware stores don't even bother to sell them separately. They come in little packs of four for about 79 cents. The Pentagon buys them for $1,118.26. Each.

Battlefield Advances

No. 1: The Gamma Goat

The army wanted an updated version of its famous Jeep—a tough, hardworking little vehicle capable of off-road or cross-country travel. Ling-Temco-Vought responded with a light amphibious vehicle that could be dropped by parachute; it was called the Gamma Goat.

By the time the army was finished fine-tuning its requirements—which means adding to them—development costs rose from $69 million to $439 million. The Goat grew too—it weighed seven and a half tons and was completed three years behind schedule. Brigadier General Vincent Ellis pronounced himself pleased. Senator Proxmire felt otherwise: "You have a program that is three years late. You have a truck that is three times heavier than it was supposed to be and does not have a bigger payload, and one that is twice as expensive as the original estimate. It seems to me that you are an easy man to please."

No. 2: Adventures in Aluminum

Navy ships are now so loaded down with advanced electronic equipment that they would be unstable at sea unless lightened topside. The Navy's solution was to use aluminum superstructures, which also cut costs.

The Navy was slow to realize that aluminum burns. One of its new cruisers, the *Belknap*, caught fire after a collision with the aircraft carrier *John F. Kennedy* in 1975. The Belknap burned to the waterline. Rebuilding it took more than four years.

The British Navy learned a similar lesson in the invasion of the Falkland Islands. A British destroyer of largely aluminum superstructure was struck by a missile; it went up like a Roman candle.

No. 3: The Bradley Fighting Vehicle

The inflammability of aluminum was something the Army missed too. Its Bradley Fighting Vehicle, an armed and armored personnel carrier, uses aluminum extensively. The Army plans to buy nearly 7,000 of them for more than $13 billion, even though a $2 M-42 grenade can turn a Bradley into a fireball (ironically, the vehicle is named after World War II General Omar Bradley, who was beloved of his troops because he cared about their comfort and their lives).

The Army rejected an early version of the Bradley as being too expensive but eventually accepted a model that cost twice as much. By 1982, Bradleys cost nearly $2 million apiece. The Bradley gets two miles to the gallon and is so large that it cannot be loaded aboard a C-141 transport plane without being partly dismantled. Under some circumstances the driver can't see where he's going, and when the flotation device was field-tested, the vehicle sank. It can't fire its missiles without first coming to a dead stop, and the launcher takes more than two minutes to load. About 9 feet tall, it will be so visible on the battlefield that it might as well wear a sign that reads, KICK ME. Not entirely deaf to complaints, the Army is trying to find a way to redesign the Bradley, and development continues. Recently, however, the Army has been accused of redesigning its tests to ensure that the Bradley passes them. For example, a flammability test was rigged by packing the vehicle with cans of water. The Army persists with the Bradley, even though all that try to use their flotation devices must, by regulation, be accompanied by rescue teams in lifeboats.

No 4: The Sergeant York

In the 1970s, the Army began its program to develop the Sergeant York, a self-propelled antiaircraft gun intended to give battlefield protection to troops and tanks against low-flying planes and helicopters. The Army chose General Dynamics and Ford Aerospace and gave them two years to produce prototypes. In 1981, the Army chose Ford's.

The Sergeant York was a tank chassis carrying radar-directed guns. The Army planned to buy more than 600 for a total of $4.8 billion. The Sergeant York failed its first tests and then its second tests. It refused to start in cold weather and broke down in hot weather. The guns jammed repeatedly, and the radar system was unable to distinguish between legitimate targets and buildings or bushes. New tests were ordered in 1985, and the Sergeant York failed again—its firing range of two and a half miles was three quarters of a mile short of requirements. (The Sergeant York was named for a World War I hero famed for his marksmanship.)

At the end of 1985, Defense Secretary Caspar Weinberger ordered the program killed—$1.8 billion had already been spent—and the 65 Sergeant Yorks delivered to the Army were to be dismantled and scrapped.

No. 5: The M16 Rifle

The infantryman has the toughest job in the military and, in one sense, the most important. His job is to capture territory. Targets may be rendered uninhabitable and reduced to rubble, but they aren't captured until they are occupied, and it is the infantry that occupies them. Given that, one would think the infantry would at least be supplied with a reliable weapon.

Not in the U.S. Army, as countless GIs in Vietnam found out. M16 rifles were so unreliable that soldiers threw them away whenever they could lay their hands on captured Viet Cong weapons. At the same time, the VC soon learned that abandoned M16s were hazardous to their health and stopped picking them up on the battlefield.

After Korea, the Army wanted a rifle capable of fully automatic fire—machine-gun fire—and it began to develop the M14. The M14 looked much like the famous M1 of World War II, but there were important differences. It was a lot heavier, larger and more complicated, and in fully-automatic fire, it was uncontrollable and dangerous.

The M16 was a fresh approach: light, small, relatively cheap, easy to maintain and build, but capable of full- and semiautomatic fire while still being easy to control. It came from outside the Army establishment, which was a strike against it. It also fired a small, light, 5.6-mm. cartridge that was significantly smaller than the 30-caliber round the Army had used for decades—another strike. The Army thought the new little bullet was practically unmanly.

But with the Vietnam War heating up and the M14 utterly unsuitable, the Army was forced to adopt the outlander M16, which was perfect for jungle fighting. To show who was boss, and to cover its embarrassment over the M14 debacle, the army demanded changes in the M16. It demanded, for example, that the M16 be capable of firing at and hitting targets 850 yards away—something only telescope-equipped snipers did in World War II and no one could do in jungle warfare, it not being possible to see that far.

The Army demanded and got so many alterations and adjustments that by the time the M16 went to war, it wasn't any good anymore. It jammed repeatedly; required constant, finicky cleaning; and then jammed some more. Soldiers began writing home to complain to their congressmen and to their families. The press picked up the story, and after a lot of asses were covered, the necessary improvements were finally made—mostly by undoing the Army's alterations and going back to the original design. All it cost was a few G.I.'s lives.

No. 6: The C-5A Galaxy

The C-5A Galaxy, the world's largest aircraft, was conceived by the Pentagon as the King Kong of transport planes—it was to have a capacity of 200 tons. Lockheed Aircraft agreed to build them for $29.5 million each.

By the time the military got through with its fine-tuning, the Galaxy was so heavy it could no longer meet its original landing-strip limits for takeoff and landing. It also cost twice the original price.

At the first official flight, one of its wheels fell off. But all in all, it worked, and was accepted for service. An Air Force general later said he was pleased with the C-5A. Then he added, "Having the wings fall off at eight thousand hours is a problem."

Somewhere in the middle of this boondoggle, a quiet, bespectacled Air Force financial officer began asking questions and complaining about unrestrained cost overruns. The Air Force transferred him out of the C-5A program, then pushed him off into a dark corner where he did no useful work at all. Finally, he was fired. The reason, the Air Force said, was to save money.

Like Two Old Prizefighters Meeting Years After the Big Bout

In 1959, Colonel Paul Tibbetts, the pilot of *Enola Gay*, the B-29 that dropped the first atomic bomb, met Mitsuo Fuchida, who led the Japanese air attack on Pearl Harbor. As Tibbetts recalled their conversation he said to Fuchida, "Boy, you sure took us by surprise," to which Fuchida replied, "You didn't do too bad yourself."

Where Do You Suppose They Sent the Battleship?

According to the Colorado Springs *Gazette-Telegraph*, an Army clerk at Fort Carson, Colorado, wanted a $6.04 light bulb, and dutifully punched a long series of numbers into his computer.

A week later the clerk was sent an item that cost more

than $28,000. It was an anchor that weighed 14,500 pounds, used for parking battleships. It was left at a shipping yard for the clerk to pick up.

After some checking it was realized that the clerk, who wanted a light bulb inventoried under number 2040-00-368-4972, had incorrectly typed a digit. He had inadvertently ordered item #2040-00-368-4772, which is the stock number for an "anchor, marine fluke."

At the Naval Supply Center, which filled the clerk's order, no one thought to ask why the Army would want a seven-ton anchor in the middle of Colorado.

News From Our Allies

No. 1

British soldiers on the Isle of Man had been told that they must salute the local fairies.

The Isle of Man, which lies between Great Britain and Ireland, has a tradition that fairies, pixies, elves and other little beings live beneath a bridge on the road between Douglas and Castletown. Local residents always raise their caps in salute to the fairies, and the soldiers have been ordered to salute also. According to an official spokesman, "The British Army respects local customs."

No. 2

Every commissioned officer is promoted directly from the ranks—there's nothing except sheer ability to stop you achieving a high position.—Advertisement for the New Zealand armed forces in the *Auckland Star*.

No. 3

Canada's armed forces held their largest field exercises in decades last year, and they threw into the field every tank in their arsenal. There were eighteen of them.

The Canadian Navy, the world's third largest in World War II, is today only a little larger than Ecuador's. It has twenty-three elderly steam-powered destroyers and frigates, many of which are more or less permanently in reserve with cracks in their boilers and hulls. Its two antiquated diesel submarines of World War II design are used as the targets in antisubmarine drills. (An amusement park at a shopping mall in Edmonton, hundreds of miles from the nearest ocean, has four submarines that it uses to give customers rides in its aquarium.)

Consequently there are also doubts, politely raised from time to time, about Canada's ability to carry out its NATO obligations.

A spokesman for Canada's defense department agreed with critics that their Navy was in "the most deplorable state of all." As for its NATO responsibilities, he said, "We can put the required number of ships in the field, and some of them are able to protect themselves."

Testing ... Testing

At one of its Southern bases the Air Force has a testing program designed to help it design stronger cockpit canopies, which can shatter when planes are struck by birds in flight.

The testing is centered on what has come to be known as the Perdue Missile, for chicken entrepreneur Frank Perdue. The missile is actually a converted cannon used to fire dead chickens at grounded aircraft at 700 m.p.h.

That sounds messy enough, but the Defense Department wanted to go a step further by opening a Wound Laboratory, which would test the effect of weapons by shooting dogs under controlled conditions.

XIII.
MARRIAGE AND ITS CONSEQUENCES

Marriage is a troubled institution these days. Though making something of a comeback, at least to hear magazines and newspapers tell it, marriage, on closer inspection, seems to be more a matter of convenience these days, or of profit, as suggested by the cartoonist whose drawing of two women talking over lunch was captioned, "I'm going to marry Phil. I think there might be a book in it."

Here, at any rate, is a chapter.

When Does the Dream Begin to Die?

A hell of a question, one that haunts all collapsed marriages. Sometimes it happens right at the beginning.

A couple who thought of themselves as in tune with the times thought it would be a terrific idea to have their wedding videotaped. The whole thing, taping and all, went off smashingly, with only two things going wrong, although neither was exactly a small point.

The father of the bride had brought an envelope with a thousand dollars in cash to pay for the reception, and the first hitch was that at the last minute he realized that he couldn't find it. A protracted and somewhat agonized search followed; it turned up nothing. Eventually it was agreed that a check could be accepted, and the celebrations proceeded.

Somewhere along the way it was decided that all the guests ought to sit back and watch the videotape of the wedding they had just attended, and that's where the real trouble started. The tape showed women crying, manly congratulations, the kissing of the bride and all that. And it also showed the father of the groom slipping the envelope full of cash into his pocket.

The marriage was annulled.

The *San Francisco Chronicle* hinted at early trouble with a subtle touch: "Haggart and his wife were married last February 28 and were separated later that month."

Another short marriage was that of David and Ruth Lucas, of Paducah, Kentucky. It was, acording to *The New York Times,* the first marriage for the bridegroom and the third for the bride.

Because of apparently irreconcilable differences and, without doubt, irrevocable actions, it was very likely the last for the bride and certainly the last for the bridegroom.

The couple was described as "perfectly happy" at the beginning of their wedding day, but before it was over, they had an argument, and Mrs. Lucas shot Mr. Lucas to death.

Mrs. Lucas is currently serving forty years for manslaughter.

Sometimes there is trouble over a long period. The Emersons of Tamworth, England, were happy enough for eighteen years, but then had an argument that resulted in total silence between them. They communicated by notes for twelve years.

Their lawyer said he didn't believe it at first but was convinced by his own eyes. "When one would come into the house, the other would leave," he said.

The rift came into the open when Mrs. Emerson was charged with theft and defended herself by explaining that her husband had stopped her allowance—even for food. The couple's last known exchange of notes came when Mrs. Emerson wrote, "I have been to a lawyer. I am going to get a divorce." Mr. Emerson wrote back, "Go ahead."

Sometimes the strife is well hidden until the bitter end. In Alton, Illinois, a woman left her ex-husband an unusual bequest from her $82,000 estate. The will read, "I give and bequest all my dresses and matching accessories to my ex-husband."

The woman's lawyer explained that the ex-husband "liked to dress up in women's clothing, and she wasn't too happy about that." The attorney said the will was the woman's "last laugh," saying the clause about the clothing "was just something she decided to put in there."

The rest of the estate went to children and grandchildren. The ex-husband planned to contest the will.

Worst Member of the Wedding

For an Illinois man it was important to have his father at his wedding, and thus it appeared particularly unfortunate that his father had just died.

But the son moved quickly. "I don't want to wait another day," he said, and arranged to have his wedding performed beside his father's open casket. The wedding vows and the eulogy were spoken on the same day and in the same room before the same audience.

The pastor officiating performed a traditional wedding service before what a press called a "hushed" group of eighteen friends and relatives.

Sometimes It Really Is Cheaper to Let a Couple of Lawyers Handle It

A couple in Switzerland decided to battle it out to the end personally.

It all began when the husband canceled one vacation trip too many for his wife. She expressed her disappointment by pouring bicarbonate of soda into the fish tank, wiping out his rare tropical fish.

A long argument followed when he found his prized species belly-up in the tank, and the result was that he grabbed a selection of his wife's diamond jewelry and threw it into the garbage disposal.

She responded by flinging all her husband's stereo equipment into the swimming pool. He then doused her $200,000 wardrobe—fur coats, designer gowns and all—with liquid bleach. After that things began to go downhill.

She poured a gallon of paint all over his $70,000 Ferrari and used another can of paint to redo the interior. So he kicked a hole in a $180,000 Picasso original she loved.

She had just opened the sea cocks of his 38-foot yacht, causing it to sink at its dock, when the couple's daughter came home and saw what had been going on. She called the police but was told they were powerless to do anything because it was not illegal for people to destroy their personal property. Eventually the family lawyer managed to arrange a truce.

Falling Apart

One divorcing couple kissed good-bye for good while falling to Earth at 120 m.p.h., thus dissolving their twelve-year marriage.

Not for them bickering and rancor. The couple decided on a civilized split and a unique one. With a lawyer and seven skydiving friends on hand for support, they flung themselves out of a plane at more than 12,000 feet; the divorce papers were handed to the wife during the free-fall.

Homewreckers

Not all divorces are so peaceful. A Washington man was mightily upset when his wife filed for divorce after they had been separated for some months. He began making a mess of what had once been the couple's happy home.

"When I got the call over the radio," said a police officer, "I thought it was the usual domestic case where the husband is tearing up the house—you know, throwing things around."

Not so. The husband really was tearing down the house. With a bulldozer.

"When I got there," the police officer said, "I made him stop for a minute." The lawman hoped the pause would give the husband time to recover himself, to look around and see the terrible, senseless, vengeful thing he was doing. To take stock, to fell a pang of regret and to decide within the fullness of his heart to do no further harm. No such luck. The man simply displayed his demolition permit, which he had bought at City Hall for $11.50, and then went back to work. When he was done with the rough bulldozing work, he applied the fine touches with a backhoe.

A man in England also took extreme action, of a somewhat cruder nature, under what he considered wifely provocation. His wife locked him out of the house, which he considered a gross offense.

So he revved up his blue Toyota, raced it across the lawn, overran the rosebushes, and slammed head-on into the house, blasting through the front wall and penetrating as far as the living room. Then he backed up and slammed in twice more before calling it a day.

"It sounded like a bomb going off," a neighbor said. "They were always having rows, but this was really something. I looked out and saw a wrecked car sticking out of their house."

Where the Hell Is Dear Abby When You Really Need Her?

A woman explained to a divorce court why she wanted to split from her husband, a dentist.

She said her husband was cheap, even though he made $40,000 a year. She said he never took his family on vacation and never bought his six children any Christmas or birthday presents. He would not fix the roof even though it leaked when it rained. He gave her a used engagement ring, formerly worn by his first wife. He never spoke to her except to give an order. He gave her only two gifts during the twenty-nine years they were married.

And one of them was a potato peeler.

Just Trying to Get Her Attention, Your Honor

In Birmingham, Alabama, a man was arrested, charged with, and finally convicted of beating his wife over the head with her pet chihuahua.

The Lure of Love Remains Strong, Nevertheless

No. 1

Pregnant and unmarried, a young woman was at the brink of the altar, separated from it by only the lack of a wedding dress. Her fiancé was more than willing to do what used to be called "the right thing," but right also seemed important to the young couple.

And so, to finance a wedding gown, plus clothes for

the forthcoming child, they took to crime. They managed to rob three banks before they were caught.

In court, exhibiting his celebrated dry wit, the judge said, "The wedding dress would come under the heading of something borrowed, I guess."

No. 2

A Long Island man became despondent after a quarrel with his girlfriend. He was so despondent that he determined to end it all in his third-floor apartment.

Suicide being one of the few courses not taught at community colleges and in adult-education programs, he had to wing it. In his first attempt, he filled his bathtub, got in and tried to electrocute himself by dropping his video-cassette recorder into the water. The attempt failed, police said, because he had neglected to plug it in.

For his next attempt he decided on self-immolation. Therefore he set fire to his bedroom drapes. Smoke spread throughout the third floor and a hundred people were driven out of their homes, but he survived and was was dragged to safety by a pair of police officers. He was later charged with second-degree arson.

XIV.
BANK ROBBERS

Bank robbers once had something of a reputation in this country. John Dillinger was a fairly romantic swaggerer; Bonnie and Clyde, otherwise known as the Barrow Gang, were thought of as something like latter-day Robin Hoods as they scorched about the landscape during the Depression, robbing banks and engaging in hair's-breadth getaways. Later there was Willie Sutton, who often got caught but who also had a genius for jailbreaks.

Then, somewhere along the line, the whole business and tradition went to hell in a handbasket. Bank robbing fell into some sort of equal-opportunity or open-admissions mode, and the field was overrun with incompetents—expansion crooks, so to speak. It got so that a self-respecting felon would almost rather go straight than associate with the oafs who were making a fine old trade into a joke.

What do we know of the modern bank robber? In *The American Journal of Psychiatry* Dr. Donald Johnston wrote that most bank robbers act on impulse and are emotionally disturbed. After interviewing numerous robbers serving time, Johnston learned that most knew nothing at all about the banks they robbed, or tried to rob—they simply barged in and demanded money. He found several men who acted out of feelings of inadequacy (two because they were unable to give money to beggars and one who felt insignificant after hearing news of the astronauts' moon landing). A man who wanted to punish himself for marital infidelity staged a holdup with an unloaded gun, so as to be sure of hurting no one, and waited patiently for the police to arrive on the scene. When they did, he aimed his gun at them and was promptly shot—but only in the arm. So he took aim again, and was shot again, and then staged an escape attempt, which caused him to be shot in the leg.

The reason he carried a gun (which he knew to be empty) was to draw fire. He wanted to be killed. He would have committed suicide, but that would have canceled his insurance (thus exposing his wife and nine children to financial risk); also, he was a Roman Catholic, for whom suicide was a mortal sin.

Rose Is a Rose, Etc.

Rose DeWolf, of Philadelphia, is a newspaper columnist who has kept track of the bank-robbing business lo these many years and has kindly lent her file for this volume.

The peerless DeWolf records the crook who robbed eight banks and got money every time, but always dropped the loot before he could get away. He kept going to banks that threw a small explosive device into the swag bag, and it was his apparent intention to keep on trying until he found a bank that didn't have any such devices.

Another crook, aware of the new security tricks, was a little smarter, though not by much. When he tried to tackle a branch of the Provident National Bank, he added a P.S. to his note, saying, "Please no explosive money. Thank you."

One bank robber wrote his holdup note on the back of his phone bill; another, who was robbing the very branch in which he had an account, was so nervous that he wrote his note on a deposit slip. And when he came to the blank marked "account number," he unthinkingly filled it in. It took cops a little longer to catch up with Nine Fingers, who shot off one of his own fingers during his getaway. The cops took the finger in for fingerprinting, naturally, and the evidence eventually nailed the suspect. The headline on that story was FINGER POINTS TO SUSPECT.

Bank tellers are told repeatedly to treat robbers as dangerous, but they frequently can't keep a straight face when the time comes. One robber was caught when a teller told him he was in the wrong line. She sent him to another line to wait and then called the cops. At Valley National Bank in Passaic, New Jersey, a teller turned away a robber three times on the same day. She would tell him "Nothing doing" each time. Finally he gave up.

A teller in Buffalo replied to the time-honored warning, "This is a stick up," by insisting that the robber hand over a note. The crook said he was noteless; this was an oral robbery. The teller then demanded to see his gun. The rattled robber said, "You're crazy!" and fled. Another teller stalled a robber by reading his note and saying, "Just a minute, I'll have to check with my superior." She disappeared for a minute to give the alarm, then returned and said she was sorry, but her boss had said she could give the robber only $150. When the crook said Okay, she counted out the money. Then she asked him to sign a receipt, which he did while the cops were walking in the door.

A crook who thought to outsmart the automatic security cameras with a disguise was also caught. He attracted too much attention when his false beard kept falling off. Another was asked to wait by a bank manager, who said he had to get the money out of the vault. The crook was making himself at home in the office, had even put his feet up on the desk, when the manager returned, accompanied by a policeman, who inquired as to what was going on. "I'm waiting for the money," said the crook.

Even customers sometimes can't take robbers seriously. In October 1982, a man walked into a bank in Syracuse, New York, with a shotgun and a demand for $1 million. Unfortunately for him, he had pushed his way to the front of the line, offending one of the customers, who knocked him down and sat on him.

Another way to not get any money is to rob the wrong kind of bank. A crook in the Federal Reserve Bank of Philadelphia was told politely that the bank did distribute money to other banks in the area but that it didn't have any cash available for withdrawals. The crook apologized and asked to have his note back.

Even those who actually get out the door, and with money, have their problems. They usually bungle the getaway. They lose the keys to the getaway car or lock them inside. In Williamstown, New Jersey, a pair of robbers didn't have a getaway car—they had to rob a bank to buy one. Cops caught up with them at a nearby dealership, where the manager was stalling them with paperwork. Some New York crooks were badly slowed down when, after leaving the bank, they had to go back and ask their victims for exact change for their subway fare. A solo operator in Oxnard, California, his kidneys perhaps overstimulated by events, left the bank and then went in search of relief. He ducked into a nearby laundromat and was crushed to find that it had only a pay toilet—and he had no change. He was arrested in what police called a "very excited state."

But even DeWolf can't catch 'em all, so to speak. Robberies, or attempted robberies, happen all the time, So, on to the late roundup.

If He'd Succeeded, Who'd Have Suspected Him?

In London, David Worrell, 25, got a twelve-year suspended sentence for his crime. The judge was lenient because Worrell failed and because he had a lot going against him.

Worrell was blind, and he tried to pull off the job armed only with his cane. He had only pretended to have a gun, and when he heard the sirens of police cars, panicked and ran smack into a door.

Silent Type

In Portland, Oregon, a 1969 robbery attempt was conducted in writing so as not to attract undue attention. The hopeful scribbled, "This is a holdup, and I've got a gun. Put all the money in a paper bag." The teller read the note and then wrote a note to the holdup man: "I don't have a paper bag."

Habitual Criminal

A New York City man was doing very well as a bank robber—he'd held up thirty-one banks, gotten money every time and was on the most-wanted list.

He was successful, said a police spokesman, because "he was sharp—he knew the ins and outs of the banking system. He knew how long it would take the police to arrive after the teller's alarm was tripped." Unfortunately the man developed several habits that led to his downfall.

He robbed banks in midtown Manhattan only, and he

robbed branches of the Goldome Bank almost exclusively. Police concluded that the perpetrator might be what is known as a "disgruntled ex-employee," and upon checking, they found that a teller-trainee had been sacked by Goldome just a few days before the robberies began. The trainee turned out to be the thief, whom the bank had fired for "lack of intelligence."

The reason he restricted himself to midtown Manhattan branches was that he was holding down an honest job at the time and could rob banks only on his breaks.

Send in the Clowns

A Delaware woman pleaded guilty to robbing a bank of $70,000. Thinking to make her approach to the teller an easy one, she wore a clown costume and posed as a person delivering a gift.

Approaching the teller in a bank is the easy part. People do that all day long; that's what the tellers are there for. It's getting away that is difficult. Especially if you are wearing a clown suit.

No Note Required

Banks like automatic teller machines because they reduce the need for tellers but also because they would seem to be invulnerable to holdups.

That may frustrate crooks elsewhere, but not in Melbourne, Australia, where thieves recently smashed into a bank with a front-end loader, which they used to rip the machine right out of the wall. Then they carted it off to a dump truck to make their getaway.

There are no reports of their capture, but their MO looks to have a limited lifespan. Cops are henceforth bound to look suspiciously on groups of men lurking around automatic tellers with significant amounts of heavy construction machinery parked nearby.

With Lightning-quick Reflexes, Our Government Closes in

The Justice Department, which apparently reads neither newspapers nor *The American Journal of Psychiatry*, commissioned a study to tell it what bank robbers are like.

The study examined the facts in 11,000 bank robberies in 1978 and 1979. The study reported that arrests are made in nearly 70% of the cases, which makes bank robbery significantly riskier than other types of theft.

When the thief actually escapes with money, the amount averages a rather pathetic $3,300.

The study concluded that most bank robbers are unsophisticated and amateurish types who just don't take the time to think the job through.

XV.
FEMINIST NOTES

Feminism flared up in the 1960s and bids fair to keep on going, despite occasional and premature burials, sometimes by its own supporters. The melodrama of bra burnings soon quieted down, and the revolution, unlike so many other revolutions, actually accomplished some useful things, although there were times when it was reasonable to ask whether the greatest danger to some feminists was chauvinists or some other feminists. Infighting is an occupational disease of revolutionaries.

The Movement, as it came to be called, also produced some outbursts of freestyle lunacy on both sides, and is largely responsible for such high-fructose personalities as Alan Alda and Phil Donahue, of whom less anon. Although the Movement continues to produce some mighty peculiar incidents, no one can say that it is all a lot of noise about nothing.

A Case in Point

The Dubuque, Iowa, Human Rights Commission lost a member when he resigned after analyzing the cause of poor mail delivery, which he divined as the fault of "all those stupid broads we have working in the post office now."

Don't Worry, We'll Get Right on It

Officials of the European Economic Council told the Irish government in 1976 to get busy and enforce the sex-equality regulations to which all EEC members had agreed. To remedy the oversight, Dublin quickly placed newspaper ads for applicants to fill a position called "equal-pay enforcement officer." The ads specified different salaries for men and women.

We Must March, My Darlings

Under continuing pressure from feminists demanding the right of full participation in the armed forces, the Army began a study to determine whether mixing men and women in combat might produce unforeseen problems. At length, the study was completed, and it concluded that there would.

The problem, according to the report, would be "sexual fraternization," which would jeopardize "expedient mission accomplishment." Therefore, the report continued, there must be guidelines on what constitutes acceptable and unacceptable fraternization. To help male soldiers adjust to the change in the old-fashioned one-sex battlefield, the Army proposes training courses in "female physiology."

Also, Somebody's Got to Carry His Books Home From School

A high-school boy in Maryland announced his desire to try out for the girls' field-hockey team, noting that he has no alternative because the school does not have a boys' field-hockey team.

And Parts of Neptune

A brochure distributed at a NOW conference read, "The feminine of history is mystery is about the sun and the moon, masculine and feminine, the two hemispheres of the brain, megaliths, earth energies, the archetypes of the psyche, Atlantis, and the planet as a whole."

Short and Sweet

He said: "No woman has been chief of a CSIRO division, and only one woman has been acting chief of a division. But this is not because we are prejudiced against women. It is because we always get the best man for the job."—The Sydney *Australian*.

Take That!

Women who have complained about sex bias in the English language are now being joined by men who have the same objections.

The Fathers' Rights Association of New York objects to the likes of *motherhood, doorman, gunman,* and *dirty old man.* Men's Rights Inc., of Sacramento and Boston, has a Media Watch that comes down hard on such offenses as an Aquafresh toothpaste commercial that, says founder Fred Hayward, "suggests that women are more competent to determine what is good for their children than men." Hayward has also complained to NBC regarding the use of the phrase *women and children* in coverage of disasters; he says it suggests they are more deserving of sympathy and promotes "a belief that male life is more expendable."

Warren Farrell of Leucadia, California, has a ready answer whenever feminists complain to him (apparently he is a target of such protests) that God is always referred to as a man. He says men should be equally upset about the characterization of the devil.

"Nobody ever called the devil 'she,' " he says.

Nothing New, Then

STATISTICS ON WOMEN:
SOME GOOD AND SOME BAD
—Headline in *Women In Communications.*

Sound Off—One, Two; Sound Off—Three, Four

Women Marines in training had been singing a little song on their marches, as trainees on the march appear to have done ever since sergeants hit upon the idea of training them by marching them. It's march, march, march and train, train, train, so to speak. Anyway, as they trooped along in their steel helmets and fatigues, their packs and rifles weighing them down, the trainees sang as follows:

I saw a bird with a yellow bill
Sitting on my windowsill.
I coaxed him in with a piece of bread—
And then I crushed his little head.

A mean marine—
A lean marine!
I guess I'm just a mean marine!

This moving ditty came to the attention of Audubon Society president Peter Berle, who shot off a letter to Marine Corps commandant.

"Idolizing people who squash birds' heads is not consistent with the goals of the Audubon Society," Berle wrote, adding, lest "a tough marine . . . consider this as another crank letter from a pansy," that his own military experiences included earning a master parachutist rating with nearly one hundred drops.

Berle went on to say, "In my experience advocacy of unsportsmanlike hunting techniques was not necessary to instill pride or toughness in troops." No stranger to recruiting techniques himself, he tried to nail the commandant as an Audubon Society member.

He didn't sign up, but a spokesman for him said that was because he is extremely busy, not because marines "favor squashing birds' heads." The spokesman added, "You can bet your bottom dollar you won't hear the women marines singing that song again."

XVI.

IS GOD DEAD, OR WHAT?

It has been about a quarter of a century since *Time* magazine dropped its bombshell, a cover article entitled "Is God Dead?" The piece caused quite an uproar with its examination of new and alternative theological systems and the continuing decline of conventional organized religions in America. The faithful were outraged that the question had even been asked; the not-so-faithful thought it was about time; and the faithless ricocheted between joy and indifference.

To date we have no answer, although we get periodic tantalizing hints. Some believers point to the drug plague, the acceptance of old-fashioned immorality as modern morality, and the growth of crime as evidence that God is alive but plenty angry. Wiseacres like to say that God is alive because we still have plenty of famines, earthquakes, tidal waves, fires and other tragedies, which conventional religions themselves have always described as "God's will." Cynics noting the emergency conversions of such folks as Eldridge Cleaver, John Z. Delorean and various Watergate criminals—to say nothing of the Bakkers and Jessica Hahn— say God is alive but is running with a bad crowd.

In any event, recent years have seen a sudden spurt of religious zeal in America—not in the organized churches, which continue to decline, but among a decidedly mixed bag of born-again zealots, charismatic preachers and fundamentalist ravers.

The importance and depth of this religious outburst is unclear. Newspaper columnist Michael J. McManus ran his own survey recently and found that most of the people he spoke to believed firmly that we should all follow the Ten Commandments but that very few knew what all the commandments were.

Here are other reports on what's doing in the World of Faith.

Personal Faith in Our World of Today

No. 1

The Southern Baptist Convention approved by a wide margin the plan to hold the group's 1989 convention in Las Vegas, an unusual site, on the face of it. The appeal of the site was explained by an SBC member who said, "There's going to be prostitution. There's going to be drinking. There's going to be gambling. That makes me even more determined to go there."

No. 2

An outing and songfest at the Mount St. Frances Seminary in New Albany, Indiana, ended abruptly with a suicide.

Witnesses said that Sister Carolina Mary, age 37, of Louisville, Kentucky, had appeared to be in good spirits when she suddenly stripped off her shoes and sweater and threw herself into a blazing bonfire of oil-soaked wood.

No. 3

Every day for nine consecutive days, an impoverished woman went to a church shrine in New York State to pray. She prayed to St. Jude, the patron of lost causes, for help in keeping her family together.

On the ninth day it appeared that St. Jude had heard her pleas: She found at the foot of the statue an envelope containing $10,000 in $100 bills. She was relieved and elated. She spent the money on furniture, put a deposit on an apartment and paid for her daughter's tuition at a beauty school.

Another parishioner had been praying for help, too, at about that time. This worshipper asked help for a successful change in career, and when his prayers seemed to have been answered, he made a donation—an envelope containing $10,000 in $100 bills. The worshiper never revealed his name, but he did call St. Jude's Church and tell the Reverend that a quick visit to the statue would produce gratifying results. But by the time he was called, the money had been found by the woman worshiper.

All that was forgotten when, almost a year and a half later, the priest learned that a parishioner had had her prayers answered with a heavenly gift of $10,000. Naturally, he called the cops.

"I'm not looking for punishment," he said, "but I do have an obligation to the parish, which is out $10,000." To the county district attorney's office, the case was not a simple one. In fact, as there was no criminal intent on the woman's part, there might be no case at all. The woman said, "I think I'm being punished for believing in St. Jude, and I still do. Somehow, I believe he's going to get me out of this."

And maybe he did. The case was eventually dropped and she went free.

No. 4

In Radnor, Pennsylvania, a woman pulled up at a stoplight behind a car with a bumper sticker that read HONK IF YOU LOVE JESUS. In Cincinnati, another woman found herself in an identical situation.

Both honked. In the cars ahead of them, both drivers replied with an obscene gesture.

Heaven Forbid

"I would have made a good pope."—Richard M. Nixon

Oh, Shut Up!

Fundamentalists in Columbus, Ohio, ever on the prowl for ungodly and dangerous books to ban, have seized lately on E. B. White's poignant children's classic, *Charlotte's Web,* a gentle tale of a farmgirl and her pet pig.

The faithful who want to rid school libraries of the blasphemous text base their demand on the fact that the book includes animals that talk. According to members of the group, who read inflammatory excerpts aloud at a fund-raising function, it is against God's will for animals to talk.

Confession Is Good for the Soul

In San Francisco a woman went to her priest for consolation and relief. She had embezzled nearly $30,000 and had to get it off her chest because she "couldn't take the pressure anymore." She added, "I needed to talk to someone, and the only person I could speak with was my priest."

It didn't make any difference to her that she had stolen the money from the church. She still expected, she said, "forgiveness, absolution and secrecy." The priest called the cops and the woman spent seven months in the slammer. The woman called a lawyer and launched a $5 million suit against the priest for violation of confidentiality.

New Godly Frontiers

No. 1

In Los Angeles a former Scientologist sued the Church of Scientology, claiming it defrauded him of thousands of dollars for Scientology courses that were supposed to give him greater intelligence and business success.

Documents submitted in the case say the Church of Scientology teaches that, 75 milliion years ago, Earth was called Teegeeach and that it was one of 90 planets ruled by Xemu, who used thermonuclear bombs to spread evil in the universe.

Press reports said Scientology members sought to prevent disclosure of the documents. Church president Heber Jentzsch said press reports distorted the documents' contents.

No. 2

In some harbor towns, priests hold an annual Blessing of the Fleet. In New England, they bless motorcycles.

One ceremony, the eighth annual for Colebrook, New Hampshire, was sponsored by the White Mountain Cycle Club. Some 3,800 cycles and riders were on hand; it took three priests an hour and a half to bless 'em all. Another, the seventh annual in Litchfield, Connecticut, attracted a parade of motorcyclists two miles long and was complete with the sort of humor the clergy is famous for. Father Ray Lombard said he would "bless sidecars, too"; another priest said the blessing was "good only up to 55 m.p.h."

No. 3

For those who cry "Gimme That Byte-Sized Religion," there is now GRAPE—the Gospel Resources and Programs Exchange.

GRAPE offers nine religious or church-affairs programs on floppy discs. One of them is called PARSEC, for Parish Secretary. It is designed to help keep tabs on church membership, donations and fund-raising efforts. Another disc contains what GRAPE says is the "first ecclesiastical computer game." It is called Pax-Man.

No. 4

Some people come out of jail ready to back to crime, but a few come out rehabilitated. One of the latter would appear to be a man who did a short stretch for writing bad checks but put his time to constructive use.

Not long after his release, he opened the Karate for Christ Martial Arts School in Grand Rapids, Michigan.

The rehabilitated man, who shatters planks barehanded while preaching the Word, says, "I believe that the Lord works through you and that karate can build your confidence. I show people that the Word of God is quick and powerful and sharper than any two-edged sword.

"With His help, you can slice through any temptation."

No. 5

Biblical scholars were well into their translating work for the Revised Standard Version when they discovered that the old Bible is sexist.

Nevertheless, according to a spokesman, the Revised Standard Version will not refer to God as Her. Translators, he explained, must remain true to the gender of the original Hebrew and Greek pronouns.

Another spokesman said it would be "impossible and dishonest" to remove all of the Good Book's male bias, but it was important to "sweep diligently through Scripture to discover female imagery for God."

Deuteronomy 2:18 was cited as an example of a text whose female imagery in the original has been altered by the sexism of later translators. The text in the Revised Standard Version still reads, "You were unmindful of the rock that begot you," but now there is a footnote explaining that "begot" could be "bore."

No. 6

Reader's Digest, drawing upon decades of experience in condensing magazine articles, novels and major non-fiction works, issued a *Reader's Digest Condensed Bible*.

One *Digest* editor explained that the original—the best-seller of all best-sellers—contained "a lot of repetition" that could be cut out. Another editor explained, "You simply take out what you can, without distorting what the author meant. Only in this case, the author has more stature than most."

Cynics suggested that the *Digest* would next turn the Bible into a TV miniseries called *The Nine Commandments*.

Just Another Example of Your Basic Church Militant

The Hare Kirshnas, formally known as the International Society for Krishna Consciousness, or ISKCON, are willing to shave their heads, dance and chant in public in loose robes and beg annoyingly in airports and other public places, but they don't put up with what they consider wackos.

Thus, one of ISKCON's founders was kicked out of the organization. He was charged with "bizarre, aberrent behavior" and with being "too spiritual, too mystical."

Like a Virgin

No. 1

In Nicaragua the Catholic Church has been looking into reports of appearances of the Virgin Mary in a poverty-stricken hamlet. Villagers who reported the appearances have described the Virgin as being "almost nude."

The tiny community of Cuapa, about seventy miles north of Managua, was overrun by pilgrims. They saw nothing, but satisfied themselves with stripping the bark from a tree under which the Virgin is said to have appeared to church sexton Bernardo Martinez. Other residents of the village said they saw the Virgin "among the electric light bulbs" of Cuapa's church.

No. 2

From Mexico have been come confused reports of a 13-year-old virgin becoming pregnant—in short, an immaculate conception. The religious excitement died down after knife fights involving the girl's defenders and men suspected of having gotten her pregnant.

No. 3

Pilgrims have flocked to the village of Rmaich, Lebanon, near the Israeli border, to see a bleeding statue of the Virgin.

Many Lebanese Christians took the event to be a miracle. "It is hard to say this is a miracle," said Archbishop Maximos Salloum of the Christian Melchite sect, "but it is extraordinary." The cleric said the bleeding could be a response to the "deep pain of the Virgin over the bloodshed of Her beloved sons in Lebanon."

No. 4

Ballinspittle, Ireland, has been overrun with tourists hoping to see a 336-pound concrete statue of the Virgin that is fully clothed and does not bleed, but moves.

A 17-year-old girl was the first to report that the statue, set in a hillside grotto, moves; many villagers and visitors soon reported that they saw it move too.

A Roman Catholic bishop called for "caution and prudence" regarding the possibility of a miracle, but business in the town soon took off as pilgrims poured in. A local committee had to be set up to provide crowd control; a bus company had to provide extra vehicles; fish-and-chip vans and souvenir suppliers moved onto the site; and the three local pubs did a brisk business. "I haven't done business like this since the Pope came to Ireland," said one vendor.

Residents angrily denied that the whole thing was a trick to promote tourism. A psychologist at Cork University said any movements by the statue were optical illusions caused by the gray background of the grotto.

Clare Mahony who first reported the statue's movements, insists she spoke the truth. "She's here, and the next minute she's swaying to and fro," she said of the statue, "and then the odd times she bows."

No. 5

In heavily Catholic Quebec, Canada, 1986 got off to a rousing start with reports of a statue of the Virgin weeping tears of blood.

Maurice Girouard, of Ste-Marthe-sur-le-Lac, a suburb of Montreal, had the statue, about two feet tall, in a private chapel in his home, which was quickly invaded by an apparently endless stream of pilgrims. Round-the-clock watches were instituted to observe any further weepings; clerics, penitents and crackpots offered interpretations of the event, but church leaders took the usual cautious line.

A brother of the Adoration of the Trinity Through Mary nevertheless took it upon himself to certify that the weeping was a genuine sign direct from God. A man who identified himself only as Dante announced that he was "a child chosen by God to lead the Lord's government. In the year 2012, God will destroy the world and only one billion people will be allowed to live. The Lord has chosen Quebec as the seat of His government. The Archangel Michael and I shall govern. I have the power." He went on to say that he was personally responsible for the departure from office of two once-popular Canadian politicians.

Girouard, who recently moved his life onto a more spiritual plane after a divorce and years of drinking, tells skeptics of many other statues of the Virgin that have been reported to bleed or sweat—in the U.S., elsewhere in Canada and in Italy, Czechoslovakia and Yugoslavia. It was in Yugoslavia, coincidentally, that he saw apparitions of the Virgin of Mudjugorje the previous summer.

After his visit to Yugoslavia he returned home and built his private chapel. Later he installed in it a plaster Virgin given to him in December by a Jesuit friend. He and his wife rectified their divorce by remarrying and taking vows of chastity and piety. "I used to drink a lot," he said. "Now I do not drink at all. Now I only eat to live; I don't live to eat. Now I enjoy *la gourmandise spirituelle.*"

In the middle of the month the weeping Virgin was carted off to a Montreal laboratory specializing in organic chemistry. The lab reported that the tears were made of a mixture of animal fat and vegetable oil.

As for Me and My House, We Will Serve the Lord ... and Mixed Drinks, Snacks and Canapes

In Wauconda, Illinois, a minister who turned his 10,000-square-foot mansion into a church, that features a sauna, an indoor pool and a bar has been ordered to stop charging admission and selling liquor.

The Universal Life Church was no hit with the neighbors, who considered it more of a swingers' playground. In court, Margaret Mullen, an Assistant State's Attorney, said the church was violating liquor-license, building-code and zoning laws. Lake County Circuit Court Judge William D. Block agreed, telling the minister and his wife they were henceforth forbidden to charge for drinks and admission and to have gatherings of more than fifty people. The ruling, said Mullen, "in effect closes the party operation permanently." The defendant, who became a minister in 1981, was ordained by mail for a fee of $30.

God Moves in Mysterious Ways, His Gastronomic Wonders to Perform

No. 1

Maria Rubio of Lake Arthur, New Mexico, was bent over a hot stove frying tortillas when she was granted a vision of Our Lord Jesus Christ in 1977.

The vision was *in* the tortilla, which developed an image of Christ. Rubio carefully preserved the tortilla for the benefit of the faithful everywhere.

Rubio says that some of the visitors to the Shrine of the Holy Tortilla, in her home in Lake Arthur, have reported miraculous cures. "A lady came in here a couple of years ago in a wheelchair," Rubio says. "She was paralyzed and promised to walk all the way from [the nearby town of] Artesia once a year if she was cured. She was, and she made her first walk last year."

No. 2

The burning question, so to speak, was enshrined in

the prose of Gloucester County *Times* reporter Joe Diemer: Could Jesus truly decide to appear in an abandoned chicken coop behind a Deptford, New Jersey, pizzeria?

The question arose in December 1980, when Bud Ward set out to take his wife to lunch, detoured to take a picture en route, and ended by starting a wave of religious feeling that swept southern New Jersey.

Ward, then Deptford Township's official fire photographer and a recovering stroke victim, felt well enough to dine out. He was driving his wife to the restaurant when, at an intersection, he felt impelled to turn left instead of right, which would have been the correct way. After making his turn he saw flames—and professional instinct took over. Within minutes he was parked near the Naples Pizzeria, on Good Intent Road, had his camera out and was taking pictures.

It was a modest blaze, quelled in about forty-five minutes with the help of fifteen firemen and three trucks, and Ward thought little of it at the time. He took only seven shots and had been ready to quit at the fourth when he felt a pain in his stomach. He dropped his film off at K-Mart and didn't see the first shots until a week later. When he came to the fourth shot, his 9-year-old daughter entered the room and said, "Daddy, why is Jesus in that picture?"

Ward, not particularly religious, said he had trouble recognizing the image at the time, but word soon spread, and many others, children and adults, identified the images as quickly as young Heather had. Soon the Pizza Jesus of Deptford Township was the talk of southern New Jersey.

Depending on who looked at it, the fourth frame showed the image of Christ in long hair and a flowing robe, or also a small girl standing in front of Jesus. Others could make out a Star of David in the background, a lamb cradled in Christ's arms, and a dove of peace above his head. Others noticed a birds' nest in a tree so close to the flames that, they thought, it should have burned, though it did not. At least one person thought he saw a third face, that of an infant, amid the flames.

Soon enough, other things began to happen. There were demands for public showings of the picture—a color slide—and for prints made from the slide. Ward, no hustler, sold some prints at five dollars each and said he was donating the modest profit to a burn center. Ward's health improved markedly (at first he would say it was coincidence; later he would say that his life had in some ways changed unexpectedly for the better after he took the picture).

John Lennon was killed three days after the picture was taken, and some people identified the figure in the photo as Lennon. Most people, however, insisted it was Christ. When the image was enlarged, facial features on the two figures appeared, or appeared to appear. Some people wanted to have the slide projected onto their bodies.

It being near Christmas, the owners of the pizzeria hung a wreath on the charred wreckage. It was quickly stolen. Souvenir hunters also began removing ashes and bits of wood at a rapid rate. There was some talk of a shrine to preserve the remaining remains. The possibility was complicated by the coop's straddling two lots owned by two different people, plus the usual red tape—parking facilities, insurance and so on—attendant on such a project.

Although Ward sent copies of the picture to many who requested one, and some people have attributed beneficial effects to the picture, Ward never attempted to tell people that it contained any particular image or figure. "I leave the interpretation up to you" is what he told everyone.

The picture was still attracting attention the following year, and Ward said he would never take another fire picture. "I had never seen a good fire, and now evidently I have," he said. The famous photo was not Ward's first brush with well-known figures. He had previously photographed the likes of Janis Joplin and Tom Jones, and until the fire picture, his favorite was a shot of Rosalyn Carter applying lipstick at a banquet tale at Auletto's Sunset Beach Ballroom.

Next Week, Macrame and the Immaculate Conception

Calvary Chapel of Laguna Beach, California, will be presenting the Master Potter, a dramatic arts ministry showing real-life conflicts through a real-life potter, a potter's wheel, actors and actresses acting out the lives of the pots from 10 A.M. on Saturday, May 11.

The potter, Jill Austin, portrays the heart of God as she throws the pots.—The Santa Ana *Register*.

Where to Wait, If Wait You Will, for the Second Coming

During World War II, large numbers of South Pacific islands, islets, and atolls were visited by the U.S. military, which brought with it the full and electrifying panoply of American civilization. Natives who had to make fires by rubbing sticks together were astounded by the miracle of the Zippo lighter; imagine the effect of all the rest—trucks, jeeps, planes, guns, machinery, refrigerators and such, to say nothing of the mighty battle fleets anchored offshore and planes roaring overhead.

Then the Navy left, taking American civilization with it, just like that. The war had ended, and men who were as gods disappeared virtually overnight—and that's the point: They *were* as gods. Soon, on various isolated islands, there sprung up what came to be known as Cargo Cults. Longing for the goods of the consumer society that had visited them so briefly, the cults worshiped and prayed for the return of the Americans and their priceless cargo. In that, all the cults are the same, as they are in their personification of the Americans in a single deity. In one place the god is called Tom Navy; in another, John Frum. Otherwise, the cults' doctrinal differences are not very great. Some have only a few relics—lighters, eyeglasses, cameras—to venerate. Others have enough helmets to wear in ritual parades. Still others have built large wooden mock-ups of airplanes. Cargo planes, naturally.

All of this poses problems for the Christian missionaries who still seek to convert the heathen and prepare him for heaven. It's not easy. Missionaries come bearing the Word, not cargo. The eager pastor can hardly get "Praise God From Whom All Blessings Flow" out of his mouth before the natives begin looking around for cargo.

One missionary who faces this problem is Father Joelson Ling, a soul-saver in Vanuatu, a nation comprising a string of 80 islands and 130,000 people in the Coral Sea east of Australia.

Cargo cultism is in rude good health in Vanuatu, according to James P. Sterba, a *Wall Street Journal* reporter who checked it out firsthand. The natives Father Ling hopes to save worship John Frum and persist in the ancient male custom of drinking kava, which Sterba says has been compared to drinking novocaine.

Kava is made from plant roots that adolescent boys chew up and then spit into a communal bowl. Water is then added, the guck is stirred up a bit and then strained. The revolting result is kava. Revolting but potent. Kava first numbs the mouth, then, bit by bit, the entire body. Vanuatuans get very relaxed on kava, relaxed to the point of immobility.

You can see the extent of the problem facing Father Ling, who is perhaps unaware of the parallels between cargo cultism and his house brand of salvation. For Vanuatuans, John Frum is still within living memory; they have seen his might and sinew; they have relics of his being; in the meantime, kava is not scarce. For the power of Christ they have to take Father Ling's word.

And Christ has been gone nearly 2,000 years. When Father Ling tries to warm them up to wait for the Second Coming, Vanuatuans tend to look at him—if capable of any response at all—and ask, "Why He no come?"

Having a Devil of a Time— Wish We Weren't Here

In 1985, Procter & Gamble, the gigantic Midwest manufacturer of Ivory Soap, Pampers and other household products, finally decided to remove its famous man-in-the-moon logo from its product labels.

The problem was that the logo had become infamous, though no one seems to know why. Still, since 1982, the company has been plagued by rumors that the logo is a symbol of devil worship. Leaflets claiming that were addressed to "all Christians" and distributed in California in 1982, resulting in 15,000 angry calls to P&G in two months. The leaflets said a P&G spokesman had bragged on a television show (variously identified as Phil Donahue's

Merv Griffin's or *60 Minutes*) that the company supported the Church of Satan with its profits.

P&G has denied the rumors repeatedly, saying no spokesman has ever appeared on any of those programs for any reason. The company even says it read through a year of transcripts for each program and found that none had so much as mentioned P&G.

The company held press conferences, set up a toll-free 800 number to spread word of its innocence and even asked religious leaders to help. They hired investigators and eventually tracked down and sued seven people who were spreading the story. The suits were settled out of court when the defendants promised to state publicly that the rumors were false. One of the defendants was a weatherman for an Atlanta TV station; he had received one of the leaflets and repeated the rumors when addressing local civic groups.

But nothing really worked. Rumors squelched in one area went underground and surfaced elsewhere, most recently in the New York–New Jersey–Pennsylvania area.

Eventually P&G said uncle. The man in the moon no longer appears on its products.

Indications That God Isn't Dead But Is Sure as Hell Fed Up

No. 1

When Principia College in Elsah, Illinois, suffered an epidemic of German measles, it posed a challenge to the students' religious principles.

There were a total of seventy-nine cases of rubeola (two-week German measles) at the college, according to Nola Kramer of the Jersey County Department of Health. A Chicago spokesman for the Christian Science Church said church members were free to make their own choice on receiving an immunization shot, but most students at the school rejected them.

Two of the students died.

A student who took the shots said he did so "for the concern of the outside community."

No. 2

Lois Sattler was sitting on Pulpit Rock in the Blue

Mountains last week thinking about God when a bolt of lightning struck her on the bottom, tearing out the seat of her jeans.—The Sydney, Australia, *Sun-Herald*.

No. 3

On the Hawaiian island of Maui, two couples awestruck by the beauty of their surroundings walked to the edge of a cliff overlooking the ocean, clasped their hands and closed their eyes to pray.

The next day, two battered survivors were rescued at the foot of the cliff, which had collapsed beneath their weight. The bodies of the other two were found by a surfer.

XVII.

YOU SAID A MOUTHFUL

A mouthful, yes, but not a brainful. And it is becoming a wearisome burden for those of us who require some clear idea of what was intended.

Edwin Newman, a former NBC News correspondent, has fought nobly to separate sense from nonsense in the use of the English language. In the 1970s, he wrote two splended, witty books on the subject—*A Civil Tongue* and *Strictly Speaking*—and if any of what follows makes your hair stand on end, you will enjoy reading them. If, on the other hand, any of the following mirrors your own utterances, you had better read them: perhaps you can still be saved.

Anger over mutilation of the language surfaces every few years, and it does less good than one hopes for. It's too easy for the protesters to be labeled rule-bound grammar-worshipers and fuddling old cranks who spend their lives tidying the commas and plumping the subjunctive mood. It's too easy for lexicographers to come grumbling out of their dens to argue that change can't be stopped because change is the very nature of a living language. And it's too common to have the educational establishment chime in with the charge that rules of grammar and usage represent some kind of oppression worked on the young by their bullying elders. "What does it matter how students speak," they ask, "as long as they make themselves understood?"

Understood by whom?

Newman, pointing with a shudder at the pretentious gobbledygook spouted by bureaucrats, public officials and high priests of the professions, noted their tendency to make language "soft and gaseous." (He must have been thinking of those fast-food doughnuts that look so tempting but dissolve into a sugary residue when you try to eat them.) He said those who speak sloppily are likely to think sloppily as well. After all, we think in words. If our language becomes limp and imprecise, our thoughts will too; we won't understand ourselves and others will not understand us.

Critics of careless language aren't trying to stop change but prevent vandalism. And it is vandalism to batter words to your own purpose against their meanings. Words are tools, and a word that becomes fashionable enough to be frequently misused is like a screwdriver that has been used to pry open paint cans, break apart crates and peel up floor tiles: worthless for its intended use.

There are few new things under the sun, but there is one new phenomenon that adds urgency to the need to protect our language. That is mass communications. Never before has man had the power to distribute so much inaccuracy and misinformation to so many people so quickly and with such little effort.

In addition, let a word be said in behalf of grace and eloquence, which should be striven for and appreciated, not regarded as frills. Anyone who can create an apt phrase or vivid turn of thought ought to do so and take pleasure in it. Literary art will occur in its own time, but speaking well is largely a matter of craftsmanship. It can be taught; it can be learned.

And so can the lightly regarded skill of plain speaking, which too many people prefer to gussy up with potted catchphrases from Hollywood and Madison Avenue: "Sit on it," "Where's the beef?" "Make my day," "I can't believe I ate the whole thing," "I could care less," "But who's counting" and other dubious canned goods are used with enthusiasm but not thought. Their appeal is a kind of external validation. Like the brand-labeled beer mugs and ashtrays college kids steal from saloons, they prove you've been somewhere. Plain speaking is snubbed, as if there were something wrong with it. There isn't. Plain speaking and plain country cooking just aren't fancy. But unlike the thick puddings of political speechifiers and the flash-frozen "gourmet" meals made of extruded foodlike substances, both go down well.

And so, a few words on words.

The Unicorn Hunters, a group of language conservationists at Michigan's Lake Superior State College, poll the country annually for vogue words and phrases that ought, by reason of excess repetition, to be outlawed. Among their targets is "Have a nice day."

The Unicorn Hunters wish no one ill, but have had it up to here with "Have a nice day," pointing out that telephone operators say it even when people call funeral homes. And they are not alone. According to a report in the *Rocky Mountain News*, they have an ally in Wyoming. A man who delivered a pizza to a trailer camp there handed over the food, collected payment and, before he parted, said, "Have a nice day."

The customer responded by beating him up.

Then He Led a Short Service at the Supreme-being Interface Facility

Many of the hostages in the TWA hijacking of 1985 were members of the same Midwestern congregation. The group was on a tour of Middle Eastern religious sites, and their pastor found it necessary to tell reporters that they had gone to the area for "a prayer experience."

Not to Put Too Fine a Point on It

We support the drive wholeheartedly. The number of ways which this facility helps our community's economy and growth are infinitesimal.—The Park Rapids (Minnesota) *Enterprise*.

Advice From the Experts

And Accelerated Utilization Of Verbal Waste Products

What words do you use on a job application when you describe some of the things you've done?

You might say, "I carried out an assignment to re-arrange office furniture to improve office efficiency."

Or you might say, "Implemented ambitious office-landscaping program effectively."

They mean the same thing, but the second example uses business jargon and sentence structure that carries a stronger message. Here is a short list of words you might use to describe yourself (if they apply): active, adaptable, alert, conscientious, creative, dependable, disciplined, efficient, energetic, logical, objective, practical, reliable, resourceful, self-reliant, sincere, tactful.

And here is a list of punch words that can be used at the first word of sentences describing your activities and elminating the word *I*. Actively, accelerated, conducted, created, developed, directed, eliminated, established, generated, guided, improved, performed, planned, proposed, reduced, revamped, scheduled, significantly, strengthened, successfully.—Advertising supplement to The Toronto *Globe and Mail*.

Transportation

Airlines almost invariably tell you that your plane will not take off on time "due to late arrival of equipment" (never "the plane isn't here yet"); if it's really going to be late, they offer "complimentary beverage service" instead of saying "free drinks." "Experiencing a little turbulence" means getting bounced around so much you have your drink in your lap. Flying is even more laid back at NASA, where "major malfunction" meant that the space shuttle *Challenger* had blown itself to bits.

An Amtrack official, unhappy about poor connections between trains and buses, said the situation would not improve because bus companies "do not like to inter-mode." And "intermodal interface" means, according to former Transportation Secretary William Coleman, that "when you get off the train, a bus is waiting."

Medicine Men

One reason a complete physical checkup costs so much these days is that it is now a "multiphasic health screen." It includes "preventive [or preventative] diagnostic tests" of your "comprehensive physiologic state." If there's anything wrong, you may have to take medication for it.

You may have an idiopathic condition, which means

the doctor doesn't know why you're sick. He may try to find out by putting you in the hospital, where you could get an additional illness that is iatrogenic—i.e., caused by treatment. If you want a psychiatrist to treat you for what Freud called a "repressed impulse," fat chance. He'll probably treat your "unconsciously maintained conditioned action" instead. That could take years.

Architects

Architects can not only build ugly buildings but often indulge in ugly talk as well. They like to talk about "vertical-access facilities" and are pleased to have found a single term that can cover both elevators, and stairs. You get stuck in one and fall down the other, and from there the differences multiply to a point that anyone but an architect might wonder at the wisdom of calling two such different things by the same name. Okay, you have a vertical-access facility. But what the hell is it?

Best to turn from this to something else. Possibly you can accept "high-rise" as a term for a tall building. But what do architects call short buildings, low-rises? No. They are "grade-related structures."

Linguists

They're the ones who'll teach you Language Arts inside of English. You'll learn to "generate text" (write) if you are already competent in "text processing analysis" (reading). Those skills will help if in college you major in the "telecommunicative arts" in the hope of becoming a news anchor.

Social Scientists

Be sure to "interdigitate" with them rather than merely cooperate—it's a matter of good "colleagueship interface relationships" and "paradigmatic behavior parameters," to say nothing of plain good manners. You could then count on them to help you in your study of "ethnically pluralistic national societal communities." Be sure that your thesis is not full of "counterfactual propositions" (mistakes or lies).

A sociologist who wanted a government grant to study what it felt like to be in love said in his application that he intended to study love's "hypothesized dependable variables." That netted him support to the tune of $133,000.

Pentagon People

You do not get to spend thousands of dollars on a coffee maker that will keep working after all those who might use it are dead unless you can deal with syllables and polysyllables.

That is true even in a state of "permanent pre-hostility," or peace. If, on the other hand, there is war, you could launch "an all-out war to win peace," and if you stick to your guns, you will get it. When all the bad guys are dead from the all-out war, peace will result, at least until new enemies are found.

But suppose there's peace and you want to do a little shooting without making a lot of trouble? An incursion wouldn't be a wise move; incursions have been inoperative since Cambodia. So, when Grenada needs a spot of invading, launch a "predawn vertical insertion," which is a form of "police action." The fellow who came up with that probably got a medal, which may be one reason the armed forces handed out more medals for the operation than there were soldiers involved. It's also important to make sure there is minimal "collateral damage," or dead civilians. Collateral is likely to be damaged, for example, when struck by "kinetic-energy penetrators," or bullets. Whether they are fired by the enemy or are only "friendly fire," the result is likely to be the same, so keep your head down.

The opposite of that is the neutron bomb, which kills people but doesn't wreck any buildings or otherwise harm property values. That's why the Pentagon calls it a "radiation-enhancement device." The Pentagon also called the Titan II missile "a very large, potentially disruptive re-entry system." President Reagan topped that by naming the MX missile the Peacemaker. He said the voting against producing the Peacemaker was like voting against arms control.

Radiation-enhancement devices being as potentially disruptive as they are, they have the odd effect of making conventional warfare look attractive by comparison. But don't fall for it. Whether you were struck by "air support," "limited air interdiction" or that old favorite, the "limited-duration protective-reaction strike," they've bombed the hell out of you, and you will be in no mood, or condition, to split hairs.

Canada in the News

The Ontario Provincial Parliament had an education minister named Tom Wells, who later went on to Intergovernmental Affairs, and not a minute too soon.

This man once explained, "We've given priorities within the learning-materials-development plan to the development of curriculum materials in these particular areas. The thrust of our multiculturalism policy is inputted to all our curriculum-guideline committees and into our evaluation and research committees."

Explaining the core curriculum, he said, "I am very clear in my mind that the terminology I have always used as mandatory subjects which are the subjects that form the mandatory core and curriculum which means a curriculum guideline with a certain common core that will be used across the province."

He tried to spread his wisdom around, once encouraging a colleague by telling him, "Don't just sort of talk in words."

Finally, A Word from Our Fund-Raiser

Our effectiveness will be directionality proportional to the involvement and the response which is received from those endeavoring to support the purpose of the foundations but in simplistic terms inspecting the situation from a negative determination it will not necessarily suggest that we have failed should our goals not be ascertained as so hopefully anticipated.

In conclusion, may I ask for your thoughtful response. —Letter from the Historic Hawaii Foundation.

XVIII.
MODERN LIVING

Modern life—what a phrase! One gets the impression from so gaudy a bauble that there is such a thing. The idea validates itself by its own terminology. We say "modern life" and assume that it exists. It seems so much more appealing than the truth, which would have to be called "the same old life."

Life really is like a chess game—it has a lot of pieces that are shoved about to create different situations, but the pieces and the rules are the same; so are most of the situations. When we wriggle into, or out of, the same old situations in unfamiliar ways, we call it "modern life" instead of "an old situation we don't recognize."

Modern life is what we're doing now that was done by someone else at some other time we don't know about or have forgotten. Those who take themselves seriously as moderns, who truly believe they are on the cutting edge of human advancement, are kidding themselves. How important, after all, is it to own a video-cassette recorder? Still, self-delusion is no crime, and it is sometimes amusing to watch.

Okay, Now Would They All Please Go There?

In a report on what's up in West Germany these days, *The New York Times* published the intelligence that there is a bar on West Berlin's Kurfurstendamn called The Yuppies Inn.

The same article reported that some young West Germans identify with tennis star Boris Becker as a symbol of the "post peace-movement generation." One has reason to worry anytime *Germans* and *post peace* appear in the same breath.

Oh, That Royal Family!

No. 1

Late in 1985, the New York *Post*, which sometimes has a fine eye for absurdities, reported that Princess Diana's stepbrother, Viscount William Lewisham, was departing New York and returning to London because "the economy has picked up so much." He had taken an apartment with upholstered walls in the Mayfair section of London.

The *Post* said the Viscount was known for eccentric behavior, which "will be missed." By way of example, it said that at a party given by millionaire publisher Walter Annenberg's niece, Dana, Viscount Billy shocked other guests after dessert by opening his shirt to pick lint out of his navel.

No. 2

Also in 1985, Prince Charles, heir to the family business, visited these shores for a round of dinner parties, of which the epicenter was Palm Beach, Florida. Some people paid $10,000 to be invited to the various dinners, and others paid $50,000 to have their pictures taken with Prince Charles and Princess Diana.

In Palm Beach, however, not everything went smoothly. One of the biggies behind the royal visit found it useful to blow town when it was revealed that her past included posing nude for pictures in a British magazine. Another society matron told the *Miami Herald* that she would not be on hand for the polo match or the dinner at which Charles and Diana were the featured attractions. She explained that she had other things to do: "That's the day I have my legs waxed," she said.

And Don't Spit on the Carpet, Your Richness

In Beverly Hills, the school board approved an addition to the school curriculum. Schools will now teach youngsters social graces.

Otherwise known as good manners.

The posh suburb has been increasingly populated by the offspring of rich Iranians, Hong Kong businessmen and oil-rich Arabs who apparently need to be taught how to make introductions, dress appropriately, shake hands and speak to "dignitaries."

School officials pronounced themselves certain that the program was necessary. "Children are woefully inadequate when it comes to manners," said a school board member at a meeting at which the etiquette program was unanimously approved. "They are lacking in all the basic social graces—how to talk on the phone, say 'please' and 'thank you,' and eat properly."

Jean Perloff, a spokesman for the school district, said, "It's less finishing-school techniques we're talking about than basic human decency."

The etiquette program was designed for the school district by a "consulting firm."

Earlier, *The New York Times* had reported that yuppie graduates of leading American universities would also have to be taught basic manners. It had been noticed that many of them were unable to eat properly when at the table with grown-ups.

Beauty Secret for This Week

Preparation H, a hemorrhoid balm, got a big boost a couple of years ago when it was revealed that George Brett, the Kansas City Royals' batting star, suffered from hemorrhoids. It was a delicate matter, one that Brett might well have preferred be glossed over, but as hemorrhoids were keeping him out of a World Series game, chances of that were slim. He later made the best of the situation by endorsing the product in advertisements.

But there turns out to be at least one alternative use for Preparation H. Fashionable women in Beverly Hills and Hollywood have been using it to eliminate facial wrinkles, and drugstores in the area reported sales were booming.

According to some who tried it, Preparation H temporarily erases wrinkles and shrinks pores. (How did anyone get the idea of rubbing this stuff on her face?)

Dermatologists say it does work, but only by irritating the skin so much as to cause swelling, thus leveling the wrinkle, and at the risk of eventually making users look a lot worse: Frequent applications can cause scaling and inflammation.

As for the manufacturer's viewpoint, a spokesman replied, "No comment. Particularly on this matter."

Rare, Medium or Well Done?

Hot tubs can be hazardous to your health. People—that is to say, mostly Californians—tend to soak in them too long and at too high a temperature, conditions made worse by the tendency to relax with booze and drugs. What happens is that people doze off and cook themselves to death.

The Federal Consumer Product Safety Commission says to keep water temperature below 104 degrees and specifically warns pregnant women (brain damage to the unborn child may result) and people with high blood pressure, diabetes or heart disease to be careful in hot tubs.

Hot tubs can also be a drag on your sex life. Many have discovered that spending a couple of hours in the tub with their intended may set the mood perfectly, but the result for them is that the spirit is willing but the flesh is weak.

Hot tubs also require firm footing. In Iowa, two radio performers suffered electrical shock when they were doing a broadcast at tubside and fell in.

A microphone, which fell in with them, short-circuited. They were treated at a nearby hospital.

Kick the Diapers and Take It Out for a Spin

A couple in New Jersey was arrested by state police for allegedly trying to trade their 14-month-old son for a three-year-old car.

The couple fell in love with the car, a 1978 Corvette priced at $8,800, at the used-car lot. The owner of the lot agreed to the trade and then called the cops.

The car dealer, whose son, daughter-in-law and grandchild had died in a fire three years earlier, said afterward that his first impulse was to go ahead with the deal. But, he said, "I knew moments later that it would be wrong—not so much wrong for me or the expense of it, but what would this baby do when he's not a baby anymore? How could this boy cope with life knowing he was traded for a car?"

When the eager couple arrived at the lot, state police

had already staked it out. When the cops moved in, the couple, said the dealer, "had the keys and papers and we were putting the license plates on. They left the baby in the showroom on the floor."

The parents were charged with child abuse, endangering the welfare of a child and putting up a child for illegal adoption, and held on $100,000 bail.

Fashion's Lowest Tide

The summer of 1985 produced a trend for fashionable New York women, who took to wearing, for reasons mysterious and obscure, fish.

Fick necklaces in the form of trout, bass and tropical species were moving well at the gift shop of the American Museum of Natural History. Some women were spotted wearing a painted fish up to six inches long on beaded necklaces. Fish sculptured in gold and silver were also spotted, as were knitted dresses sporting fish designs.

In England, little attention was paid to fish and more to top-of-the-head creativity. A punk rocker from Kent expressed his fondness for pool by having his hair cut, styled and woven into a miniature pool table, complete with balls and two cues. Green dye completed the effect.

Did She Autograph the Wall?

When the late Robert F. Kennedy's eldest son, Joseph P. Kennedy II, got married in Gladwyne, Pennsylvania, a hamlet on Philadephia's steadily decaying Main Line, Jacqueline Kennedy Onassis attended the ceremony.

En route, her limo pulled into a gas station for a routine pit stop and then left.

Not long afterward a plaque was installed at the gas station. It read, "This room was honored by the presence of Jacqueline Kennedy Onassis on the occasion of the wedding of Joseph P. Kennedy II and Sheila Rauch, Feb. 3, 1979."

The plaque was installed in the women's toilet.

Yo, Matron!

In the early 1980s, New York City fell under the spell of the break dancers, young and not always untalented street performers who performed jerky, mimelike body movements to poundingly rhythmic and ruthlessly repetitious musiclike sounds pouring out of portable cassette players. It was hip stuff, if not particularly edifying.

Not to be outdone, the wealthy suburbs of Connecticut decided to get in on the action. Clubs for the overdressed and overrich began importing genuine street-kid "breakers" to teach their martinied members how to get down and boogie.

And thus the socially unacceptable met the morally unspeakable at clubs and benefits in Greenwich and other enclaves of the well heeled. *The New York Times* reported that the King Tut was performed at the Field Club and that the Worm was featured in Bridgeport.

One of the street kids imported to teach the rich how to get with it said the Field Club gig "was like *Dynasty,* it really was. There was some serious expenses walking in." He said there had been instances of culture shock, as when the breakers—in their usual garb of sweatsuits, headbands and sneakers—turned up for an affair benefiting a Bridgeport museum.

The hostess of the affair, he recalled, was a bit disconcerted and kept saying to one of her peers, "Oh, George— keep them in one spot. Don't move! Don't move!" The woman "was embarrassed. She was like, 'Oh, my goodness, what are we going to do?' But after we danced and were a hit and she saw that we weren't going to rip her off, it was like, 'Don't go, don't go!' "

In Greenwich, a dance center more used to teaching modern, jazz and other styles opened nine break-dancing classes within a few months.

Next Time, Just Paint Them On

In San Jose, California, four firemen had to rescue a woman from a pair of jeans.

The woman, who had borrowed the tight-fitting designed jeans from her cousin, found they were a little too tight. Her skin got caught in the zipper when she tried to close the fly.

The rescuers managed to cut her free, using wire cutters and pliers, after a twenty minute sartorial struggle.

XIX.
"THE LAW IS A ASS"

Our title comes from Dickens, who wrote those words in *Oliver Twist* and who also wrote feelingly of (which is to say against) lawyers elsewhere: *Bleak House* is centered on a lawsuit that has dragged on for generations, its present litigants being people who inherited the suit from their parents. Shakespeare had a few words on the subject, most of them sour and the best-known being, no doubt, the eager "The first thing we do, let's kill all the lawyers."

Ambrose Bierce said the law was something you go into a pig and come out of a sausage; Mark Twain said a man caught between two lawyers has about as much chance as a fish caught between two cats. All in all, your *Bartlett's* and other books of quotations have little good to say about lawyers and the law, and the ill spoken of both amounts to a large selection of hostile sentiment.

Lawyers rather resent this, of course, and when the subject comes up, they are quick to remind you that it was lawyers who got justice for John Peter Zenger and Captain Dreyfus and a third person whose name escapes them at the moment but which they could easily remember given a week to think about it.

Hell, Conviction Is What Suspects Are For

Attorney General Edwin Meese, objecting to the coddling of suspects, explained, "The thing is, you don't have many suspects who are innocent of a crime. That's contradictory: If a person is innocent of a crime, then he's not a suspect."

And There Wasn't Even a Warning Sign!

In California, a man who was trying to break into a building through a skylight was injured when the skylight collapsed beneath his weight and he fell to the floor below. He sued on the grounds that the skylight was unsafe and won a judgment against the people he was trying to burglarize.

Felonious Munching in the Third Degree

In Ocean Beach, Long Island, police arrested John Clark and Gary Kumba for the crime of eating pizza in the street. Ocean Beach police have also hauled in people for outdoor ice-cream-cone eating.

They don't like to do it, but village elders insist on having a law against public eating to discourage tourists.

Let the Punishment Fit the Crime

Fame didn't do much good for the Watergate security guard whose discovery of the taped door lock led to the biggest political scandal in American history. Not long after his moment in the headlines, the man was unemployed and living with his mother in South Carolina. There he made the mistake of shoplifting a pair of sneakers to give to his son. The judge gave him the maximum sentence—one year.

Of all the others involved in Watergate, only G. Gordon Liddy got a stiffer sentence—52 months—and only John Mitchell, H. R. Haldeman, John Erlichman and R. Howard Hunt got sentences equalling the guard's. The rest did a lot better. Dwight Chapin got eight months; Jeb Stewart Magruder and Charles Colson got seven months; Herbert Kalmbach got six months; John Dean got under five months; Donald Segretti and Egil Krogh got four months.

Tricky Dick Nixon received a full pardon.

Sometimes, Though, the Anti-coddlers Have a Point

In Indiana, a 19-year-old boy stole a stereo in a burglary, but charges were dropped even though he was found with the goods and admitted the crime. The youth was caught by his father, a police lieutenant who found the stereo when he searched his son's room.

The charges were dropped when the court ruled that the father had violated his son's rights.

Deductions, Deductions

The IRS denied some of the income-tax deductions claimed by a convicted drug dealer in Minneapolis, which included the drugs, the scale used for weighing them out, packing materials, rent, phone and transportation to and from deals. The dealer thought that was unfair, took the IRS to tax court, and won.

Two Out of Three Is Good Enough

In Florida the police found a man sleeping in his car—in the driver's seat, with the keys in the ignition, but doing nothing but sleeping and with the engine not running. A deputy woke the man up and gave him an blood-alcohol test, which he flunked, and then arrested him for drunk driving.

As assistant state attorney said the charge would stick because a person behind the wheel of a car with the keys in the ignition is deemed to be in "physical control of the vehicle" even if the engine is not running and the car is not moving.

Twelve Good Men and True

In the province of Manitoba, Canada, a murder case had to be stopped in mid-trial when alarming things were discovered about three of the jurors. One was deaf as a post. He admitted to having heard not a word of testimony or evidence, and was dismissed.

Observing that such fine points apparently had some meaning, another juror decided to come forward. He admitted that he spoke French but no English, the language in which the case was being tried, and was dismissed. Then a third juror spoke, saying that he, too, was deaf, and also without English. A new trial was ordered.

*   *   *

The ability to speak English is important for jurors in Boston as well as Manitoba. In June 1985, Cat Mousam was found not to make the grade on that score and was therefore excused from jury duty.

"It's funny they didn't disqualify her because she's a cat," said Mousam's owner, David Christian.

Mousam got onto the jury-duty list in the first place because her name was on Christian's door. When people do not answer their doors in Boston, census takers often add to their lists any names that happen to be on doors and mailboxes, election officials said.

Why Some Borrowers Prefer Loan Sharks

Any condition of this Agreement which requires the submission of evidence of the existence or non-existence of a specified fact or facts implies as a condition the existence or non-existence, as the case may be, of such fact or facts and the Lender shall, at all times, be free independently to establish to its satisfaction and in its absolute discretion such existence or non-existence. —Clause from a loan instrument written in Greenwich, Connecticut.

A Tennesse man went to jail for the failure of his twenty-seven banks, but not before asking the judge to give him a break.

Sentenced to twenty years, he asked the judge for a reduced sentence. He explained that statistics showed most marriages go on the rocks when one of the partners is in jail for more than three years. The judge thought this over and reduced the sentence to ten years.

His father, a defendant in the Federal Deposit Insurance Corporation's suits against his son, launched a suit of his own. He blamed the FDIC for all the trouble, saying it was culpable for not having moved quickly enough to stop the questionable dealings.

Too Close for Comfort

A federal appeals court in St. Louis ordered a hearing to inquire into the fairness of a 1975 murder trial.

The appeals court noted that the judge in the trial was

the husband of the court reporter and the uncle of the prosecutor, who was, in turn, dating the daughter of the defense lawyer.

It Was the Nagging That Did It

In Massachusetts, a man charged with murder was found innocent by reason of insanity of stabbing to death his father-in-law, who had reminded the defendant to take the medicine prescribed for his mental illness.

And Jelly Doughnuts Are Even Worse!

Charged with following a woman home, tying her up at gunpoint, removing her blouse and bra and fondling her breasts, a cop in Tuscon, Arizona, got off lightly when his plea-bargaining lawyer arranged for his client to plead guilty to the lesser charge of second-degree burglary.

The prosecution accepted the deal because the lawyer said he could call as a witness a psychiatrist who would testify that the defendant was the victim of wildly fluctuating blood-sugar levels, which caused blackouts and violent acts, after having eaten too many doughnuts.

A Tongue-lashing Will Have to Do

In March of 1985, Mississippi got around to repealing an 1848 law that excused the killing of a servant when the death resulted from "accident and misfortune in [the course of] lawfully correcting" the servant's behavior.

The law was overlooked when the state's laws were overhauled in 1972.

Just Hope to God They Remembered To Read Them Their Rights!

In February 1984, New York City cops chased a man suspected of drug and weapons violations into an apartment on the Upper West Side.

Two women and a child were in the apartment, and while police tried to get them out of danger, the suspect and two other men were seen throwing a cache of weapons out the window. They managed to dump all of them into the courtyard below before the police could close in.

The three men were arrested and charged with drug possession, criminal possession of deadly weapons and, for throwing the guns out the window, littering.

But such is the punctiliousness of the law these days that, said a police spokesman the littering charge "may be the only one that sticks."

Okay, the Law Is not a Ass

A man accused of mooning a couple in Kentucky got base-assed justice in court.

The plaintiffs told the court they could identify the culprit by the mole—the size of a half dollar—they saw when they were mooned in the once safe environs of their own neighborhood. The defendant's lawyer said the indentification was in error—his client's buttocks were mole-free, and he could prove it. After clearing the court-room, the judge gave the defendant a chance to clear himself by dropping his drawers, which he did.

No mole, no moon, no case.

XX.
THIS SPORTING LIFE

Some people think that there just won't be any more sports now that Howard Cosell has retired. They are incorrect. Even Cosell is not crucial to the existence of sports in general or even any sport in particular. Besides, Cosell might unretire at any time. Then what will we do?

The important thing to do is to put Cosell out of our minds and concentrate on the essence of sport—the competition, the drama, the drugs—the good old thrill of victory and the agony of defeat.

Rough Diamond

In Florida, Aaro Excavating was battling Pasco-Hernandez Community College in an industrial-league softball game when a spectator wandered onto the field of play.

The unwelcome visitor was an alligator nearly nine feet long. It was also unwilling to move—the sun at shortstop seemed just right.

One of Aaro's players decided to bully the beast by backing his jeep and trailer toward it in a show of force. The alligator responded by biting off a taillight. "He was bleeding pretty good from the mouth after that," he said, but he didn't move.

The teams moved instead, continuing play on another field and leaving the visitor to the tender mercies of an alligator-control agent.

News from NFL Control

Professional fooball is known to be a physically hazardous game, but some players manage to add drama to even the easy parts.

Some years ago, a pass receiver managed to personally put his team into the playoffs with a thrilling touchdown catch near the end of the game. Then he personally put himself out of the playoffs by engaging in an end-zone victory dance so strenuous that he pulled a groin muscle. Not too long after that, another player managed to injure himself while going out for the coin toss.

The off-season can be tricky too. The *New York Post* reported that at the end of January 1985, Washington Redskin fullback John Riggins was invited by *People* magazine to sit at its table for the Washington Press Club's annual black-tie "Salute to Congress" dinner. Also at the table was Supreme Court Justice Sandra Day O'Connor and her husband, John.

Riggins had reportedly begun drinking during a cocktail hour before dinner, and at the table there was more alcohol for the guests. On several occasions during the dinner, Riggins spoke loudly across the table to Mrs. O'Connor, saying, according to another guest, "Come on, Sandra, baby! Loosen up! You're too tight!"

Some time after the main course was served, Riggings stood up and walked around the table. He knelt down, then sat down, then *lay* down on the floor and fell asleep. There he lay for the remainder of the dinner, snoring occasionally as the serving staff stepped around and over him to serve dessert and clear the tables.

No Trotting Races Today

According to a report in the *Los Angeles Times,* an Italian undercover cop foiled an attempt to make a world-champion bike racer change seats for a race.

Before the final stage of the race, the cop saw a waiter surreptitiously put something into the food of a racer. It turned out to be a liquid laxative. The waiter had been bribed by a representative of a company that sponsored one of the racer's rivals.

Keeping Amateur Sports Pure and Clean

In Montrose, Scotland, club officials banned a youth from amateur competition on the ground that he had turned pro.

The Montrose Athletic Club held a special meeting to

reconsider the banning of Andy Williamson, age 10, but concluded that it was fitting and proper.

Williamson had won thirteen cents' worth of candy for coming in second in a footrace.

Winners of the Grantland Rice Poetry of Sport Medal

No. 1

Pro football announcer and former NFL coach John Madden said that before every game he always told his Oakland Raiders, "Don't worry about the horse being blind, just load up the wagon."

He said he had no idea what it meant.

No. 2

Super Bowl-winning coach Bill Walsh of the NFL's San Francisco 49ers said, "If I have any talent, it's the artistic end of football. The variation of movement of eleven players and the orchestration of that facet of football is beautiful to me."

No. 3

Writing in the *Chicago Sun-Times,* Brian Hewitt said "One-run baseball games always make great doorstops of the second-guessers who love to throw open the gates and charge headlong into the land of 20-20 hindsight."

The Gentlemanly Game of Golf

No. 1

Shot Off Woman's Leg Helps Nicklaus To 66
—Headline in the St. Louis *Post-Dispatch*.

No. 2

Things may have changed in the recent wave of unrest in Uganda, but as of December 1985, things have improved for golfers at the course in Kampala.

Soldiers armed with AK-47s were in the habit of pitching tents on the green of the fifth hole, making it, said one Ugandan golfer to a *New York Times* correspondent, "difficult to play through."

Polite negotiations—the sort usually held when people

with niblicks are talking to people with automatic weapons—did result in some relief. Artillery pieces were removed from the fairways and the soldiers agreed to bivouac in the rough.

"They still shag balls, though," said the golfer.

No. 3

Guerrilla activity required adjustments to the rules at the golf club in Centenary, Rhodesia.

One new rule "allows a stroke to be played again if interrupted by gunfire or sudden explosion." Another enjoins players to check the greens for land mines before putting.

No. 4

Trees are scarce in Kuwait, and so is grass. So at the golf courses in Kuwait they make do with steel pipes bent into arboreal shapes and greens made of a compacted mixture of oil and sand. Players carry around small patches of artificial turf to hit from.

The fairways are a bit of a problem too—they're spotted with holes dug by lizards that run up to a foot long. If a ball goes into a lizard hole, rules allow the victim to "play a new ball from the beginning without penalty."

Biggest Flops

No. 1

There is no need to yell "Everybody out of the pool" when Canada's various belly-flop championships are held. Canadians, thought by many to be interested in no sport besides street fighting on skates, have developed a deep interest in dropping large, ungainly human beings into swimming pools.

"Passionate Peggy" Wilson won the 1985 Canadian Belly-flop and Cannonball Championship, and this mermaid is 58 years old and a nine-time grandmother. The hit of the western regional championships was Dale Henderson of Cloverdale, British Columbia.

Henderson, a cannonball artist, weighs in at 511 pounds.

No. 2

In New Orleans, lifeguards at the city's public pools

were elated when for the first time they got through a full season without a drowning. Naturally, they decided to throw a pool party to celebrate.

More than a hundred lifeguards attended with nearly a hundred guests, and a good time was had by all except Jerome Moody, 31, whose body was found at the bottom of the pool when the party was over.

Winter Kills

Sports enthusiasts who have looked with alarm at the lines of walking wounded returning from ski resorts have in recent years become interested in cross-country skiing, which—done almost exclusively on flat trails—looks to be a lot safer than downhill skiing. After all, it would appear almost impossible for a cross-country skier to fall a distance greater than his own height.

But hidden dangers lurk everywhere.

At Keene State College in Keene, New Hampshire, a skier was speeding across the soccer field when he decided to slow down by heading into the netting of the soccer goal.

When he did, the goal fell over and killed him.

Boxing—The Sweet Science

No. 1

In Miami, an amateur boxer blew a welterweight bout and then blew his top.

In the opinion of the referee, the 19-year-old pugilist was "taking too many blows," and he decided to stop the fight in the second round rather than have the fighter risk injury. He walked the fighter to his corner and then went to get the score sheet from the judge.

The 60-year-old ref's back was turned when the fighter came out of his corner and knocked him unconscious.

No. 2

Another pugilist lost a lightweight bout, and it was no consolation that it was telecast on ABC's *Wide World of Sports*—he lost a lot more than a fight, and the telecast simply enabled some of his friends to get their last look at him for a while.

He was in the ring doing his level best when the rose tattoo on his chest jogged the memory of one of the onlookers—a rose tattoo was on the chest of a man police had been looking for.

The boxer took his second loss of the day when the cops arrested him in the locker room.

Grabbers

No. 1

Before there was a Refrigerator Perry in football, there was Tab Thacker in college wrestling. Tab Thacker was so big he didn't need a nickname. Or maybe everyone was afraid to give him one.

Thacker weighed in at 390 pounds.

The New York Times reported that Thacker's normal-sized roommate said, "A lot of people are amazed when they first see Tab. They just stare and get quiet." Some wrestlers who found themselves matched against Thacker preferred to forfeit the match rather than delay, or try to delay, the inevitable. One who didn't was lucky to come out with only three dislocated ribs.

The wrestling coach at Duke University, Bill Harvey, said, "You have a better chance of moving a VW in a lot than of moving Tab Thacker."

No. 2

From the *Boston Herald* we have this one:

Steve Grabowski was a bald man who did professional wrestling for a living under the name Steve Thunder. When he invested several hundred dollars in a high-quality hairpiece, he planned to go back into the ring under a new name—Steve Gray.

He and his hair were in their first match—televised, as luck would have it—when his hair threw in the towel. It came off, and fans recognized him. They began shouting, "That's Steve Thunder!"

Grabowski/Thunder/Gray said the hair was to be part of his new image and identity, and the loss of it killed his comeback. He filed a $200,000 suit against the hair-replacement firm.

Alternative Sports

Alternative sports are informal games and competitions that have what is called a "low degree of organization." Some people like them because they are informal, some because they are simple. Some people like them because they are not high-pressure, high-stress events—no screaming fans, no vicious Little League parents, no big-money wheeler-dealers. And a few like them because they're bonkers.

No. 1

Daring made Karel Soucek, and daring unmade him. His was a short career.

Soucek, 37, from Ontario, Canada, came to fame in July 1984, when he went over Niagara Falls in a barrel. He got a few cuts and scrapes out of it, but he was the first person in twenty-three years to be able to talk about it afterward. That was the beginning of a realtionship with barrels that was to end less happily only a few months later.

Daredevils customarily go on tour doing some altered version of their original stunt. Soucek's idea was to climb into a barrel and have it dropped from a high tower into a small tank of water.

That is exactly what the plan was when he appeared at the Houston Astrodome as a featured attraction of the Thrill Show and Demolition Derby. The problem was that he missed the tank.

The drop was 180 feet, and the tank was a mere 12 feet wide and 9 feet deep. The problem lay elsewhere—the barrel itself was unstable. Workers at the Thrill Show said the barrel would start to spin when dropped. "It started spinning real bad," one of them said. "But after a while the people started getting so impatient that we went ahead and dropped him."

Instead of hitting the water, the unstable barrel wandered off course and struck the rim of the tank and then fell in. Soucek was alive when pulled out, but he later died in the hospital.

No. 2

More successful divers are the Aqua Mules of Tim Rivers.

Rivers, of McIntosh, Florida, has had his Original High-Diving Aqua Mules clambering up a ramp and diving thirty feet into a tank of water for more than a quarter of a century. He has somehow missed the big time—never making either Broadway or the movies—but he has done well enough at state fairs and the like to count himself a fortunate man.

From time to time, animal lovers sic the law on him, but without success. Before his scheduled gig at the Alabama State Fair in October 1985, Bill Carter, the animal expert of the Jefferson County Sheriff's Department, investigated carefully but "couldn't find anything wrong." He said the mules were "butterball fat and well taken care of."

"I don't care what anyone says," said John Bodie, president of the Birmingham Humane Society. "It's just not something mules like to do, and I hope there is enough outcry that we'll bring Alabama animal laws into the twentieth century."

"I don't know much about the controversy," said the fair's general manager, Jerry Robinson, "but it sure has generated a lot of interest in the mule act."

Left unanswered is the question why anyone wants to watch a mule jump into a tank of water.

No. 3

Jim and Carlota Robinson race pigs for a living. They travel about much like the diving-mules act, doing state fairs and the like all over the country. Unlike diving mules, racing pigs do not attract much hostility from animal lovers.

If there is any ill effect of the pig-racing business, it seems in any case to be on the humans and not the pigs. The human side of the act is given to, perhaps even obsessed with, making puns (about pigheaded people—haw!), wearing OINK! shirts and such. Carlota Robinson calls herself Miss Piggy, according to Charla Cribb of the *St. Petersburg Times,* who noted that she also calls herself The Pig Lady. (Cribb did observe, however, a refreshing absence of that "sooooooeeee, pig!" stuff, reporting that Carlota simply yells, "Come on, guys—let's race!")

The pigs wear racing silks and numbers, and the winner always gets an Oreo cookie. Mrs. Robinson says pig races have the advantage of being immune to fixers—each pig gets a different number for each race.

The swankest gig the Robinson's racing Pigs have had thus far was Palm Beach, most recently agog over Prince Charles and Princess Diana. Mrs. Robinson is aware of the honor involved.

"What a year Palm Beach is having," she says.

No. 4

The poor man's discus—the cow flop—has caught on in Britain. You thought it was all *Chariots of Fire* there, or what?

It was (literally) a by-product of agricultural-exchange visits of the good ol' boys of the U.S. and England. The climate of England is not of the best for cow-flop hurling—it's too damned damp, and the flops are often too wet to grip properly or even to hold themselves together. Also, a wet flop is a heavy flop, which cuts down on distance.

The result has been a revisionist trend toward plastic bags, which are an absolute necessity under some conditions. The *Times* noted that there was a side benefit to this stylistic impurity—the sport has become more popular with women, never a bad thing. (Even so, a competitor billed as Miss Surrey Dairymaid, nee Anne Brooker, wears rubber gloves, anyway.)

Britain's veteran dung-slinger, Colin Compton—the man who is known as "a legend in the Dorking region" —refuses to join those who say "Don't wrap it, bag it." He prefers his flops in their naked state, just as the Lord intended them to be. Besides, he says bags are aerodynamically counterproductive.

"He has turned it into a science," Mrs. Compton said.

No. 5

Also small and conveniently hurlable are dwarves, which has given rise to a new sport—dwarf-tossing.

Dwarf-tossing appears to have originated in Australia as a competitive event for saloon bouncers. In a well-run toss the dwarves not only wear the harnesses that are used as handholds but also crash helmets for safety, and they are flung onto mattresses. Only underhand throws are allowed.

The sport, if that's what it is, spread to England, and at one point a bar in Chicago seemed interested. Paul

Hemp of *The Wall Street Journal* said considerable controversy has been produced. Dwarf-rights groups have protested, as have a British Member of Parliament and Vera Squarcialupi, an Italian Communist member of the European Parliament, who introduced a resolution condemning dwarf-tossing. In Australia, the cradle of the sport, a crowd of protesters tried to break up a dwarf-tossing contest at a nightclub in the town of Surfers Paradise.

So far, dwarf-tossing in England involves only one dwarf, Lenny the Giant, a 4' 4" dwarf who weighs 98 pounds. Lenny told Hemp that he enjoyed being thrown and said that those who criticise the sport do so in ignorance. He is 29 and a member of a four-man comedy troupe called the Oddballs. Between throws, he gives autographs.

The All-England record in the dwarf-toss is 12' 5".

XXI.
OUR CHANGING WORLD

We may not be leading what can accurately be called modern lives, but our world is changing. Changing into what it has been at other times but changing nevertheless. Some of us get a bit breathless about our changing world because so often we seem not to be able to keep up with it or cope with it. It throws us for a loop.

Alvin Toffler called that Future Shock. Actually it's Past Shock. The fact that the past so often catches up to an unprepared world is proof of the sorrowful old line, "They never learn." "They" are us. At other times our world changes in ways that are dismaying but unedifying.

No matter what the change or what the reason, there is no reason not to sit back and enjoy it.

Farewell, O Voice With a Smile!

Communications mavens at New Jersey Bell instituted a couple of new numbers in their unceasing efforts to supply customers with new ways to reach out and touch someone.

Special numbers were set up for services called Talk Exchange, Teen Exchange, Hispanic Exchange and Senior Exchange, the idea being that customers might improve themselves, gain insights and share knowledge through group conversations. A spokesman for the company said the exchanges, set up as experiments in Jersey City, were "a new way to meet someone you don't know."

But some customers who tried the numbers found themselves barraged with foul language and racial insults.

Randy Diamond of the New York *Daily News* reported that twenty-five calls placed to the exchanges at random produced "mostly chatter among teenagers, peppered with four-letter words, slurs and even death threats."

They Used to Be Called Lawmakers

"We were looking for influential shapers and leaders who represented a choice," said Mr. Dusenberry. "Geraldine Ferraro, more than anybody else, represented choice. It allowed her to state clearly and concisely the point she intended to make, to help clarify the choice women have today." He said Mrs. Ferraro's choice of going into politics and of being a mother was analogous to the choice that the new generation of Pepsi-Cola drinkers were making in both their lives and soft drinks.—*The New York Times*.

The Great Ball of China

The old will meet the new in Peking, the government of China has announced.

A spokesman said that Club Med has been given permission to open at two sites at Peking's Imperial Summer Palace. The leases were to begin in January 1986.

Practical Skills for Modern People

Springfield, Illinois—William H. Masters and Virginia Johnson, pioneer sex researchers, will be featured speakers at the annual meeting of the Illinois Certified Public Accountants' Society, Sunday through Wednesday at the Forum Motel, Springfield.

Masters and Johnson are the authors of *Human Sexual Response, Human Sexual Inadequacy* and the newly released *The Pleasure Bond*.

The meeting will also feature technical sessions designed to improve accounting skills.—The Champaign-Urbana *News Gazette*.

Coverup

In 1970, directors of the National Nude Beach Weekend had already mailed out their invitations to the event, to be held at the Playboy Club resort in Lake Geneva,

Wisconsin, when they suddenly had to find somewhere else to strip.

The Playboy Club suddenly changed its mind and decided not to permit the Nude Weekend to be held on its premises. Playboy Club spokesman Charles Dickerman explained that it might offend the club's guests. "Not everyone will accept nudity," he said.

Salty Doings

The Playboy Club at Great Gorge, McAfee, New Jersey, was chosen as the site of the 34th annual National Pretzel Bakers Institute Convention. . . . The theme for the meeting was "Pretzels in a Changing World."—*Snack Food* magazine.

XXII.
SEX AND SIMILAR

Sex, which has been coyly peeking about these pages elsewhere, rears its ugly head here in a chapter all its own. Also its indifferent head, its defiant head, its lower-animals head, its simultaneously untranslated head and even its feet, among other heads, things and body parts. For those of you who Only Want One Thing, this is your chapter.

Premature Ejaculation

Officials at Shannon Airport in Ireland got quickly into the international-incident mode when a young Russian couple seemed ready to defect.

The couple entered a duty-free store where the man, in imperfect English, told the clerk that he wanted "protection." Immigration officials quickly took the couple into protective custody and interviewed them about their intentions. The alert ended when it became clear that the man was only trying to buy some condoms.

Do You Have a Sub-teens Model That Plays "I Want to Hold Your Hand"?

Frederick's of Hollywood, the long time mail-order purveyor of steamy silks, peek-a-boo lace and sexy satins, has produced a pair of panties equipped with a miniature battery-operated music box.

Romantically inclined customers who want to make love to a thousand violins or the nearest tinkling equivalent can choose from a selection of mood music that includes "Jingle Bells," "Love Me Tender," "Let Me

Call You Sweetheart," "Happy Birthday," "Here Comes the Bride" and "When the Saints Go Marching In."

Shafted by Discrimination

The International Prostitutes' Committee held its first worldwide convention in Amsterdam, near the Dutch capital's internationally famous red-light district.

Some 250 hookers from all over the globe said they wanted to stop being treated like criminals by society. A world charter for prostitutes was discussed, and the delegates said they would bring pressure to bear on governments, the U.N. and Amnesty International.

"Discrimination is bad enough back home as a woman," said a delegate who wore a black-cat mask and identified herself only as Linda, from San Francisco. "It's bad enough as a black woman," she continued, "but when you're a black female whore like me, it's real bad."

And Now, It's Time for Dr. Ruth

Dr. Ruth Westheimer, the pixie of prurience and broadcasting's best-known sex adviser, announced her plan to lead a tour group to India. She said she and others involved in the "sensory-religious disciplines" would visit historically and architecturally sensual sites on the subcontinent.

Dr. Ruth also writes books. Having written for adults, she turned her hand to teenagers in 1986. In *First Love,* her beginner's manual, she undertook to explain to young lovers the business of when a woman is in her fertile period and thus likely to become pregnant, and when she is not.

As numerous readers pointed out—and as some of her readers may subsequently have found out—Dr. Ruth got the critical facts exactly backward. The publisher hastily withdrew every copy it was possible to lay hands on.

Gently Hold Her Close,
Tenderly Kiss Her Hand.
Then Rip Her Clothes off

A $500,000 federally funded study of ways to reduce crime suggested that rape might be reduced by teaching rapists conventional courtship techniques.

On the Other Hand, Maybe We Could Buy Them All Some Polaroid Swingers

In a parking garage, a woman was accosted by a double flasher. She told police that the creep first exposed himself and then exposed *her* by taking a snapshot of her astonished reaction.

They *Don't* Only Want One Thing

Psychology Today magazine polled its readers on favorite activities of married couples, giving them a wide variety of choices. Forty-five percent of the male respondents said they liked sex best. The most popular activity among female respondents was reading, which pulled 37%. Sex was a favorite among only 26% of the women. It edged out sewing by one percentage point.

Sex was also outpolled by playing or performing music, gorging on Häagen-Dazs ice cream and eating Godiva chocolates.

A more specific survey was conducted by Ann Landers, who wanted to know whether her female readers would prefer just a lot of hugging and snuggling to what Ann rather shudderingly referred to, as if handling it with tongs, as "the act." The overwhelming majority of her respondents voted in favor of titillation instead of penetration. Ann said it was all men's fault.

The Respondents Win a Free Trip to Finland

Scandinavia has long had a reputation for uninhibited sexuality, but in Finland they draw the line somewhere. The Helsinki Youth Committee thus demanded the banning of Donald Duck on the grounds that he and Daisy are still not married (after half a century); that his "nephews" Huey, Louie and Dewey may not be his nephews at all; and that the three youngsters spend all their time running around bare-assed. In Finland, a middie blouse is not enough, and the Disney ducks' "racy life-style," said the worried Youth Committee, could corrupt the young.

Crimes of Passion

No. 1

In Bloomington, Indiana, a 40-year-old woman was arrested and charged with murdering her 37-year-old boyfriend.

Police said the woman, who was held without bail, killed her lover, the owner of a bowling-supply company, by dropping a bowling ball on his head while he slept.

No. 2

In Napier, New Zealand, a man was charged with killing his wife by stabbing her in the stomach with a frozen sausage.

He denied that he had murdered his wife. The jury found him innocent of murder but guilty of manslaughter.

No. 3

Gwen Owen, 62, of Sydney, Australia, was killed with the pet rock given to her by her lover.

A police spokesman said Owen's lover visited her often and had given her the pet rock about a month before. Owen's lover had disappeared, the spokesman said, adding, "We have found the pet rock and there are bloodstains on it."

No. 4

In Hollywood a man dumped his live-in girlfriend by telling her that he was off on a business trip and expected her to have cleared out of the house by the time he returned. Pretty cold, guy.

The woman left, but when the man returned, he learned that she had found what Paul Simon might call the fifty-first way to leave your lover. The house was in good order, and the only odd thing was that the phone was off the hook. When he picked it up, he heard incomprehensible babbling, so he hung up.

When his next phone bill arrived, it explained a couple of things. The strange language he had heard was Japanese, and it was giving the correct time. It had been giving the correct time long enough to run up a bill of $80,000.

Queer Doings

In the early 1980s, the staff serving Britain's Royal Family was rather suddenly thinned in a series of firings.

Best-known among those given the royal boot was the head of Scotland Yard's Royal Protection Squad and Queen's officer, which made him responsible for the Royal Family's safety at Buckingham Palace and at public events, and personally responsible for the Queen wherever she was.

He wasn't fired but was "allowed" to resign. The reason might have been that an intruder had managed to enter the palace and actually come within the Queen's presence. Some others wondered whether the forced resignation was connected to what appeared to be an outbreak of antihomosexual hostility.

A royal valet who did not hide his homosexuality was dismissed. So were the staff of the royal yacht *Brittania,* and for the same reason.

No one could account for antihomosexuality within the royal household; in fact, London homosexuals had long considered it a good and "safe" place to work, said the *Guardian* of Manchester. Not only had there not appeared to be discrimination at the palace, but also there was a famous story of the Queen Mother phoning down to her servants to bring her a drink, saying, "I don't know what you old queens are doing down there, but this old queen is dying of thirst."

It Used to Be Just the Backseat That Was Dangerous

In Ortonville, Michigan, 20-year-old William Hishke got a hell of a deal—he bought a 1968 Buick Skylark for ninety-nine cents when a used-car dealer offered it in a promotional stunt.

Five days later Hishke and girlfriend, Nicola Davis, 18, went for a spin and then parked, as couples will do, along a country road. They left the motor running and were later found dead, apparently of carbon-monoxide poisoning.

And Now You're Going to Tell Me That Cherry Coke Is the Big Hit With Virgins

When it comes to contraceptives, Coke is it, or is not it, depending more or less on your definition of *it*.

Dr. Sharee Umpierre and colleagues at the Harvard Medical School were moved to test various kinds of Coca-Cola for their spermicidal qualities, and they reported their findings in *The New England Journal of Medicine.*

The doctors said that a Coca-Cola douche was being used in some Third World countries as a form of after-sex birth control.

The researchers' findings added some fuel to the controversy over New Coke. They said Coke in any form is not effective as a means of after-sex birth control because the sperm move too quickly into the fallopian tubes, where they are fertilized. But, they said, "Our data indicate that at least in the area of spermicidal effect, Classic Coke is it."

In their tests New Coke was only 42% effective as a spermicide. Classic Coke was more than twice as effective at 91%. Diet Coke, however, was 100% effective, killing all the sperm it was mixed with in less than a minute.

The Coca-Cola Company said, "We do not promote Coca-Cola for medical uses. It is a soft drink."

Animal Acts

No. 1

Police called to investigate a disturbance in Lindenwold, New Jersey, found quite a disturbance.

They arrested a man who was having a violent disagreement with his estranged girlfriend. They said he had killed the girlfriend's pet iguana by throwing it against a wall, then tied her to a chair and tried to make her eat the late iguana piece by piece.

The man was indicted on charges of aggravated assault, criminal restraint, making terroristic threats and animal cruelty.

No. 2

At the zoo in Canton, China, elephants Yilong, 42, and Baibao, 53, had had a long and happy relationship that had produced four offspring.

But on one occasion when Yilong was in the mood, Baibao was not in the mood. And Yilong grew angry. She began butting Baibao, and finally butted him so hard that he lost his balance and fell into the moat around the elephant pen, landing on his back.

Still furious at her rejection, or perhaps spurred by an excess of passion, Yilong then fell or threw all four tons of herself on top of Baibao. The two became, shall we say, enmeshed. They struggled to unmesh themselves, and one hundred rescuers tried to help them, but before they could be pried apart, both died of asphyxiation.

The local newspaper reported that the pair would be stuffed and mounted, which, of course, is what Yilong wanted in the first place.

No. 3

In Taipei, Taiwan, the zoo's collection of giraffes shrank from four to three when the lone female of the group died.

Zookeeper Chen Pao-Chun said that as a result, the three lonely males turned gay. He said the zoo was looking into bringing in one or more females soon, because "we are running out of explanations for the children visiting the zoo."

Love Is Blind

No. -1

In Winnipeg, Manitoba, Canada, the feverishly hot sensual center of Canada, a desperate man went to court to seek relief from a woman who constantly showers him with unwanted affection, sometimes in the form of pies in the face and buckets of water over his head.

He spent eight years trying to get her to leave him alone, but she continued to send him love letters (which he either destroyed or returned) and to visit him, uninvited, at his home and workplace.

On one visit to his job, a dry-cleaning store, she threw a pie at him. It missed and she left. A week later she returned and became emotional when he suggested that she see a doctor. On another occasion she dumped a bucket of water over his head while he was talking to a customer.

The woman insisted that he telephoned her and gave her "silent kisses." The man denied it and said he did everything possible to avoid and discourage her. Before taking legal action, he had his lawyers warn her that he would go to court unless she left him alone.

The woman wrote back, saying that going to court was exactly what she wanted. "Once and for all," she said, "I would like to know where I stand."

No. 2

In November 1977, British authorities charged a North Carolina woman, a former Miss Wyoming, of abducting a Mormon missionary with the help of a male accomplice. The missionary himself said the pair knocked him out with chloroform and took him to a remote cottage where the woman chained him to a bed and raped him.

She and her accomplice fled England after charges were filed; no extradition attempts were made.

In June 1984, she was arrested outside Salt Lake City International Airport, where the missionary worked at the commissary of Western Airlines. He called the police, who charged her with harassment and disturbing the peace.

The woman's lawyer said he didn't think she had done anything criminal in shadowing the man. Also, her precise intentions were somewhat unclear. "I think her interest in him is a matter of nostalgia. It was for old-times' sake."

Police said she had kept a notebook of the man's daily activities, mapped his movements and photographed him.

Early the next month she called United Press International to give her side of the story. She said the incident of the cottage in England had come about because the man had phoned her and begged her to help him escape from Mormon control. She also said they were in love.

"We had the world on a string and were going to be

married," she said. "Then the Mormon church decided they were going to break things up because I wasn't a Mormon—I had left them because I had found out they were a cult who controlled even a person's sex drive."

She said the kidnapping story grew out of a Mormon attempt to discredit her. "The Mormons were afraid the real story would come out," she said. "I mean, they wanted people to believe I was a dizzy blonde tramp with bionic arms who could kidnap a man. And how can you force a man to have sex with you?" She said, "I'm not some tramp off the street. I'm a former Miss Wyoming. I also was a Girl Scout, but you don't read about that in the press."

She said the alleged victim's statements to British authorities about the kidnapping were made after he had been "brainwashed" by the Mormons. The Mormon Church denied any conspiracy and said that their church, as an institution, had had nothing to do with the kidnapping.

As for her recent arrest in Salt Lake City, she said it was part of a Mormon attempt to discredit her again because she is writing a book that "will blow the cover off what really happened in England. The true story has never come out before, and the true story is 'Mormongate.'"

She refused to say where she was calling from, but her lawyer said the statements made were similar to what she had been telling him in private for some time.

At the time of the kidnapping she had said she loved the man. A lot. So much that if he asked her to, she would "ski down Mt. Everest nude with a carnation in my nose."

Love Is Stupid

Despite Coast Guard advice to stay home, a British man set out into the English Channel on the start of what was to be a round-the-world voyage in search of love and romance.

Prospects did not look especially bright for the bold sailor, as his boat was a top-heavy-looking 16-footer powered only by a 5½ hp outboard motor. The Coast Guard had guessed right—the would-be admiral had to be rescued twice.

A few miles from port, the man's boat ran out of gas. He managed to get a few gallons of fuel from a passing tanker and set forth again. He was lost by then, but that mattered little, as he was also sinking. A fishing trawler tried to tow him to port, but the gallant little boat sank beneath her captain's feet. The trawler dropped him at the French port of L'Aberwrach, where he looked back sadly on the disaster.

He said he had put two years of work into fitting out the craft for his love cruise. Lost with the vessel were his cash, photographs, radios, provisions and "all twenty-eight of my Elvis Presley tapes."

It was conceivable that he might get another chance at his voyage. The foundered boat, drifting just beneath the surface, was declared a menace to navigation, and the French Navy had been sent to locate it. That gave its captain hope that the French would salvage the plucky craft and haul it back into port for him to rebuild.

He was apparently unaware that the usual practice with a navigational hazard is to sink it by gunfire.

And Sometimes It Doesn't Even Taste Good

No. 1

After what a Nassau County spokesman said was "simple gumshoe work," a detective arrested the man at his home. Police said the man allegedly broke into the home of two sisters who lived a few blocks away because "he liked their feet."

On one occasion the man tickled the feet of one sleeping sister until she awoke and screamed; he then grabbed a shoe and fled. Some time later, the man again broke into the house and this time tickled the feet of the other sister. When she woke up, he again stole a shoe and escaped.

Police said their prisoner, the son of a Baptist minister, was a suspect in five other neighborhood break-ins, each of which involved toe-tickling, shoe-stealing or both. Neighbors described the accused as "such a polite young man" who "would always have a nice word for people on the block."

* * *

No. 2

In 1985, Nassau County was again the scene of rampant foot-fetishism.

A man from Massapequa was caught by cops who called him the "Long Island Toe-Kisser." The suspect was released on bail.

Two of his alleged victims submitted affidavits describing the man's digital devotions. One woman said the man came to her door pretending to look for another family in the neighborhood and asking whether he had found the correct house. Moments later, the man grabbed her. "He slid his arm down my body and went to his knees. He had a tight grip on my legs and ankles. He said, 'I would like to kiss your toes.' This was in a passionate voice. I screamed several times."

The other woman said she had had two experiences of toe-lust, most recently when she got a phone call from a man who asked, "Can I kiss your toes?" and later appeared at her home. Both women said the man had arrived at their homes in a champagne-colored late-model Corvette.

When a detective spotted the car some time later, he moved in. The suspect was at home with his fiancée at the time.

No. 3

In Illinois, a 21-year-old man was arrested after he allegedly dipped his sex organ into a jar of salad dressing at a K-Mart store.

Remember Tom Swifties?

In December 1985, a New York dating service for herpes sufferers started a membership drive, complete with an incentive to lure new customers. Anyone signing up that month would get one free date introduction, the club promised rashly.

XXIII.
ANNALS OF MEDICINE

Doctors have come a long way in recent years—mostly downward. Long worshiped as nearly godlike preservers of life, they have lately run afoul of criticism, much of it in the form of malpractice suits, but not a little from patients who believe that even when they do their jobs correctly, they manage nevertheless to be ego-driven, bossy, cold, uncompassionate and unfeeling know-it-alls. Some charge them with being more interested in money, honors, publicity and status than in humanity. That was what Marsha H. Nathanson was getting at when she wrote to *The New York Times* to complain strenuously about the spectacle of France's Pasteur Institute suing the U.S. Government over who deserved the credit for first establishing the cause of AIDS. "Come on, children," Miss Nathanson said. "People are dying!" She suggested—something that apparently had not occurred to the medicos involved—that there were a number of reasons to shelve the argument over who gets the credit until after a cure is found.

Doctors want to see themselves in their television image, as Dr. Welby endlessly cloned. Too late for that now, guys.

Get Well Soon!

Discover magazine reported that hospitals are not good for your health.

The magazine said that 2 million people every year contract diseases while in the hospital—diseases that are not the ones they went in to have cured. *Discover* also said that 300,000 patients a year die from the diseases they get in hospitals.

Doctors like to gloss over this with the term *iatrogenic disease*. It's so impressive and baffling a term that patients seldom think to ask what it means. FYI, it means a disease that is a result of medical care.

Unkind Cut

In Michigan, a Hindu woman sued her hospital when her newborn son was mistakenly circumcised.

"The nurse came and told the mother that her son was okay," said the family's lawyer, "and that they had performed a minor surgery." Circumcision is not a Hindu custom, and the family sued for loss of religious status and "cultural damage" to their son.

Unkindest Cut

Wishing to be in the best medical shape possible for his upcoming marriage, a young Pennsylvanian went into his local hospital for a minor operation.

Somewhere and somehow in the course of his receiving the best of modern medical care, someone managed to accidentally amputate the man's penis.

The Eyes of Texas Are Upon You— and Your Bankbook Too

In December 1985, the Texas Health Department approved new rules designed to prevent private hospitals from dumping some patients—those they considered poor financial risks—on public hospitals.

Women in labor and patients in the midst of emergency treatment (even those trailing intravenous tubes) had been routinely shipped out to public hospitals as soon as private hospitals discovered that they had no medical insurance or other financial resources.

The new rules state that patients must be transferred for medical reasons only and also forbid discrimination based on age, sex, national origin, religion, economic status, physical condition and race. When patients are transferred, all pertinent medical data must accompany them; the transfer must minimize risk to the patient; the receiving hospital must approve the transfer; and the patient must be told about any free or low-cost treatment available from both the hospital he is leaving and the one he is going to. The rules provide for a variety of penalties, the severest of which is the revocation of a hospital's license.

Lest any of that seem unduly bureaucratic, harken unto the works of one spokesman. He told health officials, "We were getting outrageous cases; a heart patient in critical condition, all kinds of things."

He cited the cases of a woman in labor who had been transferred from a private hospital, and of a stabbing victim who was sent over with his intravenous tube still in place. He also told of a middle-aged man who came to his hospital with third-degree burns suffered in a grease fire, and with a catheter and an intravenous tube applied at another hospital. "The guy staggers in with all these lines hanging out of him, and a nurse asked if she could help him. He managed to say, 'I sure hope so. This is the fourth hospital I've been to.' "

The Good Doctor Prescribes

Dr. David Stry, owner/director of the Villa Vegetariana Health Spa in Cuernavaca, Mexico, has stipulated in his will that he wishes to be buried in the non-smoking section of the cemetery.—Press release issued by Dr. David Stry.

Quick, Call an Ambulance! On Second Thought, Call a Cab!

No. 1

In Dallas a woman died of a heart attack that was worthy of note. It occurred in an ambulance that was supposed to be rushing her to a hospital.

Patricia Finch said she called for an ambulance when her mother, 57-year-old Laverne Allen, became ill. Finch said the ambulance driver who answered the call seemed to be in no hurry; she said he used neither his siren nor his flashing light during the trip. Most important was that the driver stopped en route at a fire station because his shift was ending.

To some Texas ambulance drivers, the end of a shift is

the end of a shift—they go off duty and that's that. There was a delay of four minutes before the new driver took the wheel and drove on to the hospital. The patient was treated upon arrival, but by then it was apparently too late. The damage caused by the heart attack killed her some two weeks later.

No. 2

Dallas ambulances had been in the news about a year earlier, also in connection with the death of a patient. Lillian Boff, 60, had a heart attack, and her stepson called for an ambulance—but did not get one.

The stepson said that the ambulance dispatcher refused to send an ambulance until he told her what was wrong with his stepmother. The man said that all he knew was that the illness appeared to him to be very serious—his stepmother had collapsed and could not talk.

The dispatcher demanded something more precise than that. The man tried to explain that he was not a doctor or a paramedic and had no diagnostic knowledge of any kind, but the dispatcher was having none of that and still refused aid. The stricken woman died without receiving treatment of any kind.

No. 3

In New York City, a man who was injured in a hit-and-run accident got three ambulances but might as well have been in Dallas, for all the good they did him.

At about 4:30 A.M. on December 19, 1985, the Emergency Medical Service sent an ambulance to the accident site; en route, the crew noticed what they thought was a flat and called for a backup ambulance. The backup ambulance started out; its crew noticed that it was overheating.

The patient was put in the first ambulance, which set out for the hospital with the backup trailing behind. When two wheels fell off the first ambulance, the patient was transferred to the backup, which managed to get to the hospital. The injured man was pronounced dead on arrival.

While all that was going on, paramedics at another hospital, having heard the first two ambulance crews calling for help, sent their own ambulance racing to the scene. It crashed into a Volkswagen, injuring four people.

* * *

No. 4

In Brooklyn, there is a private ambulance company that advertises "High-Risk Medical Transporation."

Heroic Measures

No. 1

In Peking, Dr. Huang Xianjian has a bedside manner that owes nothing to the wimpy Doc Welby.

His patients, Dr. Huang told the *China Daily,* "must have stamina" if they are to benefit from—perhaps even survive—his "trampling treatment," which he says has cured "thousands" of people suffering from lumbago.

The trampling treatment consists of trampling the patient. Dr. Huang climbs up on the bed and then jumps up and down on their backs until they are cured. The treatment works, Dr. Huang says, but he admits it has the unfortunate side-effect of "almost unbearable pain."

No. 2

In San Francisco, police warned the public of a man claiming to be a doctor who lures women into bed with him.

"He calls the women," a police inspector said, "and tells them he has examined their blood tests and that they have a serious fatal disease, some kind of fungus." Then he tells them he can save their lives by having sex with them.

The man, who calls himself Dr. Franklin, tells the women he has a drug in his body that can cure the disease. The drug is transmitted, or injected, if you will, during sexual intercourse.

Police say one woman admitted to having paid $1,000 for the good doctor's therapy.

No 3

In France, a man obsessed with a fear of women joined a therapy group whose leader believed that Pierre Beaumard, 37, could begin a new and better life if his fears were stamped out, literally.

The cure proposed was for Pierre to lie between two mattresses and have other members of the group walk all over him. Pierre agreed, sandwiched himself between the mattresses, and was duly walked upon by four other members of the group. The results suggested that a few bugs would have to be worked out of the treatment: When Pierre was hauled out, he was no longer afraid of women, but only because he had died of suffocation.

No. 4

In Oklahoma, a woman sued her ex-husband, a psychiatrist, for subjecting her to experiments while treating her for physical and mental problems at the private mental-health hospital of which he was medical director.

The treatments, she said, included injecting her with her own urine. Her lawyers also claimed that the ex-husband convinced her that her physical and mental problems resulted from the foods she ate and from the wearing of clothes made of synthetic materials.

The jury awarded the woman at total of 6.5 million in compensation and punitive damages.

Heroic Alternative Measures

No. 1

Terry Bradshaw, his injured right elbow threatening to end his career as quarterback of the National Football League's Pittsburgh Steelers, underwent bird therapy in the hope of a cure.

The bird—a mynah bird owned by Collin Kerr of Toronto—was claimed to be successful in helping athletes. Kerr said the bird was insured for $12 million through Lloyd's of London and had a record of 2,003–78–1 in helping people who believed in its ability to heal them.

The avian therapist and Bradshaw had a half-hour session in the Steeler offices in Pittsburgh. According to Kerr, "The bird sat on his hand, where Terry was hurting. He [Bradshaw, not the bird] said it felt very warm; he felt it healing."

Bradshaw later retired from professional football.

No. 2

A British farmer is the latest in a long line of people who have found a cure for baldness.

John Coombs says the answer is to have a cow lick

your head. Specifically he recommends his cow Primrose, who cured him by accident. Coombs said that Primrose, attracted by cattle-food dust that had settled on his dome, gave him a licking one day, and a few weeks later he noticed hair growing on a spot where there had been nothing but a gleam for years.

"There may be some scientific explanation," the farmer says. "It could be the lactic acid on her tongue that's the magic ingredient." Coombs invited other bald men to visit Primrose, adding, "I must warn them, she has a very rough tongue."

Complete Dental Care

A 71-year-old dentist in Canada denied indecently assaulting a 14-year-old patient by touching her breast.

In his testimony the dentist also said a person has six lungs; that a schizophrenic (which is how he described the 14-year-old) is a "person of below-average mentality"; that nail-biting and smoking are the result of sex problems; and that he was the "number-one man in Canada" for something he termed psychosomatic surgery.

"If a patient comes to me with a nail-biting problem," he explained, "I psychosomatically cut off all their fingers and transpose new ones. When they come to, they have new fingers and never bite their nails again."

The defendant, who claimed to treat people for such other problems as migraine headaches, obesity, bed-wetting and insomnia, said he anesthetizes patients with "animal magnetism, mesmerism and acupressure." He said he puts patients into a state of regression to learn all of their problems.

"I learn all their guilty secrets. My patients are born again. Their guilt is all removed," the dentist said. He said some patients, upon realizing what they have revealed, go into a state of "abreaction" and may become violent. "They yell and scream," he said. "That's what happened here. This girl [the accuser] tore the notes out of my hand and ran screaming out of the door."

The dentist said that in his treatment he puts his hand on the heart and lung area, beneath the patient's left breast. Earlier he had said he didn't know where the breasts were located.

Asked whether his treatment included rubbing his hands

on a patient's chest, the dentist became angry. "Don't use that word," he shouted. "That's smut . . . *rub*. That's a dirty word. I try not to get mixed up with the sexual parts of the body."

Some Real Gassers

No. 1

A Long Island dentist gassed his 19-year-old nurse to the point of unconsciousness with nitrous oxide (laughing gas) and then removed her clothes and had sexual intercourse with her.

The nurse was unaware of what had happened until she came to and found herself naked and the dentist only partly clothed.

The dentist was not charged with rape. He pleaded guilty to sexual misconduct, facing a maximum sentence of a year in jail and a $1,000 fine. The innocuous charge also made it possible for him to keep his license.

No. 2

An accountant-turned-burglar on Long Island got into a dentist's office in Wantagh, New York, but couldn't get out. Police found him zonked out on the floor, still inhaling laughing gas. He said later that he had first used laughing gas two years previously, when he worked at a hospital, and had become addicted to it. His only intention on breaking into the office was apparently to steal a few whiffs and get happy.

XXIV.
THE LITERARY LIFE

What has happened to literary standards? the purists cry. Probably nothing, but there is a persistent belief, doubtless rose-tinged, that writing was better and more serious in times before our own.

It sometimes seems that way, but mostly because the pure rubbish produced in earlier times has not survived to shame the good stuff produced alongside it. It's true that Henry James took a hard line back in the days when he wrote book reviews for the *Times* Literary Supplement. Once asked to cut three lines from an article of some five-thousand words, he did so but wrote back to the editor, "I have performed the necessary butchery. Here is the bleeding corpse."

But in those palmy times there were, believe it or not, Harlequin Romances under other names, and other books carelessly and hastily flung together. No need, then, to apologize for the present in the face of the past.

Of course, that's only if we're talking about writing of a literary or at least subliterary type. If we're talking about the appalling effusions of sports stars, movie stars, TV stars, politicians, feel-good philosophers, management seers and religious loonies, that's different. There are lots more of all of the above "doing" books today than there were in former times. But in their case, of course, we are no longer talking about writing.

A lot of strange stuff gets printed, anyway. Here are a few samples (and other things) by (or involving) some of the mortals of the written word.

Books Received

Practical Infectious Diseases
The Care and Feeding of Stuffed Animals
Wife Battering: A Systems Theory Approach
Theory of Lengthwise Rolling
The Sex Life of Flowers
Bicycles in War
Honeybees from Close Up
New Trends in Table Settings
Lithuanians in Canada
Politics in the Tokugawa Bakufu, 1600–1843
The Grimke Sisters from South Carolina
Prince of Librarians
A History of the Z. Smith Reynolds Foundation
Health-seekers in the Southwest 1819–1900
The Foreman: Forgotten Man of Management
The Curse (whose publisher ballyhooed it by exclaiming joyously, "At last—a book about menstruation that is truly fun to read!")

Is That Why Sly and Sasha Stallone Named Their Son Seargeoh?

Godfather, author Mario Puzo's latest novel, *The Sicilian*, was about an outlaw named Giuliano. From start to finish the hero's name was misspelled "Guiliano." A spokesman for the publisher explained that it wasn't really a misspelling but a deliberate change that would make the name easier for Americans to pronounce.

Bedtime Story

According to one standard reference work, "Freudians have made much of the symbolism of the *Alice* books, written by Lewis Carroll, a.k.a. Charles Lutwidge Dodgson, an Oxford mathematics scholar, ordained deacon and amateur photographer. No doubt they made even more of the symbolism when photographs by the author of *Alice in Wonderland* were published. Carroll/Dodgson's favorite subject was naked little girls between the ages of 6 and 12.

Even a Moose Gets Tired
of Reading Sometimes

After reading eight times in three days to audiences near Sudbury, Ontario, Canada, a large moose appeared at the window whenever I spoke.—Report by a poet in *Books in Canada*.

Our Spirited Publishers

Michael Korda, chief editor at Simon & Schuster, "owns six tailor-made suits—three from New York's Melendari, three from London—in dark-color twills and tweeds, wools and linens, all with suppressed waists. . . . The same spirit that led him to participate in the 1956 Hungarian Revolution for three weeks prompts him to sew riding-club badges on his jeans jackets or don a Stetson hat or a pair of black Paul Bond cowboy boots with sharkskin heel protectors." —Article in the Sunday *New York Times Magazine*.

If Not Invited to the
Hamptons for Labor Day . . .

Every year since 1978, the Pulp Press of Vancouver, Canada, holds its Three-Day Novel-writing Contest, open to all comers.

It started in a bar after "one dimly lit beer too many," says Pulp Press editor Steven Osborne. "As I recall, someone mentioned that Voltaire wrote *Candide* in just three days. One of us—it could have been me—said he could do a better job than Voltaire in the same amount of time." And so Osborne and seven friends locked themselves away for seventy-two hours to see whether any one of them was up to the challenge.

"None of us came up with a novel that weekend," Osborne recalls, "but we knew a good thing when we saw it, so we set up a national competition for the Labor Day Weekend." They're still doing it. And so, those who wish to fling themselves at a typewriter for three days of exhaustion and the hope of fame—2,000 copies of the winner's book are printed by Pulp Press—can enter at bookstores in the U.S. and Canada. The entries can be written anywhere but must be sent in with a witness's affidavit swearing that the novel was written in three days. No manuscript longer than 716 pages will be accepted, nor any shorter than seven words.

Once all the novels are in, Osborne and a dozen other judges have to read them. "Just imagine what it's like going through a few hundred manuscripts in two months," he says.

How to Talk About Artists

One senses his careful and knowing approach to the reality of a piece of paper.—Alma Houston, in a book about the Inuit artists of Cape Dorset.

The Way of a Man With a Phrase

No. 1

Ask an artist, even one as optimistic as bill bissett, about the Canada Council, and you conjure up a tight-rope walker balancing in the passing lane of a three-lane high wire.—*Books in Canada*.

No. 2

It stung—and it was meant to sting. The police were under a more than usually heavy barrage from the press at that time, and public opinion was running high. Casey had a good deal on his shoulders. He had to beat off the rotten politicians snuffling for plums as a hog roots for truffles, on one hand, and on the other endure the high-minded and utterly ridiculous suggestions of a citizenry determined to tear down the walls at one clean sweep and wreck one of the most efficient police machines in history in order to feed the populace bountifully on the cake of reform.—Helen Reilly, *The Line-Up*.

No. 3

She sings, oh Lord, with a rowdy spin of styles—country, rhythm and blues, rock, reggae, torchy ballad—fused by a rare and rambling voice that calls up visions of loss, then jiggles the glands of possibility.—*Time* magazine.

No. 4

A round of raucous, good-humored toasts echoed across

Silver Bank as emotions that had been corsetted over months of arduous toil rose to the surface and—fueled by champagne—breached.—*TV Guide*.

No. 5

The Assemblymen also were miffed at their Senate counterparts because they have refused to bite the bullet that now seems to have grown to the size of a millstone to the Assemblymen whose necks are on the line.—Joseph F. Sullivan, *The New York Times*.

No. 6

It is the lot of such people, if to be opposed, then also to be invigorated by opposition, beholding their enemies in an eternal vigil, like the lifeless cobra in whose eye the murder's image is forever embedded, and they actually crave to hate that constant hallucination of face—whether smirking through the attack it signals or the absolution it seeks—which becomes, in fact, almost a badge for those enemies, for one attributes to them not that state of normal human happiness, shot through with the common moods of mankind, that should move us to entertain for them a feeling of kindly sympathy, but a species of arrogant delight that merely pours oil on the furnace of our rage.—Alexander Theroux, *Revenge*.

No. 6

How simplistic it would be to imagine that Genevieve, while being a faithful wife, was sexually attracted to Robert! A psychoanalyst might confirm it, but Genevieve would retort that Freud was out, as out as rococo or as Louis II of Bavaria. As for Robert . . . —Francoise Mallet-Joris, *The Underground Game*.

(Of this a reviewer in *The New Yorker* wrote, "Many portions of this book, if read slowly aloud, could be used to wring confessions from crooks.")

Last Word

Upset by the clever puns and wordplay used to introduce Letters to the Editor published in New York's *Village Voice*, a reader in San Diego wrote, "Dear Sir: As one of your earliest subscribers, I feel that I am entitled to challenge you to run this letter without one of your cutesie-pie headlines."

The Village Voice ran the letter under the headline: FUCK YOU.

XXV.

THEY GIVE
GOOD HEAD

Headline writing is often the most challenging and sometimes the most enjoyable part of editing a newspaper.

What makes it hard is the need to condense the most important part of a story into a very few words and a very small space. Every letter has to be counted; the spaces between the words have to be counted; time is usually short. Headline writers are permitted a few luxuries. Within limits, usually pretty firm ones, they can bend the rules of grammar a bit, get away with some unusual constructions and use occasional abbreviations. Those freedoms sometimes help, but every now and then they merely help the editor get into trouble.

Everyone who goes to a journalism school learns about some legendary heads. There's one about the madman who escapes from an asylum and rapes a woman (NUT BOLTS AND SCREWS), the shipwreck survivors who regret their having argued over taking turns at the oars (RAFT RIFF-RAFF RUE ROW ROW) and the newlywed who saves her husband from the attack of an angry donkey by beating the animal with a stick (BRIDE OF THREE WEEKS BEATS ASS OFF HUSBAND).

All of those are undoubtedly phonies; they're too pat. They reek of contrivance. But the rare pleasure in headline writing comes from having put all the facts together in a way that captures the essence of the story and something more.

Variety has two famous heads to its credit. One was for a story reporting that rural moviegoers were not going for dopey films about country bumpkins: STICKS NIX HIX PIX. The other was on the great stock-market crash of 1929: WALL STREET LAYS AN EGG. The New York *Daily News* hit it perfectly with its head for a story on President

Gerald Ford's refusal to help the city during the worst stretch of its financial crisis: FORD TO CITY: DROP DEAD.

The rest of the time there are a lot of plain, ordinary heads that are serviceable but unremarkable, and more than enough heads (one a month is plenty) to give editors nightmares, or to amuse or offend the public.

Here are the best of the worst.

CENTER TO AID
VETERANS BEING
RESURRECTED
—The *Louisville* (Kentucky) *Times*

SOFTWARE TRANSFORMS APPLE IIE
INTO A TYPEWRITER
—*The New York Times*

FORD, REAGAN NECK IN
PRESIDENTIAL PRIMARY
—*The Ethiopian Herald*

AIR FORCE CONSIDERS
DROPPING SOME
NEW WEAPONS
—*The New Orleans Times-Picayune*

HEW IS TOLD
TO 'JUSTIFY'
SEX-POT STUDY
—*The Hot Springs* (Arkansas) *Sentinel–Record*

PRODUCER FINDS ART OF PRODUCING
LIES IN SHOW BUSINESS
—*The New York Times*

FRANCISCAN SISTERS
BALL TOMORROW
TO AID THE POOR
—*The Brooklyn Daily News*

MBA STUDIES MUSHROOM
—The Youngstown (Ohio) *SBA News*

GUARD SHOWS ITS MEAT
—The New York *Daily News*

TWO WOMEN IN LINE
FOR REAR ADMIRAL
—The Tampa (Florida) *Tribune*

PONTIFF MUM ON
GAY HIRING
—The New York *Post*

STIFF OPPOSITION EXPECTED
TO CASKETLESS FUNERAL PLAN
—The *Toronto Star*

BRITAIN'S UNIONS
RESIST PAY PLAN
—*The New York Times*

UNIONS TO COOPERATE
ON PAY POLICY IN UK
—*The Wall Street Journal*

EARTHQUAKE, VOLCANO AND FLOODS
MAR EASTER HOLIDAY
—The *Toronto Star*

ARE A BIG PROBLEM
ARE A BIG PROBLEM
—*The New York Times*

MAN ROBS,
THEN KILLS
HIMSELF
—*The Washington Post*

ART AND ANTIQUES ON DISPLAY:
ESKIMO OBJECTS TO HERALDRY
—*The New York Times*

BAN ON SOLICITING DEAD IN TROTWOOD
—The Dayton (Ohio) *Daily News*

FOOD-FOR-NEEDY CENTERS
TO LOSE AID FOR ABUSES
—*The New York Times*

FIREBOMBING JURY TAKES WEEKEND OFF
—The Hartford (Connecticut) *Courant*

PABLO PICASSO
IS DEAD AT 91
ROOF COLLAPSED AFTER WARNING
—The New York *Daily News*

CHOU REMAINS
CREMATED
—The Peoria (Illinois) *Journal Star*

DR. TACKETT
GIVES TALK
ON MOON
—The Indiana *Evening Gazette*

CODFISH SLOW TO ARRIVE FOR TOURNAMENT
—*The New York Times*

PATTY HEARST MUST SUBMIT
TO PSYCHIATRIST, JUDGE RULES
—The Philadelphia *Evening Bulletin*

STRAY DOG BELIEVED
FROM OUT OF TOWN
—The Pittsfield (Massachusetts) *Berkshire Eagle*

FRIED CHICKEN
OFFICIAL IMPROVED
—*The New York Times*

13,500 CUBAN TROOPS
STILL REPORTED IN CUBA
—The *Miami Herald*

FRUIT PIZZA:
NIGHTMARE
OF NAPLES
—The Los Angeles *Times*

FIRST LADY LOOKS TO
PARENTS ON DRUGS
—*The New York Times*

NIXON SENDS TUGS
TO AID OF JERSEY
—*The New York Times*

BOATING WHILE IMPAIRED
WINS HOUSE APPROVAL
—The Asheville (North Carolina) *Citizen*

SCIENTISTS TO HAVE
FORD'S EAR
—The Portland (Maine) *Evening Express*

MOON CHURCH TOLD
TO PRODUCE WOMAN
—*The New York Times*

SAUDIS MOVE
TO ENSURE
CRUDE PROFIT
—The New York *Post*

JELLYFISH
STRIKE AT
ROCKAWAY
—The New York *Post*

CARNIVOROUS
PLANTS TALK
AT BROADMOOR
—The *Wellesley* (Massachusetts) *Townsman*

WOMAN OFF TO JAIL
FOR SEX WITH BOYS
—The *Kitchener* (Ontario) *Record*

WATER CAN EASE
THIRST OF PLANTS
—The Austin (Texas) *American Statesman*

DISABLED FISH IN POLLUTED WATERS
—*The New York Times*

$15,000 AWARD TO WIDOWER FOR LOST BRAIN
—The *Chicago Tribune*

DISCORD AMONG SIKHS
BLOCKS UNITY
—*The New York Times*

BRITISH VIRGINS ARE JEWELS OF THE CARIBBEAN
UNTAINTED BY COMMERCIALISM
A MUST STOP FOR SAILORS
—Travel-story head in the Chicago *Sun-Times*

JUSTICE DELAYED IS
JUSTICE DEFERRED
—The San Fernando Valley *New Californian*

MARCOS' OPPONENTS CHARGE
AIM IS THEIR 'EXTERMINATION'
        —*The New York Times*

MOM BLOWS LUCY'S DATE
—Head on the "Dear Abby" column in The *Parkersburg* (West Virginia) *Sentinel*

XXVI.
BATHROOM STORIES

Actually, it is the British who are famous for their devotion to bathroom jokes. Throw out a line about a funny smell, indoor plumbing or various bodily functions and you will knock a British audience to pieces. Heaven only knows what howlers those royals, always fond of a few yoks, pass among themselves.

Americans, on the other hand, merely love bathrooms.

Tubs, basins, toilets, fixtures—they love all that stuff, too; they spend billions on it every year and never once laugh. On the contrary, they are serious, tedious and earnest about bathrooms, which of late have become the "hot" room in the home for yuppies and others I don't want to know.

The kitchen has been done to death; it is no longer hep. Christ, doctors do over their kitchens, trucking in restaurant ranges the size of aircraft carriers, refrigerators that cost $5,000 apiece, and exhaust systems driven by fans capable of lifting small aircraft off the ground and gliding them to Nutley, New Jersey. Thus the bathroom is the new frontier of conspicuous consumption.

There are tanning lights galore, Jacuzzis of all sizes, heated towel racks and innumerable electrical grooming aids backed up by racks of oils, ointments, unguents, sprays, perfumes, colognes, soaps, shampoos, conditioners, toners, firmers, shapers, filers, pluckers, massagers, polishers and the like in such gorgeous array as to make the whore of Babylon fling herself under a bus in envy and despair.

That, to Americans, is civilization. Americans have sometimes used bathrooms as the measure of other civilizations: Squeaky cleanliness is next to godliness. Sanitation is not to be dismissed, but it is not all. After World

War II, great hordes of Americans went to Europe to see museums, castles, the cradle of Western civilization. They came home telling their friends, "When you go, take plenty of toilet paper."

Knock, Knock, Who's There?

In Merano, Italy, an 80-year-old man was taking a bath when he suffered a hernia and found the he was unable to get out of the tub.

To summon help from his neighbors, he began banging on the bathroom wall. He finally caught their attention after four days.

Canny Scot

Howls of pain emerged from the bathroom of a bar in Bangor, Scotland, and customers ran to help. They found a fellow customer glued to the toilet seat.

An ambulance crew managed to pry him loose from the seat, which had been covered with glue by practical jokers.

Women's Rooms, San Francisco Division

No. 1

In the women's room of the bar in a San Francisco hotel, astounded and occasionally revolted patrons discovered an octopus lying on the floor. Actually, it was clinging to the floor, no doubt in terror, with its powerful suction cups. It was, so to speak, a big sucker—it weighed forty-five pounds—and it took six people to get it out of there.

No. 2

At a city Hall of Justice, many women workers were angry because a man kept using their restroom.

The man, a probation officer awaiting a sex-change operation, had been given permission to use the women's room. Known as Victor-Victoria, he was taking female hormones and wearing dresses, but the women said they couldn't feel at ease because he still had a male sex organ.

(A similar problem faced a Londoner who liked to be known as Dena. He, too, was dressing and acting like a woman while awaiting a sex-change operation, but his use of a public women's room went beyond mere complaints to his being arrested. So he went to the men's room and was arrested for that, too. A rare case of a man's literally not having a pot to piss in.)

And Some People Complain About Pay Toilets!

Lockheed, told that it had been charging too much for toilet-seat covers for the Navy's airplanes, sought to wash its hands of the matter by turning it over to another contractor.

In late 1985, Lockheed was still trying to find a manufacturer to bid on supplying the toilet-seat covers for less than the $640 each Lockheed had charged.

Another Challenge for Mr. Tidy-Bowl

Sheriff's deputies had begun to think of one California man as a bit of a crackpot. Several times he had complained to them about a snake he said was living in his toilet. Every time they checked it out—no snake.

But one day he called and asked them to come over as fast as they could—the snake was there right that very minute, looking him in the eye. The snake slid back down into the plumbing as soon as it caught sight of the law, but the deputies had seen enough to vindicate his mental stability, and they called for professional help.

Animal-control officers arrived shortly, dismantled the toilet, and fished out a five-foot boa constrictor. Boas, they said, were water-loving snakes, and this one might have been flushed down another toilet.

More on Pay Toilets

A woman was seated—securely, she thought—in a stall in the women's room of a shopping center in Canada, but not for long.

Soon she realized that another woman was trying to get her attention. Looking up, she saw a hand appear over the top of the stall door. There was a gun in it.

A woman's voice then told her to surrender all the money in her purse. In no position to negotiate, the victim forked over $5, and the robber left.

Police said the robbery was a first as far as they knew.

Don't Flush for Everything

One newspaper reported the story of a Brooklyn cop who was suspended for sixty days. The charge: using "excessive force," which included trying to drown a judge in a toilet bowl.

The officer had arrested a man, his son (both judges with the Department of Motor Vehicles) and a third man after an auto accident. Punches were thrown at the scene, and things got worse back at the police station.

There, the officer grabbed the elder judge at one point and said, "I'm going to show you what it's like to drown in a toilet bowl." He was pushing him toward the toilet when the judge's screams for help brought two other officers to the scene in time.

The three men won a $230,000 settlement from the city.

Exploding Toilets

No. 1

In the women's room of a service area on the Garden State Parkway in Sayreville, New Jersey, a woman felt a slight electrical shock when she tried to flush the toilet. And that was the least of it, according to The New York *Daily News*.

The next thing that happened, said parkway operations manager John Simonse, was that the toilet "literally blew up. It blew into little pieces."

The woman was not injured, Simonse said, but "a little shook up, to say the least," as was a woman in an adjoining stall. They were treated for anxiety at a hospital.

All restrooms at the service area were closed for some sixteen hours while state police investigated. They found nothing that might explain what had happened.

"It's a mystery," Simonse said. "Investigators found no bomb parts or any explosive devices in the stall. We just don't understand it."

*   *   *

No. 2

A woman who was applying hairspray some years ago ran into a little mechanical difficulty: The aerosol container refused to stop spraying. The woman solved the problem by simply spraying the stuff into the toilet until the container was empty. Then she left the bathroom.

Shortly afterward, her husband entered the bathroom and seated himself on the toilet. He happened to be smoking at the time, and when his cigarette burned down to a stub, he did the natural thing—he parted his thighs and dropped it into the bowl.

The toilet exploded.

XXVII.

CLUBS YOU COULD JOIN

People are always joining clubs of one sort or another, and what is remarkable about the clubs they join is their attempt to encourage brotherhood through exclusion, much like college fraternities (whose members have the excuse that they are still children). "Brotherhood is for people like us," is their message, "and there are blackballs for the rest," which is rather like restricting brotherhood to identical twins.

Women are forever trying to get into men's clubs, often because clubs dominate some professions, and to be denied membership limits professional advancement. Men sometimes defend the exclusion of women by saying they never try to get into women's clubs, leaving unstated the fact that membership in sewing circles and ladies' auxiliaries would seldom be of any value to them. When sex is not an issue, class usually is. People join country clubs to be spared the rigors of public tennis courts, golf courses and swimming pools, where they might run into fruit vendors, mechanics and doormen.

But though its value is dubious, the urge to club is a natural form of clannishness, and thus there are even clubs for those who wouldn't be welcome in other clubs. One need never be alone.

Low-Key, Low-Profile, Low Pulse Rate

"Dare To Be Dull" is the challenge of The International Dull Men's Club, whose founder and president, Joseph Troise, may have succeeded in creating the sole men-only club that women will not try to get into.

Troise, a free-lance writer and auto mechanic in Boulder, Colorado, says he is trying to "reach out to all the other people out there who actually like lime Jell-O and washing their own car but until now have been afraid to admit it."

The club, according to *New York Times* correspondent William E. Schmidt, was founded in 1980, and, by late 1982, had grown to 1,000 members and several chapters in the U.S.

Troise says dull men lead safer lives and never suffer from the stress of having to constantly appear interesting or trendy, and that the dull do most of the work of keeping society together. "It is the dull who run our elevators, drive our cabs, type our reports, do our accounting and brush the branches, so to speak, over the trail of our past deeds. Behind every flashy facade sits a humorless and fastidiously competent drone who keeps the whole damned ship afloat."

To be dull, however, is not necessarily to be inert. Troise and others in the club have in fact participated in numerous uninteresting activities.

J. D. Stewart, a statistical analyst for Eastman Kodak and head of the club's chapter in Rochester, New York, planned to compile a vast register called *Who's Nobody in America*. It would include everyone who is not in *Who's Who in America*. That, according to Stewart, would give his volume something like 230 million names.

The chapter in Carroll, Iowa, established a Museum of the Ordinary. Its exhibits included ashtrays from all fifty states, a display of bowling balls and a collection of hubcaps.

Troise, who says the club's slogan is, "We're out of it and proud of it," has also considered established a dating service for dull people. He said it would organize social outings such as a bus tour of New Jersey golf courses. The dating service was tentatively named Club Dead.

Smart Move

In Toronto, a group of Canadians who felt oppressed by the existence of Mensa, the organization for people with high IQs, responded by starting an opposition club of their own.

Their organization, called Densa, attracted the not-very-bright. The club, organized in a very informal manner, did not engage in touring shopping centers or visiting parking lots, which might have been too much of a mental strain for the membership. Mostly they preferred to drink beer and be dense together.

The New Religion

In California, a man interested in spirituality as well as sociability announced the founding of the First Church of Monday Night Football.

No tithes or donations are required, dogma is limited and the only sacred ritual is to sit before the TV set during Monday nights in the fall to watch ABC's weekly telecasts. The regulations, blessedly few, are the Seven Commandments. Their number comes from the points awarded for a touchdown and conversion.

Even Joining Isn't Necessary

Bruce Chapman of Cincinnati, Ohio, has created the International Organization of Nerds. His title is Supreme Archnerd.

Chapman, who founded the ION in 1984, said he has about 3,200 members, including President Reagan, Cardinal O'Connor and Johnny Carson. Like most ION members, they did not join the club. It joined them.

The club does admit applicants, but Chapman says about 90% of its members were nominated by other people and became members whether they liked it or not. The Supreme Archnerd says anyone who wants to give the gift of membership should write to the ION at Box 118555, Cincinnati, Ohio, 45211.

News From the World of Cults

The Church of the SubGenius is open to people who want to join a cult with the inconvenience of having to work like dogs in some obscure South American country and then be forced to drink cyanide-grape Kool-Aid.

According to a report in *The New York Times*, the Church of the SubGenius is variously described by its members, known as SubGenii, as a "cult," an "uncompetitive, collaborative network of individuals who are sensitive, creative and sweet to each other," and an "inherently bogus religion." Nevertheless, it has a bible, *The Book of the Subgenius,* published by McGraw-Hill.

It also has an exalted, mystic leader, J. R. Bob Dobbs, who is known as the High Epopt. He is elusive. "No one has ever really met Bob—he's a mystery wrapped in an enigma," says one SubGenius. But his teachings are revealed, or intuited, in any case. Bob's chief tenet appears to be that the SubGenii "must have slack," says a member. In short, leave them alone, don't bug them, give them a break, get off their backs.

Sometimes SubGenius services or ceremonies of some sort are held. In 1985, a "devival meeting" at the Stone Bar in San Francisco's North Beach section came to the unwelcome attention of the police. There had been songs by the Zombies-for-Bob Choir, music from The Band That Dares Not Speak Its Name, and a watch-smashing to free people of their "time addiction." The police got involved when one of them thought he saw a SubGenius loading an M16 automatic rifle. On investigation it proved to be merely a plastic prop.

In Dallas, at the Republican National Convention in 1984, SubGenii staged a rally. What they rallied around was "nothing in particular." That led a Cleveland Sub-Genius to start a program called *The Bob Dobbs Radio Revival on Cleveland's WRUW-FM. Since then at least three other radio stations have carried SubGenius programs: KNON-FM, Dallas, Texas; KPFA-FM, Berkeley, California; and WSMU-FM, East Orange, New Jersey.*

The organization has grown to some 5,000 SubGenii since its founding in 1980. Those who wish to be ordained as high priests or priestesses can have the matter taken care of for a fee of $20.

XXVIII.
NAMES AND JOB TITLES

Names. You are probably waiting with a certain resignation to have the old Shakespeare quotation from *Romeo and Juliet* thrown at you, but a paying reader deserves better than to be hit over the head once again with that line, which has been used in every newspaper feature article involving an unusual name.

So we will pass on directly to titles, of which Daniel Defoe said, "Titles are shadows, crowns are empty things." Nice, and apt for what follows on both.

Call Me Madam

In that great warren of bureaucracy known as the federal government, any number of people work—or, at least, are employed—and it seems as if every one of them must have a title and a rank and a grade. Titles are very important in Washington, D.C.

The Assistant Administrator, Management and Administration, Federal Energy Administration, announced to overjoyed employees that new job titles would be available to those who needed them. The new titles were: Deputy Assistant Associate Administrator, Assistant Deputy Associate Administrator, Associate Assistant Deputy Administrator, and Associate Deputy Assistant Administrator.

Those needing titles were to work it all out with the Deputy Associate Assistant Administrator of Management Nomenclature.

In the Veterans Administration there is a job called Director, Broadcast Services, Special Assistant to the Associate Deputy Administrator.

The Agency for International Development has an Administrative Assistant to the Assistant Administrator for Administration.

When You Call me That, Smile

When it comes to titles, the royalty goes to royalty. Kings and such are top dog and get to call themselves whatever they like, and get to make everyone else call them that too. (The correct way to put it is "style themselves," whence the term *self-styled.)*

Every emperor of Japan is the Son of Heaven, a fairly grand bauble, but styles and titles get far grander than that, enough to make Elizabeth II—by the Grace of God, of the United Kingdom of Great Britain and Northern Ireland, and Her other Realms and Territories, Queen, Head of the Commonwealth and Defender of the Faith— look a bit common.

King Haile Selassie of Ethiopia was known as King of Kings, Elect of God, Conquering Lion of the Tribe of Judah.

The Shah of Iran—officially the Shahanshah—was styled King of Kings, Light of the Ayrans, Shadow of the Almighty.

Nepal's King Birendra Bir Bikran Shah Dev inherited the titles Incarnation of Vishnu, King of Kings, the Five-Times Godly, Valorous Warrior and Divine Emperor.

Best of all was King Sobhuza II of Swaziland, who was not only well decorated but something of a personality as well.

When King Sobhuza died at the age of 83 in 1982, he was the first sovereign since Queen Victoria to rule for 60 years. (Sobhuza had hoped to outdo her 64 years on the throne). He was survived by his number-one wife, Mdlovokazi, the Great She-Elephant, and more than 100 other wives, as well as more than 600 children and 3,000 grandchildren. Sixty-seven of his sons and 18 of his daughers were listed in Burke's peerage, and all in all, the question of the succession was a bit muddled.

King Sobhuza came to the throne in the 1920s, and he retained a large measure of royal power right up to the end, long after the Kabaka of Buganda and the Mwami of Burundi and the Sarduana of Nigeria had disappeared.

Sobhuza II was styled the Lion of Swaziland, the Bull, the Great Mountain, the Inexplicable.

He was listed in the phone book as "His Majesty."

The Game Of The Names

The name Ivan (a form of John) is as common in Russia as Joe is elsewhere. It became popular under the czars, when the Russian Orthodox Church required parents to use the names of saints. As it happened, there were plenty of saints but a superfluity of St. Ivans. There was a St. Ivan available on 170 days of every year.

New York Times correspondent Seth Mydans reported that things changed radically after the Revolution. Parents began appropriating word and slogans, even inventing names, to get into the Revolutionary spirit. After a while it appeared that a certain amount of competition set in—who could name the most revolutionary name?

In a burst of creativity, thousands of new names were produced. Kids were named after prominent topographical features, elements (those named Radium and Helium were often called Radi and Heli for short), and trees and flowers.

Children were named Anarchy, Utopia, Diesel, Electrification, Hammer-and-Sickle, Artillery Academy, Diesel, Hydroelectric Station, Catch-Up-and-Overtake and Hypotenuse. There was a fad for acronyms: Vilior, for Vladimir Ilyich Lenin, Initiator of the Revolution, and Lorikerik, for Lenin, October Revolution, Industrialization, Collectivization, Electrification, Radiofication and Communism.

More recently, and with the encouragement of the government, the trend is being reversed, Mydans reported. Government experts are available to help with the selection, and now names like Aleksei, Dmitri, Yelena and Olga are making a comeback at the expense of, say, Turbine and Central Chemical Warehouse.

Meanwhile, Back in the Free World

Here, too, names live and die by the whims of fashion. These days it appears that all children have to be named Kim or Scott, or must have ordinary names that are flagrantly misspelled (e.g., Nansi and Dorthi) or decorated with capital letters stuck in the middle, as in JaNette. Among the names that have pretty well petered out since the mid-1800s are some that were the product of religious devotion and others that appear to be flat-out mysteries. Currently lying fallow are the likes of Abishag, Amorous, Babberley, Brained, Clapham, Cotton, Despair, Dozer, Energetic, Feather, Ham, Increase, Lettuce, Minniehaha, Murder, Salmon, Strongitharm, Tram, Uz, Water and Wonderful.

XXIX.
PETS AND WILDLIFE

Americans love pets. Americans love pets so much that they spend more on them every year than they do on starving homeless people in their own country.

Landmarks in Pet Care

No. 1

In Stuart, Florida, get in touch with H. C. Hoffner for the last word in gifts for your pet.

Hoffner sells used fire hydrants.

According to the *St. Petersburg Times,* Hoffner started in this line two years ago by snapping up a lot of hydrants being unloaded at a public auction. He sold them all for $25 apiece and has said since "I could have sold a hundred." His own dog is among the satisfied customers.

Hoffner plans to buy more secondhand hydrants whenever they become available. Not all of his customers have dogs. Danny Roberts gave his a new paint job and planted it outside as a lawn decoration, but, he says, "Some of the neighborhood dogs who come around use it."

No. 2

A New York pet psychologist was called in to help a saloon owner's pet dog, which had become a problem drinker. The dog, a chihuahua, would bark for booze, and wouldn't shut up until it got some. It preferred creme de menthe.

The psychologist put doggie on the wagon by feeding it pills that induced vomiting when mixed with booze, and after a few miserable experiences, the dog swore off the stuff.

For working on such problems he gets $45 an hour.

* * *

No. 3

One newspaper reports that drinking dogs are a severe problem in Denmark—bad enough to inspire a woman to start a drying-out tank for dogs.

"Scandinavians just think of themselves as hearty drinkers," she says, "and that goes for their dogs, too. They think that getting a dog to like a saucer of beer is a big joke, and before they know it, the poor animal has become an alcoholic. That's where we come in."

She says dogs are easier to cure because their dependence is merely physical, not, like humans', psychological. The cure is total abstinence, and she says that after three or four weeks on the wagon, her patients will stay off booze for good.

"We're not as famous as the Betty Ford clinic," she says, "but we're doing just as valuable a job."

No. 4

In class-conscious Palm Beach, Florida, Wendy Fielding founded a company called Rolling In Dough to cater to the tastes of upper-crust dogs.

The *St. Petersburg Times* says Fielding, who is also a sculptor, bakes what amount to designer dog biscuits shaped like tiny 1954 Bentley automobiles. Known as Molly's PBDB's, they may be the first cars that dogs can chase and eat.

They sell for $3.50 per quarter-pound package.

No. 5

Pet Medical and Health Products of Princeton, New Jersey, has invented a cure for doggie breath.

The product is a pet mouthwash that comes in a spray bottle. Company president Bill Papciak, who introduced the blend of plaque-reducing and bacteria-killing agents at a pet-industry trade show, says pets don't object to being sprayed. He says it works on cats, too.

No. 6

Getting dogs and cats to play by themselves should be less of a problem from now on, says *The New York Times*.

Harold A. Adler of Westlake Village, California, was granted a patent for an electronic ball that is activated by a collar carrying a tiny radio transmitter. When a pet wearing the collar gets close to the ball, the transmitter causes the ball to start rolling.

The *Times* said the electronic ball "frees the pet owner from the sometimes-onerous duty of entertaining a bored, unhappy pet."

No. 7

Bar Mitzvahs and Bas Mitzvahs are important religious rituals that mark the thirteenth birthdays of Jewish boys and girls. Although they are often accompanied by celebrations, their chief purpose is to mark the transition from childhood to adulthood.

In Pennsylvania, a woman decided to hold a Bas Mitzvah for her dog.

She said she and her dog, Shana Raquel, would wear matching peau de soie dresses for the event, which would span two days, culminating in a black-tie dinner for 125 guests, some of them flown in from Europe.

A local paper reported on her plans, eliciting protests from Jewish leaders. As a result, she ordered what she called "tremendous security" for the party, and decided to stop calling the event a Bas Mitzvah, although invitations using the term had already been mailed.

"It's such a cruel world, and it's going to be a beautiful party and a lot of fun," she said.

Dead Pets

No. 1

One day actress Barbara Bain got her copy of the Sunday *Los Angeles Times* delivered as usual—the delivery boy heaved it up onto her front lawn in the time-honored manner.

On this particular day the bulky paper landed on her dog, killing it outright.

Bain told the competing *Herald-Examiner* that the *Times* "offered to make restitution," but said, "How do you put a price on a pet you've had for fourteen years?"

No. 2

At the Houston Zoo, a few folks visiting the reptile house began to notice something odd about the coral snake on display.

They noticed that it didn't seem to be alive. An investigation proved that it was actually a rubber dummy.

Curator John Donaho admitted the deception, saying, "We have had live snakes in the exhibit, but they don't do well. They tend to die."

No. 3

New York's *Daily News* said a hunter in Georgia's Chattahoochee National Forest made an unusual find late in December 1985. What he found was a torn duffel bag with forty plastic containers of cocaine and a 175-pound black bear, stoned and stone-dead.

Gary Garner of the Georgia Bureau of Investigation said the cocaine was probably dropped during a smuggling attempt. "The bear got to it before we could," he said, "and he tore the duffel bag open, got him some cocaine and overdosed." By the time authorities got to the scene, there was "nothing left but bones and a big hide."

Garner said he belived the smuggler involved was a man who some months earlier had jumped out of a plane near Knoxville, Tennessee, with seventy-five pounds of cocaine strapped to his waist. The escapee not only lost the duffel bag to the bear but lost his life to his parachute. It failed to open fully, and he was killed on impact.

No. 4

Released for a day's romp in Pembrokeshire, England, in June of 1953, a homing pigeon did not home, as expected, that evening. Nor the next. The bird did not return, in fact, until eleven years later. It was dead as a smelt by then and had been sent home in a paper carton by mail.

From Brazil.

No. 5

A Connecticut lawmaker offered a bill outlawing the throwing of uncooked and instant rice at wedding. He says the rice is dangerous to pigeons and other birds.

The pigeons eat the rice, which then swells up inside them. Some die of bloating; others explode.

(In Toronto, a newspaper columnist latched onto a similar idea. He said people plagued by mice stop trying to get rid of them by using poisons. He suggested using instant mashed-potato mix instead, which would result in mice blowing up all over the place.)

No. 6

New York Times correspondent Iver Peterson reported the tribulations of the Wyoming Fish and Game Department and the black-footed ferrets it had captured for their own protection.

The ferrets, said to be the rarest mammals in North America, were among the few survivors of a species that had nearly been wiped out as ranchers killed off the prairie dogs the ferrets preyed on for food. Six ferrets were captured and sent to a laboratory at the University of Wyoming, where it was hoped they could be bred, although ferrets had never been bred in captivity. Instead, half of them died and the rest fell ill of distemper, which is as dangerous to ferrets as it is to dogs.

Six more ferrets were captured and put into strict individual isolation in the hope that this latest attempt to save their lives would not prove fatal to them.

There had already been an attempt to breed ferrets in captivity. It took place in the 1970s and led to the extinction of the North Dakota ferret colony.

No. 7

A New Jersey man operated a pet cemetery, where he sold small but nevertheless final resting places for pets, mostly dogs and cats—6,000 of them, he said in 1981.

Economy burials cost $85 and fancier burials ran up to $650, which included a coffin, one of the best plots and a stone with a bronze marker. Business wasn't bad.

But in August 1985, New Jersey's Department of Environmental Protection said it had discovered an open pit at a home site owned by the man. The pit contained hundreds of pet carcasses.

The New Jersey Division of Consumer Affairs launched an investigation; in the meantime, *The New York Times* said, the environmental agency fined him $25,000 for operating an illegal landfill.

No. 8

British animal lovers were outraged to learn that the production of *Santa Claus—The Movie,* starring Dudley Moore, required the slaughter of ten reindeer.

Parts of the movie were filmed in Norway, where a herder had sold thirty reindeer to the production company. When location filming was completed, some of the animals were slaughtered for their skins.

Nearly Dead Pets

No. 1

A Wisconsin dance troupe was rehearsing its performance of *The Nutcracker* when it came undone owing to a combustible bunny.

The New York *Post* reported that the group had a crowd-pleasing trick of pulling a live rabbit from a flaming dish before its awed audiences. But during a dress rehearsal the rabbit caught fire and fled across the stage. The director said, "Some of the hair got caught, but we put the fire out right on stage. We just wrapped a coat around the rabbit and took it to a vet. It's fine."

No. 2

In Sheffield, England, a parakeet had to be rescued from a toilet.

Bertie escaped from his cage and flew out an open window. A strong blast of wind apparently hurled him to the ground, and his owner, upon finding his rigid little body, assumed he was dead.

She was flustered by the event. "I was in such a state when I found Bertie outside," she said. "I did not know whether to put him down the john or the garbage chute."

She chose to flush little Bertie, and it was fortunate for him that the home was not equipped with a garbage disposal, as the disconcerted woman might have used that instead.

Some time later she heard chirping sounds coming from her toilet. She called plumbers, who, after taking the toilet apart, found Bertie moist but safe in an air pocket in the pipes.

She was so upset by having nearly drowned her pet that she felt she couldn't keep him any longer. She gave him away and got a kitten to replace him.

Pets and the Law

No. 1
A New Jersey woman was savagely attacked by a Siberian husky that had escaped from its pen. The woman's son came to her defense, killing the beast with an ax. The local ASPCA came to Fido's defense, hauling the man into court on the charge of cruelty to an animal.

No. 2
Burglars in a town in Texas broke into a man's home and made off with $9,000 worth of property, never noticing that a witness was there the whole time.

The victim's parrot, Baby, watched the proceedings, and several days afterward began saying, "Come here, Robert, come here."

Baby had never said those words before, and police used them to track down the burglars, one of whom was named Robert. They were arrested in another burglary.

No. 3
Do not leave your chimpanzee at home alone where he may become bored and lonely. And may do something about it.

That is the lesson to be learned from a New York woman and her chimp, Bongo.

Bongo, a trained performing chimp, had been left at home by his owner. He broke open a liquor cabinet and downed a quart of vodka and two bottles of beer, crashed through a window, and swung from tree to tree down 205th Street in Jamaica, Queens. Along the way he broke a few more windows and bit a neighbor on the toe.

The police arrived, but got nowhere. They called for backup—wisely, because Bongo, at 150 pounds, was said to have the strength of several men. One officer suffered a scratched arm when the lonely chimp "repeatedly embraced" her. He did not ask her to sing "Melancholy Baby."

The ASPCA and a police emergency unit arrived, its owner had come back in the interim, and just as well. "That's a real ape, and we just don't have the facilities to handle that powerful an animal."

The woman got a summons for failure to control Bongo,

and the much-hugged officer was treated for her scratches. The neighbor refused treatment for her toe.

Pets and Extreme Cases

No. 1

An orangutan being prepared for stud service lost his job when he gave birth. The event proved Eric, of Chicago's Lincoln Park Zoo, to be unfit for the task.

A spokesman said that had Eric actually been sent to China, as planned, "We would be more than a little embarrassed." At any rate, he said everyone was very pleased with the birth, which was the goal of the trip, except that Eric was expected to give rather than conceive.

No. 2

In New Jersey, an odd crime occurred, one that might be called cattle pre-rustling.

A dairy-farm owner reported the theft of several 150-pound cans of frozen bull semen, worth $50,000. The owner of the farm said hard times in the dairy industry were to blame.

No. 3

For Sale—purebred male Bug, 14 months old, loves children, excellent pet, clean, intelligent, $75.—Classified ad in the St. John, New Brunswick, *Evening Times-Globe*.

No. 4

People who want to keep king cobras as pets should get in touch with the University of Utah, the Salt Lake City Veterans Hospital and the city zoo.

Researchers there have managed to find a way to remove the cobras' venom ducts by surgery. The researchers told a national conference of zoo officials that all snakes in the Salt Lake City zoo have had the operation, and that keepers who have been bitten since now suffer only "painful fang wounds."

No. 5

In *How to Shoot an Amateur Naturalist* Gerald Durrell reports on "the excellent Frog Watch conducted by the Royal Society for Nature Conservation. In Britain you can phone a frog—that is to say, there is a special hot-line telephone number broadcast on local radio and printed in the local paper, by which you can report your first sighting of frog spawn in ditches, garden ponds or the dwindling number of natural ponds. Experts then mark this on large-scale maps of the area and thus gain a picture of the extent of the amphibians' breeding grounds . . . but . . . toads present a very difficult problem. . . . When they are grown-up and the breeding season arrives, they hop off in their thousands to the pond or lake where they were born.

"Of course, in many cases they have to cross roads or even motorways to attain their objective and so many thousands are killed annually by cars. In the Netherlands, where they seem to deal more sympathetically with their wildlife, they have created underpasses for migrating toads. There is . . . a move afoot to help remedy this with the slogan "Help a Toad Cross the Road." People empathetic to toads . . . take buckets, dustbins or other containers to those points where the toads habitually cross and as the vast concourse of amphibians arrives they bundle them into the buckets . . . and take them safely across. . . . It is to be hoped that the Boy Scouts give up their time-consuming traditional task of helping old ladies across the road and concentrate instead on the toads."

Pet Menaces

No. 1

A potential killer goose stalked a city park in North Mankato, Minnesota, according to the *Weekly World News*.

The avian attacker, who weighed a hefty thirty pounds, chased a crowd of nursery-school three-year-olds in the park, knocking some of them down and beating on them with its wings.

The goose was removed from the park by a local farmer, but the kids' teacher reported that some of them still woke from their naps screaming, "The goose! The goose! He's going to get me!"

*   *   *

No. 2

In Meridian, Texas, killer hornets drove a farmer to his doom.

Attacking in vast numbers, they caused him to jump from his tractor to avoid further stings. He was run over by the mower he was towing.

No. 3

It was the *Weekly World News* that asked the dread question, "Can your pet give you AIDS?"

At a symposium of more than a hundred veterinarians and animal researchers at the University of California, the conclusion was, "It's possible, but we just don't know."

No. 4

Catfish have been known to grow to up to a hundred pounds, but killer catfish were unknown until last year in Eufaula, Oklahoma.

The near-victim of the Lake Eufaula Monster was an 11-year-old boy whose story of "the one that got away" is traditional in most respects except that he got away from the fish.

"He was screaming 'Daddy, he's got me!' " said the boy's mother. His father jumped into the water to help the boy, who had been pulled beneath the surface twice, apparently by a large catfish.

"There was a mouth print [on the boy] and teeth marks all the way down his leg from his knee to his ankle," said his mother.

XXX.
TOYS THAT KILL

Beware of toys. Rambo toys are bad enough, but other playthings contain dangers far beyond the madness that overtakes parents trying to put the damned things together on Christmas Eve.

Killer Snowball

In Telford, England, an event straight out of animated cartoons occurred, but with fatal results.

Seven-year-old Tony Bowers and two friends were celebrating winter by rolling up a giant snowball, snowman-style—rolling it along the ground and letting it grow bigger and bigger. Such fun!

But the snowball got out of control. It ran over little Tony, burying him, and then raced down the hill with Tony trapped inside.

Rescuers arrived on the scene too late. Police said the snowball was five feet in diameter and weighed several hundred pounds, Tony included.

Blowguns of Doom

In Orange, California, police seized more than 300 blowguns, equipped with sights and shoulder mounts, that were advertised as "toys or for fun."

The Case of the Fatal Skateboard

A retired industrialist and a friend were killed in a buggy accident when the horse bolted and the buggy's occupants were flung to the ground. The victims were

Edward Galli, 74, and Wilma Turner, 66. The buggy's driver was unhurt.

Police said the horse bolted after being frightened by a skateboard.

XXXI.
TOYS THAT HARM

Toys that don't kill aren't necessarily safe, either.

This Was No Paper Tiger

In Canada, an innocent-looking paper airplane left a family homeless, said the *Weekly World News*.

A seven-year-old boy, having nothing better to do while waiting for his toast to pop up, made a paper airplane. When he sailed it through the air, it came to a landing on top of the toaster, where it caught fire. He grabbed the burning plane and tried to throw it outside, said his mother, "but it was burning his fingers and he dropped it just inside the back door."

"He came in, woke us up, and said 'Daddy, it's getting really hot in there. I think there's a fire,' " said the boy's father. "When I got into the back room about ten seconds later, the whole wall was already in flames and spreading quickly."

The fire destroyed the family's apartment, doing damage to the extent of about $35,000.

XXXII.

TOYS THAT SHOCK, OUTRAGE, AND DISGUST

And then there are the toys that grossly offend.

Bad Mouth

A talking toy designed to help preschoolers learn to talk taught a 20-month-old girl to talk dirty, according to the *Weekly World News*.

A mother bought her daugher a Mattel See and Say, which speaks the names of common farm animals when its string is pulled. But this little girl got something extra—dirty talk about bodily functions and private parts. Her mother said, "I couldn't believe my ears when I heard that toy talk. There's no denying it—the cussing is as clear as a bell." She said she really became angry when her child "ran up on the couch and jumped up and down and screamed [expletive deleted]!

"We're a Christian family," she said, "and that hurt."

A spokesman for Mattel said the words built into the See and Say could be compressed or deleted in a way that makes the resulting words sound obscene. But he said that to his knowledge that had happened with only one or two of the 50 million See and Says sold.

Mattel offered to replace the See and Say, but the mother refused the offer and said she was considering a lawsuit. "The damage is done," she said. "My child goes around calling it her [expletive deleted] toy, and I'm worried sick that she's going to bring it up around other people, or, worse, in Sunday school."

XXXIII

POLICE BLOTTER

As noted elsewhere, policemen have a tough job. It is sometimes their own fault, as we shall shortly see.

In the sixties and seventies, cops were widely vilified by young people, who called them the fuzz and pigs. The cops responded in a number of ways, very few of them intelligent. The best way was a bumper sticker that read, HATE COPS? WHEN YOU NEED HELP, CALL A HIPPIE.

The best respresentative of the worst responses was Chicago's Mayor Richard Daley, by whose order the 1968 Democratic National Convention was turned into a battle zone. As the good mayor explained, "The policeman isn't there to create disorder. The policeman is there to preserve disorder."

Perhaps the sort of thing he was getting at was the initiative of the six Chicago cops who were arrested for selling drugs out of their squad cars while on duty. Or the two Miami cops who were accused of selling automatic weapons and Miami Police badges to criminals.

Scientific Explanations

No. 1

When the District of Columbia was swept by a wave of weekend robberies, a reporter asked Police Chief John B. Layton whether he had any explanation for the outbreak.

Layton said he did indeed know what was behind it. "The biggest factor," he said, "is the inclination of certain individuals for acquiring funds by illegal means."

No. 2

An undetermined amount of money was found missing

from a dollar-bill changer at the Mrs. Wash Laundry at Washington Plaza, police said. A rear door was forced open to gain access to the premises.

The incident, which was reported Sunday morning at 6:50, led police to believe the breaking and entry occurred some time earlier that morning.—The *Middletown* (Connecticut) *Press*.

One Way to Preserve Disorder

Cuyahoga County was forging ahead with its justice center, a complex that included a jail, courtrooms and police station, but it was costing a lot of money.

As the cost climbed from $61 million to $135 million, the size of the jail steadily diminished. It was supposed to have a capacity of 1,200 but ended up being big enough for only 800.

As a result, the jail was filled and overfilled by 1980. There was no room to put anyone, and so, although there were nearly 5,000 suspects wanted on felony charges, deputies had to be told to cease looking for them.

Of Course, They Could Always Buy One Secondhand

New York's Onondaga County would like to sell you its jail. Or rent it or lease it. Anything to get rid of it.

With a new $12 million prison having been completed recently, the old prison, a 1902 structure built of local limestone and set on a 23-acre site outside of Syracuse, has become redundant. Leaving it abandoned would require guards to protect it from vandals, and tearing it down would cost $750,000.

It's very roomy at 200,000 square feet, and airy, too— the vaulted ceilings are 45 feet high in some spots. Donald Lawless of the county management and budget division said the steel bars would be relatively simple for a developer to remove.

Investigation by Excavation

Two brothers took a forced vacation from work at their gas station in Brooklyn in 1985. The FBI was digging up the spot beneath the gas pumps.

According to *New York Times* reporter George James, the FBI expected to dig up three bodies of people formerly connected with the Gambino organized-crime family. The FBI, using heavy construction equipment, dug and dug and dug. They found nothing but dirt.

"They came with a search warrant," said one brother. "Of course, I was scared." The FBI told him, "It was nothing to do with me," but he checked with a lawyer anyway. The lawyer told him to cooperate.

The digging became something of a neighborhood event, with residents and local businessmen watching its progress every day as the gas pumps, a 4,000-gallon gas tank and many tons of dirt were removed.

The FBI told the brothers that the property, which they have leaved from the gas company for seven years, would be restored and that they would be compensated for lost business. Still, they weren't entirely at ease about the whole affair.

"My customers stick with me," he said. "They know I'm a family guy. Still, it looks bad for this business, you know."

Make-work Project

A Boston police officer was indicted in connection with twenty-nine acts of arson committed in 1982.

A U.S. Attorney said the officer, who pleaded not guilty, was one of a group of men who wanted to become firemen, and said they had set the fires "to increase the public demand for firefighters and other public-safety personnel."

Fighting Fire With Fire, So to Speak

New York's *Daily News* reported Italian police used explosives to blow open the doors of a car they suspected of containing a bomb.

The car, a $100,000 armor-plated Mercedes-Benz 500, was found parked at Rome's Leonardo da Vinci Airport. It did not contain a bomb.

The driver of the car returned later and explained to police that it belonged to U.S. General James Brown, commander of NATO air forces in southern Europe. The car had been parked while the driver helped the general gets his bags to the airport's VIP room before departing on a flight to New York.

Undercover Operation

A New York jail opened 1986 with a panty rebellion.

According to *The New York Times,* prisoners at the jail get their uniforms from the county—underwear, too, if they like. Many of the women prisoners did like, and when the jail ran out of panties, they didn't like.

What really upset them was the jail's offer to supply them with men's boxer shorts. After their indignant protest, a jail officer ordered an emergency purchase of cotton panties, and the rebellion subsided with officials promising that supplies would be plentiful in the future.

"We're prepared now," said a spokesman.

Cops' Worst Enemies

No. 1

In New York city a police officer shot himself in the foot while tracking down a gunman in the downtown section.

The gunman turned out to be an actor delivering a "Rambo-Gram." He had added authenticity to his costume by carrying a prop rifle.

No. 2

In her eleven months on a California town's police force, a 24-year-old rookie has earned the nickname Calamity Jane.

First she grappled with a drunken driver, who tried to take her gun. The driver got a broken nose; the cop got a broken finger and a wrenched back.

On her first solo patrol two men she stopped to question attacked her. One put a gun to her head; the other stabbed her in the chest. She was protected by her bulletproof vest but was cut seriously on the hand.

Shortly after returning to duty, she was investigating a freeway accident when she and the driver involved in the accident were hit by a car that ran through the warning flares that had been set out.

When she later chased a car stolen by teenagers, the

kids smashed the car into a wall at 60 m.p.h. and she crashed right behind them, suffering a bruised heart, blurred vision and a broken sternum.

McKeown had also had a tough time in police academy, where she dislocated a shoulder and was bitten by a rattlesnake.

Of her eleven months on the force, only two were spent on active duty. The rest of the time she spent recovering from injuries.

Next Time, Send a Rambo-Gram

A Florida man was arrested while delivering flowers to his girlfriend.

He mischievously put a bag over his head to add a fillip to the delivery. "He was just going to be cute and come back and say, 'Flowers for you,' and then take the bag off," said his girlfriend. "Whoever called the cops was really stupid."

In any case, the sheriff's department sent six cops to the scene with a helicopter backup, and he was pinned to the wall before he even got into the office.

A coworker said he realized that a mistake was in the making but that when he went outside to explain to the police, they weren't in the mood. "All I heard was a guy say 'Don't move!' "He was about twenty-five feet away with a shotgun that looked like a cannon.' "

Cops and Animals

No. 1

Laddie and Boy, two British police dogs specially trained to sniff out illegal drugs, were forcibly retired in 1967, despite being in the early stages of their careers.

During a raid they happily allowed themselves to be petted and scratched by two suspects being questioned by one of the investigating officers. Eventually they drifted into a very relaxed state and finally fell asleep, not to wake until the officer moved to make his arrest. At that point Laddie growled ferociously, and Boy bit the officer in the leg.

*   *   *

No. 2

In Northern Ireland, according to *The New York Times*, you have to watch what you say to a cop even more carefully than in most other places.

Police Sergeant Fred Taylor told the court that he spotted a group of youths blocking a sidewalk, and went over with his German shepherd to tell them to move on. Among the crowd was 18-year-old Lawrence O'Dowd, who looked at Taylor and then looked at his dog and said a four-letter word. The word was *meow*.

O'Dowd was immediately arrested and charged with "using abusive words and engaging in threatening behavior." The court fined him the equivalent of $126.

No. 3

In North Humberside, England, police swung into action to nab a sex pervert making an obscene phone call.

An operator working the 999 emergency line alerted the police when she answered a call and heard only heavy breathing. Phone-company personnel managed to trace the call, and the police hurried off.

The *Weekly World News* said that on arriving at the address given, the cops found that their sex fiend was a dog that had managed to hit the 9 button three times while playing with the phone. He was still happily chewing and licking the handset when they arrived.

No. 4

In Regensburg, West Germany, a policeman who grabbed a suspected shoplifter found himself under unconventional attack.

The New York *Post* said the suspect retaliated by turning loose his pet rat, which scrambled onto the officer's head. The officer managed to subdue both and arrest the suspect.

Open-and-Shut Cases

No. 1

Police in Indiana responded when a woman reported finding the dead body of her husband in the basement of their home.

Near his body police found a carpenter's hammer. An

autopsy revealed that the dead man, a cancer patient, had been struck on the head thirty-two times with the claw end of the hammer. Police ruled the death a suicide.

The coroner said it was a homicide. "No way in the world they are going to convince me this was a suicide," he said. Some time later the prosecutor's office, apparently agreeing with the coroner, reopened the case to further investigation.

No. 2

Maryland State Police investigated the death of John Paisley, former deputy director of the CIA's Office of Strategic Research. Paisley's body, with a bullet hole in the head, was found in Chesapeake Bay.

The police ruled the death a suicide.

Some people had nagging doubts about their conclusion. They wondered how and why a right-handed man would shoot himself in the left side of the head. They also wondered how the victim managed to do it after tying himself up and attaching weights to his body to make sure it sank. The police offered no speculation on those questions.

XXXIV.

SAMARITANS AND SUCH

Army Intelligence

No. 1

In Portugal, Army brass looked closely at the case of a 12-year-old boy who had been shot by a sentry. The sentry testified in court that on the night in question he had issued the usual challenge prescribed by regulations, but said the boy had ignored the challenge, whereupon he fired.

During the trial it was decided to reconstruct the incident. A civilian played the role of the boy. He was shot too.

No. 2

The Minneapolis *Star & Tribune* reported that an American soldier in Panama City, Panama, was demonstrating how a friend had been killed in a recent accident.

During the demonstration, which took place on a fifth-floor balcony of a hotel, the soldier lost his balance and fell to his death.

Police to the Rescue

New York's *Daily News* reported that Officer Ken Ambrose of Altamonte Springs, Florida, went to the aid of a stranded motorist.

Ambrose pulled up behind the motorist, leaving his patrol car on the railroad tracks. While Ambrose was helping the motorist, the crossing gate at the track automatically lowered itself. Moments later a freight train roared down the track and destroyed Ambrose's car.

Zap!

In New Jersey, three men went to the rescue of a skunk that had become trapped in a length of irrigation pipe. Thinking to jolt the skunk loose by giving the pipe a few sharp raps on the ground, they hoisted it into the air.

The skunk was virtually blasted loose when the pipe struck high-tension overhead electrical wires, killing two of the men outright and leaving the third with severe burns.

Claim Validated

A meat cutter at a Swiss hotel filed an insurance claim after losing a finger in a piece of machinery. The insurance company sent an adjuster to investigate. Once on the scene, the adjuster asked to be allowed to operate the machine. When he did, he cut off his own finger.

I Remember Mama

The children of a New Jersey woman had a severe argument over the use of the family vacation cabin. So great was the rift that the children stopped speaking to each other for several years.

The brother and sister finally made up when they were thrown together in the process of settling the estate of their uncle.

During the proceedings the brother asked after their mother, a recluse with emotional problems who had been living alone at her home in Duluth, Minnesota. "So, where are you keeping Mom?" he asked.

"We thought you were taking care of her," his sister answered.

Later, the old woman was found dead in her living room. She had been dead for a year.

The Cat's Pajamas

During the London firemen's strike of the late 1970s, the British Army was called in to protect the city and handle various emergencies.

One of the lesser emergencies was the traditional one—a

cat stuck up a tree—the subject of innumerable kitsch calendar paintings but still of import to those involved. And so the old woman with the imperiled cat called the fire hall for help.

The Army responded immediately, arriving in splendor with a gleaming fire truck and rescuing the cat with efficiency and speed. The old lady was delighted—here was yet another example of Old Blighty muddling through under the worst of circumstances—and she invited the rescue team in for a spot of tea. They got along famously; then at last the heroes said their good-byes and left.

As they drove off, they ran over the cat.

XXXV.
THE WORLD OF WORK

Work is the subject of many misconceptions. It is widely believed that people hate it, but when any politicians deign for a minute or two to listen to the poor, the poor say, "We want jobs." There are utterly lazy people who go through life working as little as possible, but by and large it is seldom that you will find able-bodied men and women demonstrating for welfare. They want jobs.

What about the people who hit it big in lotteries? Some of them win millions and thus are guaranteed an enormous annual wage for doing absolutely nothing for the next twenty years. What do the winners have to say to that?

Almost invariably they say that it isn't really going to make much of a difference. They might get a new car or pay off the mortgage; usually there are a couple of minor luxuries—a new winter coat, for example—that they can now buy right away. But, they say, they're going to go to work tomorrow just as they always have.

This is not to suggest that people don't get fed up with working from time to time. Every now and then they are given cause to hate their jobs with passion, and it's a response well expressed by Johnny Paycheck's song "Take This Job and Shove It." And by some of the incidents noted below.

No Sex, Please—We're British

British auto workers, seeking to celebrate Christmas on the night shift, smuggled liquor into their plant and got drunk. That led to dancing on top of some cars, the capsizing of a pair of tow trucks, the trashing of an office and the savaging of five cars, three of which were so badly damaged that they had to be scrapped. One worker was stripped naked and covered with axle grease from head to toe. A company spokesman said the employees were "quite irresponsible."

Farewell Performance

In Dublin, Ireland, an actor was appearing on stage in one of the musical theater's best-loved offerings, Gilbert and Sullivan's *HMS Pinafore*.

Many a would-be star would have given anything to trade places with him, but he was not sure. Nagging doubts—the worst kind—apparently assailed him. And in one performance, right in the middle of "I Am the Ruler of the Queen's Nav-ee," they got the better of him.

He stopped singing; the orchestra stopped playing. Then he said, "Oh, dash this. I'm going home." He got down from the stage and walked up the aisle and out of the theater, removing his costume en route. He said later that he was investigating other lines of work.

Men at Work

In Florida a 71-year-old man went down to the beach to sunbathe. He set up his lounge chair, sprawled out in comfort and took a little snooze.

On the same beach was a man employed by the city's public works department. He was engaged in clearing the beach of storm debris and was possibly somewhat preoccupied, because he ran the old man over with a bulldozer.

Not as Dumb as They Look

In Somerville, South Carolina, nearly a hundred public school teachers whose starting salary is hardly $12,000 a year got on line to apply for another job.

The local post office had announced that it was looking for a janitor, a job that paid nearly $20,000 a year.

Don't Be the Type Who Spends His Whole Life in the Office

The owner of a Rhode Island factory didn't know when he was lucky. The day after he escaped being killed by an explosion in his building, he went back to the scene of the disaster.

The wrecked building fell on him.

Modern Times on the Assembly Line

The Gary (Indiana) *Post Tribune* reported on difficulties at the Brigend, Wales, car-engine assembly line, owned by Ford.

The Brigend facility, only three years old, is as modern as Ford could make it and is considered one of the most advanced and highly automated assembly lines in all Europe. There is the slight problem of its tending to come to a dead stop from time to time for reasons no one can explain. It happens several times a day.

Although no explanation for the halts could be found, a solution was.

Every day, one of the approximately forty workers on the line is selected to serve as the kicker. When the line comes to one of its baffling halts, the kicker goes to work, wielding either a steel-toed boot or a large hammer. That seems to do the trick.

A Ford spokesman said, "The plant is supposed to be the most modern in Europe, but with so much automation, it seems there is more to go wrong."

Deadlier Than in Wales

The summer of '85 was a memorable one for workers at a Big Three auto plant in Michigan. It was, you might say, worth your life to work there.

Black widow spiders had invaded the assembly line.

It was, in the end, no mystery. The spiders would come scampering out of dashboard parts made in Mexico, and the workers would scamper out of the plant.

A spokesman said the plant in Mexico would be fumigated and liberally supplied with no-pest strips. In the meantime plant executives with ice water in their veins were put to hand-inspecting all dashboard parts, while others heated the assembly-line racks with blowtorches to fry any lingering spiders.

Yes, This One Is Ready to Take a Man's Job, All Right

A robot was employed to serve wine at a restaurant in Edinburgh, Scotland, as possibly the world's first tin sommelier.

On its first shift the robot, wearing a black hat and a bow tie, spilled wine, knocked over furniture and terrified customers when it ran amok. The next day, for reasons that remain unknown, the restaurateurs gave it another try. The robot's head fell off, winding up in a customer's lap.

The supplier of the robot, in London, is suing the Edinburgh firm that bought it and sold it to the restaurant. The Edinburgh firm is not entirely averse to paying up, but it says it won't have the money until the restaurant pays for the robot, and it doesn't dare send a bill for the robot until the thing works properly.

The Nose Knows

According to the *ContraCosta Times* of Oakley, California, a testing lab called Hill Top Research in Cincinnati, Ohio, devotes itself to seeing how well products work before they go on the market.

One of the products tested recently was a new deodorant soap, using subjects hired from outside the company. The subjects were paid to wash up and let Hill Top's researchers give 'em a whiff.

It is a demanding business. A tester who had been working with Hill Top for thirty years was rejected for the armpit test because she didn't stink enough. She said, "I was really disappointed. I'd been looking forward to it."

Another said, "I feel we're helping science. I think it's a great thing."

XXXVI.
THE RED MENACE

Americans fear nothing more than the Red Menace. Americans are so afraid of commies that they will do anything, no matter how contrary to their own principles, to hold the red tide at bay.

Americans have befriended, supported and even created tyrants who have robbed, oppressed and murdered their own people in the name of anticommunism. It's a dirty job, but somebody has to do it. Besides, it pays well. For thirty years the Duvalier family owned its personal Caribbean country, and they got the top cut of all U.S. aid delivered to Haiti. Similarly with Ferdinand Marcos, surprise winner (but not for long) of the 1986 election in the Philippines.

In the long run, observers of the titanic East-West struggle for men's hearts and minds, as they like to say, are betting on the commies. They'll win in the end by frightening Americans to death.

More on the Red Menace follows.

Plus 10,000 Copies of *Jane Fonda's Work-out*

The drought in Ethiopia produced a famine that killed thousands, perhaps hundreds of thousands. Ethiopia's Marxist government did what it could to help itself, largely by shipping minorities it didn't like out of their home regions and resettling them in distant areas where they would die more quickly. The government also arranged for much of the food shipped in from abroad to rot on the piers.

The USSR joined the many nations involved in the international relief program.

Soviet Sport magazine and Tass, the official Russian news service, announced a foreign-aid program that would send aerobic-dance instructors to the starving Ethiopians.

"In Ethiopia," Tass said, "there are now a great many who want to practice rhythmic gymnastics. Soviet specialists who have been specially invited will help set up aerobics sections in this African country."

By February, Soviet relief efforts had intensified. Sources in Nairobi said the latest shipment of Russian aid comprised 150 loudspeakers.

They were to be set up in famine-relief camps to enable refugees to hear broadcasts from Ethiopia's government-controlled radio station.

Up the Revolution!

One response to Russia's colossal alcoholism problem would be to ban booze, and, said The New York *Post*, prohibition has actually been considered by "Kremlin bosses."

The Soviet Communist Party's Central Committee was said to have received an "avalanche" of letters from citizens still in a condition to write. Dr. Boris Iskakhov, speaking for a committee on alcohol abuse, said the letters were about a 1985 law imposing antialcohol measures. "A majority supports these measures, and others which are planned," Iskakhov said, "but there are also letters threatening sabotage and strikes if the sale of vodka and wine is banned."

Alternative Solution to the Drinking Problem

Galina Parfenova, director of a Moscow alcoholism center, got into trouble with party bosses, the *Weekly World News* reported.

Parfenova was caught using her patients to do work, free, on her country cottage. She used state vehicles to ship the free labor force to and fro. And when it was chow time, she fed them food cooked at the center by cooks on the state payroll. Her assistant handled the deliveries.

She also told the workers that in return for their work

she would get them released from the center sooner than specified by the medical authorities.

Latest Outrage Perpetrated by Godless Brutes

The *Post* also reported tragic news from Yalta, where a Russian film company was making a movie version of the famous Walt Disney cartoon *Bambi*.

Three of the four deer used in the filming were eaten for dinner.

The deer mysteriously vanished from the set where *Bambi* was being filmed in the Crimea, and an investigation by local police revealed that the deer had be snapped up by a trio of "notorious freeloaders" who slaughtered the deer and made them the main course of a birthday dinner.

But at This Rate They Will Have One Hell of a Foreign-trade Deficit

West Germany's Frankfurter Allgemeine Zeitung broke the story of four lost Russian tank troopers in Czechoslovakia.

Ota Filip, a Czech expatriate, wrote that in the fall of 1984, during maneuvers conducted by the Warsaw Pact nations, the tank crew managed to get lost in rural eastern Bohemia. Citing a smuggled report from Czech police, Filip said the lost troopers and their tank clanked into a small village at about 9 P.M. and parked behind the local tavern. A little more than two hours later, they were observed leaving.

They were not seen again until two days later, when they were found asleep in the woods. Their tank was nowhere to be seen. Authorities questioned them about the whereabouts of their tank, which was a matter of some interest to them.

"Tank? What tank? Oh, that tank. Well, it was here only a few moments ago, as we recall." All in all, the four soldiers were unanimous in that they couldn't imagine what had happened to their tank.

The mystery clarified just a bit about ten days later, the police said in their report. The head of a local recycling center told the cops that he had just bought a rather large quantity of high-quality steel from a man who owned a tavern not too far away. The police then interviewed the tavern owner, who said yes, he had indeed bought a tank recently. He didn't have it anymore, however—he had dismantled it and sold it as scrap to a recycling center. Four nice Russian fellows traded him the tank for two cases of vodka.

They were such likable allies in the struggle for world communism that he had thrown in a few pounds of herring and pickles "as a gesture of comradeship," he said.

XXXVII.
ROMANCE OF THE MIDDLE EAST

The Middle East! Think of it—with all its sun and sand, its beaches and its mindlessness, it's just like California, but with perpetual violent death added. Small wonder that UN experts trying to pin down some of the demands and aims of the innumerable Arab splinter groups were forced to conclude that many of them had no idea of exactly what they were fighting for.

As for the Camels, Forget About Them Too!

Mohammed al-Fassi, a billionaire oil sheikh, announced his intention to give the City of New York a donation of $200,000 to help out during the municipal financial crisis, but suddenly changed his mind when the city did not provide him with a motorcycle escort from Kennedy Airport to his hotel. "He was indeed intending to give $200,000 to the city," explained Ali Gamil, the sheikh's spokesman. "However, he does have certain protocol that he expects to find everywhere. He did not find it here."

A Horse! A Horse! My Strife-torn Middle Eastern Battleground for a Horse!

The crowds grew restive at Beirut's racetrack when one race began with the four favorites falling right at the start, and when a 91-to-1 long shot was declared the winner, they rioted. Knocking down fences and police barricades, they were wrecking the place until track officials withdrew the result and announced that all bets would be returned. That pleased everyone but a man who had put a few bucks down on the long shot; he threatened to blow up the track unless he was paid his winnings. He seemed a lot easier to deal with than the mob, so the police threw him out.

A few minutes later a rocket grenade sailed into the infield and exploded, causing no injuries but ending racing for the day.

And My Best for a Happy Hanukkah

Eyewitnesses during the hijacking of the cruise ship *Achille Lauro* were agreed that terrorist gunmen beat Leon Klinghoffer, an elderly stroke victim who was confined to a wheelchair, then shot him and threw his corpse into the sea.

Smarting under accusations of terrorism, a PLO spokesman opened December 1985 with the explanation that Mrs. Klinghoffer had thrown her husband overboard and blamed the terrorists so she could collect her late husband's insurance.

Beneath Their Rebellious Exterior Lies an Enduring Love of Law and Order

Shiite Moslem Amal gunmen and Druze Progressive Socialist Party terrorists were bombarding each other with tank and mortar fire on November 25, 1985, despite their leaders' declaration of a cease-fire and the threat of the death penalty for those who violated it.

The following day, Issam Aintrezi, a Druze chieftain, posed for the cameras, smoking a cigarette and nonchalantly holstering the pistol he had just emptied into the comrade-in-arms whose corpse lay at his feet. The dead man had refused to surrender his weapon for the duration of the cease-fire.

Extra! Extra! Terrorist Blows Own Ass Off!

Israel Army Radio carried the report of a Shiite bomber who had ridden an explosive-laden donkey into the Druze town of Hasbaya with ear-splitting consequences. An Israeli army spokesman said the rider probably intended extensive bloodshed, but the explosives carried in the donkey's saddle baskets went off prematurely, injuring only one civilian while launching donkey and rider into the better life to come.

It's Not a Fun Place to Be Anymore, Anyway

In Tel Aviv scientists reported mass suicides by field mice, which have been flinging themselves off the Golan Heights.

They said they had seen two mass suicides, in which groups of field mice jumped into streams and drowned. After one mass jump by the mice, scientists counted 150 tiny corpses at the foot of a cliff.

The experts say they estimate that 250 million mice live along the Israeli-Syrian cease-fire line, and there is a strong possibility that there may be too many of them. They believe that hurling themselves off cliffs is the rodents' instinctive way of solving an overpopulation problem.

Lights, Camera, Action!

For any remaining innocents who doubt that Arab terrorists posture for the media, this: "Watch this," an Arab gunman yelled to a French television crew as he raised his machine gun and fired a couple of quick bursts into the air.

Christian gunmen immediately replied with a barrage of rockets and mortar rounds in the middle of a two-day-old truce. When the barrage ended, an hour later, the tally was fifteen dead and twenty-seven wounded.

XXXVIII.

BUSINESS—BIG AND OTHERWISE

"The business of America is business," said Calvin Coolidge, then lapsed into another of his famous and greatly appreciated silences; he didn't say much, Silent Cal, but he was dead right. America is about business as Britain is about the class system, and that is why America is the land of opportunity. Anyone can succeed in business; no one can correct his parentage.

On the way to that ideal, things fall apart, the center does not hold—often enough, anyway, that business is thought of as a curse as often as it is hailed as a blessing. Yes, it creates jobs; it also creates unemployment, steals tax money and steals jobs (often enough, the new factory is simply replacing one that was closed elsewhere). Business's conception of public responsibility is often a wonder to behold: In the early 1960s American pharmaceuticals manufacturers were told by the government (which isn't always wrong) not to put a birth-control drug called Thalidomide on the market because of its dangerous side effects.

The manufacturers thought they might as well make some use of the stuff: Blending public-relations savvy with the use of the public as unwitting guinea pigs, they shipped Thalidomide to doctors all over the country and told them to give it away as samples. In this manner the U.S. managed to produce as many birth-deformed "Thalidomide babies" as had Britain, where a less attentive government had permitted the sale of Thalidomide for some years.

Here are some more notable business achievements.

Big Wheels

Dr. Lawrence Peter codified the Peter Principle—the idea that in a hierarchy a person tends to rise to his level of incompetence. That is, he keeps getting promoted for good work until he reaches a position in which he can do real damage. An example is in the American and British auto executives invited to look at the VW Beetle just after World War II.

How they laughed and sneered! The American, representing Ford, ironically, said the Volkswagen was no good; the Brit said it didn't even meet minimal automotive standards. The Beetle stayed in production for many years, however, long enough, in fact, to displace Ford's Model T as the best-selling car in the world. During the same period, the British auto industry went from failure to failure and today hardly exists.

But no sooner had the Beetle conquered the world than VW decided to dump it. Actually, the decision was made long before—the company merely waited until the Beetle had outsold the Model T and then dumped it for something more modern, more stylish, more in tune with the newly perceived wants of the American motorist, who, as it happened, didn't want it. VW's Rabbit was a failure. A brand-new plant built in Pennsylvania to make Rabbits had to be shut down. Eventually the Rabbit itself was abandoned, and VW went on to something else.

That's not to say there's any lack of love for Beetles. Americans miss them and so do the Germans. The last batch of Beetles was sold in Germany in 1985. They had been imported from a plant in Mexico.

But if companies can reach levels of incompetence, so can whole industries: The U.S. auto industry concluded in the early 1960s that it was making exactly the kind of cars that Americans wanted and would continue to want, and that Japanese manufacturers had no hope of getting a measurable share of the U.S. market.

Next Year, a Pig With Wings

The Ringling Bros. and Barnum & Bailey Circus fooled children of all ages with its claim to have a real unicorn on display. Critics immediately charged the circus with conning the public. "As far as we're concerned, it's a unicorn," the circus said. "A unicorn is an animal with one horn."

To the U.S. Department of Agriculture, which conducted a careful examination, the unicorn is a mythical beast and the circus's animal is a surgically altered goat.

Cringe Instead, Then Offer a Low Bow

A friendly hello won't get you onto the fast track at one New York bank. The company told its workers to "avoid saying hello. This elsewhere pleasant and familiar greeting is out of place in the world of business."

Nonworking Number of the Year

Citibank wrote a New York man to say he had no money in his account to cover the automatic mortgage withdrawal, would have to pay a fine and should immediately call the bank at the number provided.

He called, was told it was the wrong number, and was given another number to call. The man was growing annoyed. He had already checked his records and found that although he had deposited money to cover the mortgage, the bank, according to its own statement, had put the money in the wrong account. The woman at Citibank he spoke to verified his statement on her desktop computer and said everything could be straightened out and the fine would be canceled if he would go to his bank and get a note from the branch manager confirming the error. The man angrily refused, and after some heated negotiations the woman apologized and said she would handle the matter internally. Still furious, the man demanded to know why an organization as large as Citibank couldn't even manage to provide the correct phone number on the letter. The woman said the number had been changed after the letter had been entered into the computer, and no one could figure out how to change the computerized entry. Every week, she said, dozens of people got the same wrong number because her superior had forbidden her to correct the numbers by hand before the letters were mailed.

The man then called her superior, a vice-president, who confirmed that his personnel had been instructed to sent out phone numbers they knew were wrong because "handwritten corrections don't look very professional."

Two days later, the same man spent ten frustrating minutes at his branch failing to get through to Customer Service on the courtesy phone, giving up when another customer told him the phone wasn't working. When the man suggested that an out-of-order sign be hung on the phone, a bank officer replied, "When people don't get any answer, they figure it out for themselves."

Like Father, Like Son

Big companies spend a lot of time worrying about their images. One of them was RCA, which—deep into space satellites and other leading-edge technology—decided to get rid of Nipper, the familiar white dog who peered quizzically into the speaker horn of an old-time Victrola above the slogan, "His Master's Voice." The company got itself a glitzy, forward-looking new logo and was still patting itself on the back when the first waves of customer resentment began to roll in. And they continued to roll in, too—people didn't like the idea of the faithful hound being put to corporate sleep. RCA held out for a while and then surrendered. Nipper was resurrected by popular demand.

RCA is the parent company of NBC, which also decided to update its image, which was less work than producing better TV shows. NBC, the leader in color TV (because RCA made the sets), used a colorful peacock logo. By the mid-1970s, however, color was so common that NBC thought the peacock a bit dated. So they wrung the bird's pretty neck.

It was not a precipitate action—NBC had been planning it for a long time. It had paid a fancy design firm to come up with a fancy new logo. After 18 months and $6 million, the firm turned in a large, ugly, stylized letter *N*. The network was delighted, thought not for long. Shortly after the $6 million *N* was unveiled, a tiny PBS station in Nebraska announced that it had been using the very same logo for almost a decade. NBC brought the peacock back a little while later.

The Others Can Take Their Chances

On discovering that more than 500 of its pacemakers might contain faulty transistors, the American Pacemaker Corporation began a recall program. That was in June of 1979, and it was already a bit late—all of the suspect devices had been installed in the bodies of people with weak hearts. The company told doctors that the pacemakers should be removed in such cases where removal was "consistent with good patient management."

Dumb-Is-It

Frederick Koch, of Guilford, Vermont, was fed up. He knew very well how to pronounce his own name ("coke"), but people kept saying "kotch" instead. And so he found his way into Windham County Superior Court, where he had his name legally changed to "Coke-Is-It." People sometimes act rashly when angry.

How the news got beyond the borders of Vermont is unknown, but it did, penetrating all the way to Atlanta, Georgia, home of the Coca-Cola Company, which immediately sued Mr. Coke-Is-It for trying to grab a trademarked phrase.

After much discussion and who-knows-what in the way of law bills, Coca-Cola finally agreed that Mr. Coke-Is-It could call himself whatever the hell he wanted to.

Self-made Millionaire

Thirty-year-old Keith Gormezano created a business empire almost overnight. He became the chief executive officer of at least five companies. One of them, La Beacon Presse, had earnings of $666 million in 1985, getting it the number 35 slot on *Inc.* Magazine's list of the nation's fastest-growing companies.

Gormezano did all that, the Seattle *Post-Intelligencer* said, with a little imagination and no money. He was a magnate because he said so.

He is a publisher, but only of *The Beacon Review*, a tiny literary magazine that pulls in about $200 a year. He otherwise supports himself as the manager of a small apartment building. His financial empire is phony.

But not criminal—he did not attempt to make money

with his scheme. Occasionally his spreading fame caused people to send him money for La Beacon Presse books, but he always sent the money back.

The ersatz tycoon, who spent about five years and $900 pulling the leg of a credulous business community, said it was easy. He simply filled out forms and financial documents, and was very closemouthed about details. When pressed, he replied with that old standby about not releasing the information because the company was privately held.

Half an Hour Later, You're Furious

Small businesses also overreach themselves, which is why police in Iowa are looking for a man who was doing a mail-order business in satellite-TV dish antennas. He was charging $525 apiece and sending his customers stamped-steel Chinese woks.

Y'All Can Shove It Up Your Garage

A 26-year-old maid in Houston was thrilled to learn that she had won a car in the prize drawing advertised by a local department store, but only briefly. When she went to collect her prize, she was handed the keys to a battered six-year-old station wagon that had 89,000 miles on. It also had a broken dashboard, one door that refused to open, no hubcaps and no rear seat. The store's employees pointed out that the ads for the drawing specified only a "late-model car."

We Also Have an Emergency Shipment of Push-up Bras

In 1985, Americans responded generously—as they usually do when donations of food clothes and money are needed in the wake of natural disasters.

One of the worst of the tragedies occurred in Colombia, where floods and mud slides killed hundreds of people and buried whole villages. The aid was offered freely, quickly and in large amounts.

And then there was the shoe manufacturer who used the disaster as the chance for a tax write-off by shipping to Colombia his excess inventory of women's high-heel shoes.

XXXIX.

VEHICULAR DIFFICULTIES

There was a time when owning a car went beyond personal pride to family pride. When a husband brought a new car home, it was a ritual for the whole family to pile in for a slow drive around the neighborhood for the purpose of showing it off. It was a mild form of boasting, and a shared one—the neighbors would come out to wave their congratulations or run down to the curb to kick a tire. Somebody in the neighborhood had "made it," at least in a small way, and everybody was happy for him.

These days the owner of a new car hopes he won't have to take it to the shop too often, because even a simple tune-up will trash a week's wages, and the car won't run very well anyway. When he complains, the mechanic will cheerfully explain that the car can't possibly be made to run any better, and will blame it all on the emission controls.

But there are less mundane problems with motor vehicles, as noted below.

Low-speed Champion

A British man wanted to have his car repainted and sought the advice of a friend. The friend recommended a particular garage, saying, "They're slow but thorough."

The job wasn't finished five years later. Being an unusually patient man, he would call now and then, only to be told his car was "nearly ready" but not yet complete. "I am very painstaking," explained the garage owner. "When I have finished, that car will be the best-looking one in these parts."

At Least No One Will Steal His Radio

Beach County, Florida, determined to build an artificial reef off its beachfront—artificial reefs attract large quantities of fish and also help reduce beach erosion, and they are easily and cheaply built simply by dumping old cars into the sea.

Hairdresser Greg Hauptner decided to donate a car to get the project rolling. As onlookers, many wearing tuxedos, cheered and applauded, Hauptner's car sank into the sea. The car was a $25,000 Rolls-Royce complete with AM-FM and citizen's band radios. Hauptner presided over the sinking in a black velvet designer jacket and suede jogging shoes.

Fast, Fast, Fast Relief!

A 46-year-old Cocoa Beach, Florida, accountant was feeling a bit stressed one day, a condition she remedied by setting her office on fire and then ramming her car into another car, plate-glass store windows and a gas pump. According to Sergeant Gerald Van Landingham, the woman appeared calm when arrested. He added, "She said, 'I went out and got rid of my frustration.' "

If It Feels Good, Do It

Complaints of a disturbance brought police to the home of a Washington woman. There they found her car in rather dilapidated condition. Nearby, a broken baseball bat lay on the ground, possible evidence of foul play.

But the woman said she did it all herself and was glad of it. "I feel good," she told the cops. "That car has been giving me misery for years, and I killed it."

And One Free Game to ...

The Los Angeles bus driver who parked his vehicle and went off to loosen up with a session at a video-game at a nearby store. A few minutes later the bus loosened up too, rolling 150 feet and crashing through the front of the store, destroying much of it.

Low-mileage Special, Very Clean

In Mayaguez, Puerto Rico, a Volkswagen Beetle owner has solved his own housing shortage by ceasing to drive his car. He has, instead, moved into it. On the hood is his sink—a pail with a faucet piped to it—and a shower fitting. On the roof is an attractive potted plant.

Why Not Just Say "Fuzz" And Be Done With It?

When the Green Bay, Wisconsin, Police Department ordered license plates for its unmarked cars, all of them arrived bearing the letters *PD*.

Painful Reverses

No. 1

A British man lost no time in driving his mother-in-law to the market, but she was in such a hurry to shop that she tried to get out of the car before it had stopped moving. She fell out, and he inadvertently ran over one of her legs. Shoppers running to the rescue yelled for him to inch forward so they could pull the women free, and when he did, he ran over her other leg.

Though notably the worse for wear, the injured woman nursed no grudge. "He doesn't make a habit of running over me," she said. "Normally he's a grand son-in-law."

No. 2

An octogenarian couple were driving in their pickup truck when they struck a dog in the road. The husband immediately stopped, and his wife jumped out and ran back to see to the dog. Police said that the husband then "looked in his rear-view mirror and thought she was motioning to him to back up." He did, but "in the meantime she walked behind the truck and he backed over her. She started to holler and scream, then he put it in forward to drive ahead and drove over her."

The dog survived.

Plane Lands Atop Car

On Interstate 475 near Flint, Michigan, a twin-engine private plane made a forced landing.

No one was injured, but several were surprised, chief among them a woman who said, "I didn't hear, see or feel anything until the plane landed on top of my car."

One Leather Flying Helmet to ...

An elderly couple from Florida were out for a drive, seeing the sights. At the same time an executive aircraft was coming in for a landing at the local airport.

Unfortunately, they were both trying to use the same strip of concrete.

The airplane would seem to have had the right of way, because the concrete in question was indeed a runway and not, as the confused driver thought, a highway, but the air-traffic controller in the tower chose not to debate fine points and waved the plane off.

A wise choice, since he had radio contact with the plane and not the car, and since contact with the car might not have done any good—the man kept on driving all the way to the end of the runway, across a grass-coverted buffer strip, over the seawall and into Tampa Bay.

XL.
NOTES ON DINING IN

According to food-industry analysts, we are rapidly approaching the time when half of all meals eaten by Americans will be eaten somewhere besides home. Though there has been something of a "gourmet cooking explosion" in this country over the past twenty years, it is more hype than fact, and greasy spoons, coffeepots and fast-food vomiterias outnumber real restaurants to a degree beyond the ken of advanced computers.

Half of all meals to be eaten outside the home! But why? Some hints follow.

Budget-stretcher of the Year

Ecology writer Douglas Elliott says an excellent way to cut waste is to eat animals killed by cars on highways. He says "road kills," as they are known to connoisseurs, are safe if completely cooked.

Birds of a Feather

In England, four mortuary attendants were hauled into court for selling turkeys they had stored beside human corpses.

They had kept about thirty turkeys in the deep-freeze and had sold them to people and restaurants for Christmas dinner.

Mr. Potato Head

In the summer of 1985, baseball great Yogi Berra was in Fargo, North Dakota, to play in a golf tournament. For unknown reasons, but possibly spurred by Berra's reputation for coining memorable bon mots, someone ventured to observe that potatoes were a major crop in North Dakota. Berra retorted dryly that all the potatoes grown in the state couldn't fill his front yard.

Slow to boil, the Red River Valley Potato Growers Association simply simmered for a couple of months over the slight. Then they acted. And thus, one fine November morning, Berra awoke in his Montclair, New Jersey, home to find that he had twenty-three tons of potatoes in his front yard. "Maybe I should ask for turkeys next time," he said.

Vintage Stuff

Bloomingdale's, the department store for people with too much money to spend, began selling ice last year at $7 a bag. The store announced that it was imported ice, direct from Greenland. Very pure—it came from glaciers and was 100,000 years old.

Let's Really Hear It for ...

"Cranberries, often relegated to a secondary role at the Thanksgiving table, are capable of stardom." —Nancy Harmon Jenkins in *The New York Times*.

Phantom of McDonald's

A California man is the creator of the Breatharian Institute. His advice: Don't eat food, which is "another type of drug." Eat air instead. He claimed to have eaten nothing but air for the past eighteen years and said disciples of Breatharianism could nourish themselves handsomely on deep breaths and nothing else. He was willing to teach anybody how to do it for a $300 fee.

Some may entertain doubts about this; one of them was, in fact, his partner, who said that soon after the two met, "I saw him eat an omelet. I was so shocked. He thought he was safe, and started eating around me all the time. He sneaks into fast-food places and eats just like the rest of us. Worse, because he has to do it in places open late at night."

Mmmmmm-mmmmmm, Good!

According to the label on a frozen lemon-pudding cake, this down-home desert contains sugar, water, enriched bleached flour (wheat flour, malted barley flour, potassium bromate, niacin, reduced iron, thiamine mononitrate and riboflavin), eggs, vegetable shortening (made from partially hydrogenated soybean oil and/or partially hydrogenated palm oil with or without mono- and diglycerides and polysorbate 60 as emulsifiers), vegetable oil (made from partially hydrogenated soy and/or cottonseed and/or palm oil), vanilla-pudding mix (sugar, modified tapioca starch, dextrose, calcium carbonate, sodium phosphate, hydrogenated soybean oil, di- and monoglycerides, salt, nonfat dry milk, artificial and natural flavors, artificial color), dehydrated blend of (whey, sodium caseinate, nonfat dry milk, lecithin, calcium phosphate, and calcium oxide), yogurt, baking powder, (sodium acid pyrophosphate, sodium bicarbonate, monocalcium phosphate, calcium sulfate) nonfat dry milk, invert sugar, corn syrup, lemon emulsion (concentrated lemon oil, propylene glycol, polysorbate 80), concentrated lemon juice, salt, butter, emulsifier (hydrated mono- and diglycerides, polysorbate 60 (8%), and sodium stearoyl-2-lactylate (4%), with phosphoric acid, sodium propionate and sodium benzoate added as preservatives), tart-o-cream (calcium sulfate, monocalcium phosphate, fumaric acid and starch), annatto, cellulose gum, icing emulsifier (water dispersion of polysorbate 80 (20%), monodiglycerides, lactostearine, cellulose gum, and sorbic acid as a freshness preserver, and vanillin and ethyl vanillin.

Modest Little Wines With Great Charm and a Hint of Prestone

Importers of a well-known Italian wine had to recall a shipment from stores when government testers discovered the wine contained diethylene glycol, a chemical used in antifreeze.

Earlier, U.S. government inspectors found that dozens of Austrian winemakers had deliberately adulterated their wines with ingredients that did not come from grapes and that could have caused illness or even death.

In a move to protect the credibility of the Austrian

industry, the Austrian government announced a series of stiff new regulations to guarantee the wines' purity; numerous winemakers vigorously protested.

Royal Pain

The Prince Spaghetti Company ran an advertisement promoting "Prince in Concert"—i.e., Prince Spaghetti in concert with a variety of pasta sauces. Lawyers for the rock star Prince immediately announced that he would sue. The spaghetti company wondered whether the name of the man who kissed Sleeping Beauty would have to be changed to "_____ Charming."

Next Question

1: Is red wine ever used to cook fish? *A.* Very delectable just as is, or as a court bouillon flavored with the usual herbs: bay leaf, parsley, and thyme. Use a not-too-sturdy wine because it will overwhelm the fish, particularly if the fish is delicately flavored, such as sole. Do the cooking in a nonmetallic pan to avoid imparting a flavor. —*Good Food* magazine.

R.I.P., with Sodium Benzoate as a Preservative

James Dewar, inventor of the Hostess Twinkie, died June 30, 1985 at the age of 88. Dewar took his steps into gastronomic immortality in 1930, while looking for a way to lift the spirits of Americans depressed by the Depression. He wanted something sweet and cheap; so did Hollywood, which invented Shirley Temple films instead, leaving Dewar a clear field.

His idea—a cakelike substance injected with something resembling cream—was the first step; next came the name. He happened to notice an advertisement for Twinkle Toe Shoes and was divinely inspired. He said later that he merely abbreviated the name so it would be "zippier for kids."

When Twinkies celebrated their golden anniversary, in 1980, Dewar was moved to a mild defense of his invention. 'Some people say Twinkies are the quintessential junk food," he said, but I believe in the things. I fed them to my four kids, and they feed them to my fifteen grandchildren. My boy Jimmy played football for the Cleveland Browns. My other son, Bobby, was a quarterback for the University of Rochester. Twinkies never hurt them."

Recipe Continues in Volume II

Craig Claiborne and Pierre Franey tell you how to make a fruitcake in one and a half pages. Irma Rombauer and Marion Rombauer Becker, in their famous *Joy of Cooking,* give full details for six varieties of fruitcake in two pages.

The Department of Defense can give you a recipe that takes eighteen pages. The recipe tells you to use, among other things, vanilla extract "in such quantities that its presence be organoleptically detected, but not to a pronounced degree." Once the mix is blended, then what? "The blended fruitcake batter, sufficient to yield the specified weight, shall then be deposited into cans with liners and disks" to bake at 375 degrees (no more!) or otherwise cooked in a manner "to meet the requirements of [section] 3.5."

When you are finished, you do not have any old fruitcake. You have a genuine U.S. Defense Department MIL-F-14499F. So chow down.

XLI.

A GUIDE TO DINING OUT

Would you like to dine by candlelight with a Spanish ambivalence? Then try La Tajada Room, which offers such attractions in Cedar City, Utah. Perhaps you will wish to run to Huntington, Connecticut, where the local newspaper reported "The Huntington House is open daily for luncheon and dinner. After Labor Day the Sunday brunch featuring over forty different items and complimentary champagne will once again be avoidable."

Such are the pleasures that lure folks out of their homes to dine at fine restaurants of the sort Calvin Trillin called "The Maison de la Casa House." Trillin made that up, though it is fairly representative of some of the more pretentious suburban, red-flocked-wallpaper restaurants. More in touch with the real world was a place in Idaho called Smokey Joe's Grecian Terrace.

These—and more—are what we celebrate here.

How About a Little Grated Banana, Sir?

Two monkeys who went over the wall at the San Francisco Zoo have proved elusive, though they have reportedly been seen swinging through trees nearby. Eventually, however, help was brought in—a psychic.

The psychic reported that the monkeys were eating ravioli in an Italian restaurant and didn't want to go home.

Don't You Have Any Slugs?

On a royal visit to Bélize, a former British colony in Central America, Queen Elizabeth II paused before tucking into her dinner of local specialties. "What kind of meat is that?" she asked Dame Minito Gordon, wife of Bélize's governor.

The answer was roast rat, specifically a rat called a gibnut—the world's largest rat. Those who were close enough for a good look reported that the Queen tended to toy with her food rather than chow down with royal gusto, and apparently did not call for seconds.

Don't You Have Any Gibnuts?

In Philadelphia, a meat wholesaler pleaded guilty to charges that he had sold meat unfit for human consumption.

He admitted that he had bought the meat from a pet-food company—whose owner also pleaded guilty—and then resold it to military commissaries, schools and hospitals at the rate of more than seven tons a week for more than three years.

And There'll Be More Free Meals to Come!

Frank Hackett, sheriff of Kennebec County, Maine, had more arrest warrants than he could afford, his slim budget giving him little means to cover his large, rural territory. He also had more brains than most criminals.

"Up here we've got an old custom of the bean supper," Hackett said. "When some organization like a church puts on a bean supper, it seems everybody comes out of the woodwork." And so he sent several of the people on his personal most-wanted list a letter from a phony cable-TV network, inviting them to a bean supper to celebrate their being chosen from a computer list to take part in a documentary about "growing up and living in one of this country's most beautiful and rural areas."

Hackett printed the stationery, wrote the letters and then had his brother in New York mail them from there. Six of those invited showed up and were arrested. Fourteen others, hearing about the sting operation later, and apparently daunted by the ingenuity of the tenacious Hackett, simply gave themselves up.

Nosing Out

One state representative who opposed a "gross" and possibly unhealthy activity proposed to make it a crime for any person to "blow his nose in a loud, obnoxious or offensive manner" in the presence of other customers in a restaurant. "Some people don't have strong stomachs," he said, saying also that nose blowing spreads germs. "If we can tell people they can't smoke in a restaurant, why can't we tell them they can't blow their noses?" he asked.

Hey, You Guys, Save a Little for Her Majesty!

A New York man laid a wager on an entrant in a mouse race staged by the local tavern, then boldly played for higher stakes: If his mouse lost, he'd eat it. The mouse did lose, and the man, after resorting to the usual condiments (salt, pepper, ketchup), took his snack break. The tavern owner reported, "He said the tail was wriggling in his throat. It took him two swallows."

No betting was involved for an army sergeant at a Michigan college. A military instructor, he had pedagogical motives when, during a lecture, he bit the head off a live chicken and then drank its blood. It was much the same for a Florida high-school football coach. He had just made the point that winning required total abandon and a willingness to do anything when he spotted one of the small green amphibians with which Florida is littered and scooped it up off the ground. Soon it became a ritual for the coach to bite the head off a frog before every game.

Thanks, But I'll Try the Dining Car

A teenager who hopped a freight in Buffalo, New York, got trapped aboard the train and could not get out until four days later, in Massachusetts. He had nothing to eat all that time, saying that although he'd thought of eating some of the dog food with which the boxcar was packed, he changed his mind after reading the ingredients on the labels.

All Right, Then, It *Is* Fit for a Dog

A high school cook sued over an article in the school newspaper. The article, written by tenth- and eleventh-graders, bore the headline STUDENTS REBEL AGAINST NEW SCHOOL COOK. The story said the food in the cafeteria "contained hair" and was "not fit for a dog."

The cook had been hired in January and fired in March, before the article appeared, because of numerous student and faculty complaints, a decline in cafeteria business, and for storing food improperly. Nevertheless, the jury awarded her and her husband $10,001, of which $1 was for libel.

This Suds's for You

"It was a challenge to myself to come up with the brew, and I did it as a service to my customers," said Roger Nowill, humanitarian and owner of a Sheffield, England, pub called the Frog and Parrot. The brew, a bitters, took three and a half years to make, but it was evidently worth it. The result is claimed to be the world's strongest beer, containing five times the alcohol of normal beer.

It is so strong that Nowill serves it only in small one-third-pint glasses, limit three to a customer. The brew is called Roger and Out.

Just a Perrier and Lime for Me, Thanks

A Illinois restaurant reopened—after a final inspection by the city public-health administrator—only a month after it had been labeled the source of a spate of botulism cases. The restaurant had closed after thirty-seven weekend patrons entered hospitals; the toxin botulin was found in twenty-five of them.

Upon reopening the restaurant, one of its partners said, "Our standpoint on the whole incident has been, 'Hey—it happened! It's a one-in-a-million thing.' "

The botulism was linked by the Federal Center for Disease Control in Atlanta to the restaurant's patty-melt sandwich, a hamburger with cheese and sauteed onions on rye bread.

Well, Would You Call It Food?

On an American Airlines flight from Toronto to L.A., a stewardess announced over the intercom, "In just a few minutes, we'll be serving all of you nutrition."

I'll Have the Angel Pie, Thanks

A clipping from an Ohio newspaper is headed SHOW-CASE MENU SHARED AT LUNCHEON and begins "beautiful red roses in wine bottles. . . . sparkling wine in champagne glasses. . . . Fare that was a delectable change of pace from the usual chicken. . . ."

The delectable fare included a cheese soufflé with mushroom sauce, princess salad and angel pie. The ingredients listed for princess salad were 1 7-ounce bottle of Seven-Up; 2⅓ cups small marshmallows; one 3-oz. package of lime gelatin; 2 3-oz. packages of cream cheese at room temperature; ¾ cup chopped pecans; I cup crushed pineapple, drained; ⅔ cup mayonnaise; ½ pint of heavy cream, whipped.

The Towering Inferno

A plum pudding burst into flames in the Tower of London on Christmas Day, sending more than twenty firemen speeding toward the ancient fortress and dungeon. A spokesman for the Whitechapel Fire Station said that the pudding caught fire in a microwave oven. There were no injuries and no serious damage was done, but the remains of pudding, intended for the Tower's famous Beefeater guards, amounted to no more than a "black, shriveled lump."

Peking Stuck

Minim's of Peking, a French bistro created by Pierre Cardin, opened in the Chinese capital, bringing French chefs and French food to whatever Chinese could afford it. The sparkling table setting and Art Deco decor drew crowds of Chinese gawkers but mostly foreign customers—the Chinese noted quickly that the restaurant, which Cardin said was intended to "improve cultural relations" between France and China, was too expensive, a single meal costing up to a week's wages for an average worker.

Nevertheless, the French designer said his "mission" was to open a chain of Minims throughout China.

Two Napalms and a Nerve Gas, Please

Rambose, a Houston nightclub, features such decor as a jeep, a grenade launcher, camouflage netting and machine guns; waitresses wear fatigue uniforms and ammunition bandoliers, and the background music is a blend of Bruce Springsteen and low-flying jets.

Psychologist Joyce Brothers offered the penetrating insight that the clubs owes its existence to the *Rambo* craze, and owner Carlos Tamborrel says his customers are mostly off-duty cops, Viet vets and would-be freedom fighters. "The people have a lot of fun with it," he said.

Left Without Tipping

A customer complained to the waiter about the food in a fast-food restaurant and shortly thereafter began wrecking the place. He admitted to causing $200 in damage, but said he was provoked by the waiter, who responded to his complaint by taking two bites out of his chicken, putting it back on the plate and saying, "It tastes all right to me."

Black Coffee and a Couple of Hooters, Please

Despite protests from neighbors and city officials, Fort Lauderdale, Florida, became the site of what may be the world's first topless doughnut shop.

Bon Appétit!

The Department of Agriculture held a contest to name its new cafeteria in Washington, D.C., and the winning name was the Alferd Packer Grill. A plaque, paid for by donations, was quickly erected—and almost as quickly removed.

Though Alferd E. Packer had earned a place in history as a nineteenth-century pioneer and mountain guide, he was also convicted on five counts of cannibalism in 1874, the latter distinction being the source of objections to the cafeteria's name.

At his first official luncheon in the cafeteria, Agriculture Secretary Bob Bergland said the name was appropriately bipartisan because "the judge who sentenced Mr. Packer allegedly said to him, 'There was only six Democrats in all of Hinsdale County, and you, you man-eating son of a bitch, you ate five of them. I sentence you to hang by the neck until you are dead, dead, dead as a warning against further reducing the Democratic population in this county."

The publishers of the Denver *Post*, however, helped Packer escape the noose and even get a parole. Packer then lived in Denver until he died in 1907.

The registration rolls for Hinsdale County in 1976 showed a total of 239 Republicans and 35 Democrats.

XLII.
TAKE-OUT FOOD

Some people compromise. They wish to eat at home but do not wish to eat anything they are guilty of cooking themselves, not even a microwaved tub of Le Menu or some other blast-frozen, chemically coordinated, mechanically extruded foodlike substance. For these people there is take-out food, a form of comestible unique for having packages that are sometimes as tasty as the contents.

Crummy Deal

Bakers at a grocery store in Taylorsville, Utah, baked a chocolate-chip cookie that weighed 184 pounds. They immediately claimed a world record. For the gang in Denver that baked a mere 119-pounder, that was the way the cookie crumbled.

And the Entire Salmon Population of the North Atlantic

Chicago's Michael Bretz baked what he claims is the world's largest bagel. He planned to spread it with ten pounds of cream cheese.

Hey! You Forgot Your Duck Sauce!

In Mesa, Arizona, police said a man fled empty-handed after an unsuccessful attempt to hold up a Chinese restaurant. The would-be robber handed a note demanding money to an employee who could not read English. He thought it was a take-out order.

How About Some Nice Chicken Soup?

The burglar who robbed Delle's Delicatessen in Hempstead, Long Island, did it the easy way: He simply threw a rock through the plate-glass window at 4:25 A.M. and then proceeded to help himself to a twenty-five-pound ham, a roast beef and a couple of armloads of cold cuts.

The noise woke owner Paul Delle, who lived upstairs. Delle ran down to see what was happening and saw the crook sprint off at high speed. "I yelled to him to freeze or I'd blow his head off," Delle told police, "and he turned around, still running, to see if I had a gun. I didn't." But while he was looking over his shoulder the crook ran straight into a telephone pole. Delle then sat on him until police arrived.

Charged with third-degree burglary, the suspect also picked up a contempt-of-court charge when he made an obscene reference to the judge.

Everything on It, Including Larceny

To judge from the increase in pizza crime, those who order take-out pizzas prefer to have them delivered while those who bake them would prefer to have them picked up, and with reason.

In Birmingham, Alabama, a delivery girl was accosted by a woman she described as weighing almost 200 pounds; the woman asked whether the steaming box in the girl's arms was the pizza she had ordered. Told that it was, she said she'd go upstairs to get the money. A few minutes later, she returned with a gun.

A delivery boy arriving at a college dormitory in Minneapolis was jumped by a masked man who made a grab for the pizza. A scuffle ensued, aggravated by the arrival of the hungry customer. Both customer and delivery boy were bitten during the fracas, but eventually the masked man fled, leaving a somewhat dilapidated pizza behind him.

Theft-of-pizza also occurred in Flagstaff, Arizona, and El Cajon, California, where you might expect tacoburgers to be a more likely target. One pattern emerges: pizza thieves tend to be very hungry, almost invariably targetting pizzas that are large and heavily laden with extras, though how they recognize them is uncertain (perhaps the sight of a stooped-over delivery boy is the tip-off). In any event, the pies snatched in the above case included a large-with-everything-on-it-but-anchovies (with a street value of $17), one decked with pepperoni, cheese, and extra onions, and a 16-inch jumbo with pepperoni and peppers.

And You Can Always Choose a Used Bag

Jane Brody, author of *The Good Food Book,* boasts that she can get breakfast in her hotel room without calling room service. "I may even take a doggie bag of an in-flight meal that seemed edible and nutritious but was served at a time I was not ready to eat," she say, adding, "the air sickness bag, believe it or not, is a handy waterproof container."

XLIII.
THE CRIMINAL ELEMENT

Young people seeking fulfilling careers in our fast-paced, modern world of today should not look to crime as a means of livelihood. Heaven forfend! Crime does not pay, we have been told many times. Criminals are usually oafs who lack the brainpower to succeed in conventional walks of life. Criminals always meet evil ends. And, as a rule, those statements prove true—except for big-time drug dealers, rich people who murder their wives, corporate price-fixers, real-estate moguls, politicians, major-league ballplayers, Mafia big shots, celebrity lawyers, movie stars, union bosses, government bureaucrats, religious gurus, record-industry biggies, fancy art dealers and Richard M. Nixon.

That's why we have the policeman, whose lot, according to W. S. Gilbert or Arthur Sullivan (whichever one wrote the lyrics) is not a happy one. To the cops, who work hard, risk their lives, and are underpaid and frequently abused—only to see the crooks they arrest today go free tomorrow—we fervently wish more of the following.

Self-catching Crooks

No. 1

A man who was making a living rifling parking meters was doing so well for himself that he felt able to help a friend who had been arrested for committing a more conspicuous kind of crime, and he went to police headquarters to provide the bail money.

He was arrested himself when police suspicions were aroused as he handed over the money—$860. All of it in nickels and dimes.

*   *   *

No. 2

In St. Louis, a 16-year-old boy broke into a car and stole a pair of pants. As the pants were new, bearing a price tag marked $35, the youth thought to get a refund by returning them to the store that sold them.

So far, so good. But the woman he asked for the refund happened to be the store's security chief—and the owner of the car.

No. 3

In New York, a man who robbed a supermarket was successful until he left the store. He failed to make good his escape, partly because he was still wearing his gorilla mask and partly because his loot consisted of an enormous bag filled with $5,000 in coins.

No. 4

Helen Tanzosh, a New York City employee, was still having her lunch when she realized that her purse, which she had placed beside her, was missing—and she quickly recalled that moments before, a man had placed his coat next to her chair. Mrs. Tanzosh, however, was no low-level functionary. She was director of employee management for the New York City Police Department, and she happened to be having lunch with Police Commissioner Benjamin Ward, who made the arrest personally.

No. 5

In Homestead, Florida, four gunmen got off on the wrong foot when, seeking a stash of cash and drugs, they barged into the home of two sexagenarian mango farmers. The victims told the gunmen that they had neither the $65,000 nor the heroin they were ordered to hand over, but they willingly gave the men some nitroglycerin pills.

Unconvinced, the gunmen decided to show the couple they weren't to be trifled with, one of them snapping the clip out of his pistol in the process, another ripping the phone off the wall, only to learn it was an electric can-opener. The victims were handcuffed and pushed them to the floor; when friends of the victims arrived; they too were forced to the floor. One of the gang demanded their car keys. "You've already dropped them," the victim said. "Oh," said the gunman, who retrieved the key ring but could not identify the ignition key.

At length the four desperadoes concluded that they were in the wrong house and decided to reduce their aims to simple robbery. They grabbed such valuables as the mango farmers had—including a ring, which they slid off after carefully soaping the woman's finger, and fled. On the way to their car, they dropped the ring. In the car, they got lost while trying to locate the Florida Turnpike. Finally, they saw a tollbooth ahead; naturally, they roared through without stopping.

Also naturally, it was not a tollbooth. It was the guardpost at the entrance to Homestead Air Force Base, where they were immediately picked up.

No. 6

A car thief in Suffolk County, Long Island, was being chased by a squad car when he made a wrong turn into a parking lot and crashed into three cars and one building. He was immediately surrounded by forty policemen. The thief had crashed into police headquarters.

"We're still trying to figure out how he did it," said a police spokesman, who noted that the building "is easily recognizable," because "there are always at least fifty police cars parked around it at any one time."

No. 7

Chicago police were in hot pursuit of a man who had run a red light, and by dint of skillful maneuvering were soon closing in on him: Two squad cars were on his tail and a third was being positioned for a roadblock.

Undaunted, the fugitive crashed his van into the roadblock, drove around it, and made his last mistake by attempting to escape on foot. He ran straight into traffic court.

No. 8

When a 14-year-old Detroit boy decided to buckle down to a little car theft, he also buckled up, just as safety experts advise. The lad and four pals were having a pleasant little joyride until a police car got on their tail and followed them into an alley. Panicked, the boys stopped, deciding to ditch the car and run for it. Three of them did, indeed, elude the cops, but the driver was arrested on the spot while still trying to unlatch his safety belt.

No. 9

Among the job qualifications some car thieves overlook is knowing how to swim; another is being able to tell the difference between a car that can be stolen and a car that is worth stealing. The 22-year-old Brooklynite who is the star of this piece overlooked both, and the result was a career as short as it was moist.

The thief, dazzled by the sight of a car that was without its owner but with its ignition keys, simply hopped in and drove off, not stopping to think that his prize was a homely Plymouth all of eleven years old—and certainly unaware that it was capable of a top speed of only 35 m.p.h. on a fast day.

When the owner realized what had happened, he quickly found a police car. Lieutenant Robert Truebert gave chase and radioed an alert. Soon thereafter, Officers John McLoughlin and Thomas Crimmins spotted the lumbering Plymouth; in deference to its age, they engaged in what can only be called warm pursuit. The thief threaded his way through a maze of narrow streets and then turned west on Atlantic Avenue, which is a wet-end street. It ends, in fact, at the East River.

The car was limping downhill toward Pier 6 when it ran out of pavement and then, according to Truebert, "hit the drink and sank like a ton of bricks."

The suspect bobbed to the surface a few moments later, spouting water and those three little words, "I can't swim." Fortunately for him, the cops had a rope handy, and they were able to haul him out—and haul him in—in one simple, labor-saving operation.

No. 10

Killers also catch themselves, as in a case in Miami, Florida. According to testimony at their trial, two young men were driving around looking for someone to rob; having found a victim, one let the other have his pistol, which was used to shoot and kill an elderly man. The victim's family offered a $10,000 reward, a matter of some interest to the thieves, as the robbery attempt netted them no money at all.

In fact, authorities said, the reward was so enticing that the owner of the gun tried to get it by fingering the triggerman.

Self-convicting Crooks

No. 1

A woman in Spring Valley, California, pleaded innocent to car theft, but not for long. The plaintiff pointed out that the jacket worn by the defendant had been in the car when it was stolen.

No. 2

In Tulsa, Oklahoma, a man elected to defend himself before the law when he was accused of a purse-snatching episode. His defense came undone when he fixed his accuser with a pentrating stare and demanded, "Did you get a good look at me when I took your purse?"

No. 3

In Oklahoma City, a 47-year-old suspect being tried for armed robbery decided he needed a better lawyer—himself. He gave his counsel the sack and was doing well enough in his own behalf until the man whose store was robbed identified him as the robber. The suspect accused the manager of lying and then, losing his cool just a bit, shouted, "I should have blown your head off."

Trying for a quick recovery, he added, "If I'd been the one that was there."

The jury had its work cut out but managed to deliberate for twenty minutes before bringing in a verdict of guilty.

Out-of-court Settlements

No. 1

A thief in Taipei, Taiwan, was in the midst of stealing racing pigeons when he fell from the roof of a five-story building, killing himself and the pigeons he landed on.

No. 2

Seduced, as they say, by the dark side of the force, Andrew Thronton, 41, left narcotics work with the Lexington, Kentucky, police for what is known as the private sector, or dope smuggling to the cognoscenti. He planned to put his Army paratrooper training to work by parachuting himself into business with $4,500, a pair of pistols, a couple of knives, ropes, food, night-vision goggles and 79 pounds of cocaine.

Tony Acri of the Federal Drug Enforcement Agency said smuggling via parachute had its points: "Number one, a parachutist is not picked up on radar . . . during a night drop there's not much noise and it doesn't arouse suspicion." He also noted two potential drawbacks: (a) "you fall on somebody's house" and (b) "your chute doesn't open."

Entrepreneur Thornton drew one from Column B late one night, landing in a neat but deceased pile in the backyard of Fred Myers, who lives near Knoxville, Tennessee. Myers noticed the body when he happened to glance out his window the next morning.

"I never had a landing in my yard before," he said.

Crooks Charged With Breaking and Sort-of Entering

No. 1

A New York burglar failed to loot a supermarket in 1969, under humiliating circumstances. Mounting the roof, he found the skylight too small to slide through—but by just the tiniest margin. A light bulb glowed in what passed for his brain: Stripping off his clothes, he threw them through the skylight, planning to go in right behind them, now that he was skinny enough to make it.

But he wasn't.

No. 2

In Jacksonville, Florida, the target was a pharmacy, the means of ingress a chimney. This time the would-be burglar was stuck for six hours after his rope snapped while he was lowering himself into the premises. After the cops winched him out, it was observed that he never had a chance in the first place: The fireplace had been sealed years before.

*   *   *

No. 3

It didn't work in San Diego, either. Again the rope broke, and the crook plummeted thirty feet closer to his goal—the rich treasures of the Sumitomo Bank. However, he got stuck in the ventilating shaft about twenty five feet shy of his goal and was left, according to police, "just kind of hanging around," his legs dangling from the ceiling.

To make matters worse, the crook had started his job at about 10 P.M. on a Friday night and was not rescued until the janitorial staff found him on the following Monday.

No. 4

We take you now to West Palm Beach, Florida, where a fellow sought to rob a Greek restaurant by entering through a ventilating shaft only nine inches wide. The accused thought he could make it because, though a substantial 5'9", he weighed a mere 140 pounds.

Scrawny, but not scrawny enough. He got stuck anyway, though he did get far enough along to suffer cuts and abrasions from the blades of the exhaust fan.

No. 5

All of the above clowns were lucky by comparison to the burglar who got trapped in a ventilating shaft in Brooklyn. His legs didn't dangle for the janitors to observe, and no one heard his shouts. He was found only during renovations, and by then he was dead—neatly dried out and mummified by what police estimated were several years of, so to speak, forced ventilation.

Guilty of Gross Incompetence

No. 1

A Los Angeles woman got a broken arm when she was mugged, but she came through the incident smiling because, unlike most dog owners, she was a devoted pooper-scooper. She smiled because she liked the idea of the mugger's grabbing greedily into her little plastic bag, which she had used to clean up after her dog. "I only wish there had been a little bit more," she said.

*   *   *

No. 2

An English thief hoping to loot supermarket tills concocted a plan based on the well-known fact that the hand is quicker than the eye. At the checkout counter of a Southampton market he gave the cashier a £10 Sterling bill to pay for his groceries. When she opened the register, he scooped out the cash before she knew what was happening. What he got for the £10 (about $25) he gave the cashier was a haul amounting to just over £4 (about $10).

No. 3

In Brookfield, Connecticut, a hitchhiker who wanted more than a free ride grabbed a motorist's wallet. A little later he discovered that the wallet contained identification papers but no money. Then he discovered that he'd left his own money—$70—behind in the car.

On top of all that, he got caught: He telephoned his victim and offered to exchange the wallet for his money. The victim said sure, and then called the cops.

No. 4

Thieves in Brooklyn successfully looted a restaurant wine cellar of $30,000 worth of French wine. "I guess they took the French wine because they probably thought French is always better and more expensive," said the restaurant's cellarmaster. He noted, however, that the crooks had left behind a hoard of premium American wines worth more than three times as much as the French—and they didn't even get the *good* French. They overlooked a case of 1961 Château Lafite worth $550 a bottle.

No. 5

In 1971, a trio of thieves planned to rob a post office in Essex, England, and spent hours going over every detail except that fact that the post office had been closed for twelve years. Charging in with shotguns at the ready, the crooks learned the place was now a general store. As it was morning at the time of the raid, no business had been conducted, and the bandits netted about $15 for their trouble.

* * *

No. 6

Whittier, California, police were after the man who tried to rob a gas station of $600 and left incriminating evidence behind. Trying to prevent the robbery, an attendant got into a fight with the robber and bit off his thumb. The crook dropped the money and fled, bleeding. The police took the thumb in for fingerprinting.

No. 7

A federal district judge in Baton Rouge, Louisiana, gave the defendant five years on probation but only because he was, the judge said, "the most inept counterfeiter I ever heard of."

The judge based his remark on the defendant's practice of cutting the corners off $20 bills and pasting them onto $1 bills, thereby counterfeiting twenties at a cost of $21 each.

No. 8

An earlier counterfeiter managed to make a long and successful career by balancing incompetence with an unusual lack of greed.

In the late 1930s, Edward Mueller was a retired building superintendent who lived alone with his dog. Needing to eke out his savings, he did odd jobs for neighbors and worked as a junkman, pushing a car along the streets, picking up this and selling that. Still, he needed more money, and he turned to counterfeiting.

He remains the only man on record who counterfeited $1 bills. And he didn't make many of them—just enough so he and his dog could get by: fifteen a week, tops. He traveled all over New York City to make sure he never stuck anyone with more than one bogus bill. It was a lot of work.

His bills ranked as the worst counterfeits ever passed. His plates were extremely crude, and he used a cheap hand press he kept by the kitchen sink. The portrait of Washington had only one eye—the other was just a hole—and Washington's name was misspelled. But who looks at $1 bills?

Mueller was known to the Secret Service as Mr. 880—for his file number at the department—and, according to writer St. Clair McKelway, he was the object of a manhunt "that exceeded in intensity and scope any other manhunt in the chronicles of counterfeiting."

It took the Secret Service longer to catch Mr. 880 than any other counterfeiter—ten years.

Even then, he was caught only by dumb luck. A fire broke out in the apartment next door to Mr. 880's; firemen broke into 880's pad so the blaze could be fought from two sides; while they were at it, they threw out the window almost everything that was inflammable. Among the things that landed in the vacant lot next door were 880's faithful press and a fresh run of his appallingly bad $1 bills.

The bills were discovered the next day by some boys playing in the lot. How bad were those bills? So bad that the kids thought they were play money. The kids' parents, however, thought they were counterfeit, and that led the Secret Service at long last to Mr. 880, then 73 years old.

He was sentenced to nine months in prison, but the judge was informed that if the sentence was increased to a year and a day plus a fine, the old man could be paroled after only four months, and so the sentenced was increased. The fine that accompanied the sentence was $1. The Receiver of the Court handed over a receipt after looking at the bill with a critical eye—the first time anyone had taken a hard look at a bill from Mr. 880.

Today the old man's memory is enshrined principally in *Mr. 880*, a movie made by 20th Century-Fox in the late forties. Every now and then it turns up on late-night TV. Check your listings.

No. 9

A guest at a Florida resort hotel called the security guard with an unusual request. He said $1000 worth of cocaine had been stolen from his room, and demanded either the return of the drug or $1000 in compensation. "I'll get back to you," said the guard, who called the sheriff.

Oddly enough, the cocaine was recovered. The guard and a deputy sheriff then took it up to the guest's room, where the deputy was introduced to the guest, in case he hadn't noticed his badge, gun and walkie-talkie. The guest took the cocaine and complained, "It's mine, but there's a lot missing." Asked to sign a receipt for the cocaine, he cheerfully did so, and then was arrested and led off to jail.

"That's the last time I'm going to trust a security officer," he said.

Still at It, Despite All

No. 1

Jailed for drunken driving in Winterset, Iowa, a prisoner found himself longing for his girlfriend after two months in stir. Finding a weak point in the fence around the exercise yard, he slipped out one day and spent a Saturday evening as he did in the good old days—in the warm arms of his lover. Returning the next morning, he triggered an alarm and was nailed while trying to break into prison.

No. 2

An inmate at a medium-security prison near Indianapolis, Indiana, is addicted to pizza and imprisoned because of it. He is serving a fifteen-year term for robbing a Pizza Hut in May 1981. He was arrested for that robbery while eating pizza at another pizzeria (one he hadn't yet robbed) and was at the time on parole from a previous pizzeria robbery.

Most recently he was given liberty to leave the prison to fetch New Year's Eve treats for his fellow inmates—three dozen pizzas. He did not return, but his freedom was short-lived: He was caught at a phone booth at a nearby Pizza Hut.

A prison official said the man had been chosen for the errand because he had been a model prisoner: "He'd gone out last year to help, and was considered trustworthy. Needless to say, we'll take a second look at these inmates who've been screened."

Imagination—a Saving Grace

No. 1

In Los Angeles, a man suspected of phoning bomb threats to public places was tracked down and arrested. When permitted to make his legally guaranteed single phone call, he phoned a bomb threat to the Los Angeles Airport.

No. 2

Vandals in Larchmont, New York, broke into the office where Howdy Doody—a famous puppet star of 1950s TV—was stored, and tore the freckle-faced has-been limb from limb. Parts were strewn all over the office. The dismembered marionette was permanently damaged, and there was no insurance. Howdy was formerly insured for $100,000, but the policy had lapsed while Howdy was unemployed.

No. 3

A Culver City, California, woman boarded a commuter-packed city bus and, brandishing a pistol and claiming to be "a U.S. marshal, late for work," forced the driver to race ahead at high speed and run six red lights. Police said later that the woman did, indeed, have a badge on her coat.

It read, SPACE PATROL.

XLIV.

STATESMANSHIP AND DIPLOMACY

Sir Henry Wotton (1568–1639) said, "An ambassador is a honest man sent abroad to lie for the commonwealth," a remark so apt that he got hell for it when he returned to England. In diplomats, statesmen and politicians, honesty is not a long suit; they are not forthcoming except perhaps in their memoirs, which represent a last chance to grab undue credit or spread undistributed blame at a time when they are safe from punishment and the damage they did is safely done.

How Bloodthirsty Brutes Are Changed from Terrorists into Freedom Fighters

The U.S. State Department no longer uses the word *killing* in its reports on human rights. The word has been replaced by *unlawful or arbitrary deprivation of life*.

The department's Assistant Secretary for Human Rights, Elliot Abrams, told reporters being briefed on a report on worldwide human-rights practices that "unlawful or arbitrary deprivation of life" is "more precise."

But We've Already Had Nobody Presidents

A person who goes by the name of Wavy Gravy in San Francisco proposes that Nobody run for president because, for example, Nobody understands the economy, and because "When you count up all the people who didn't vote in 1976 and 1980, it's clear that more people voted for Nobody than for any of the other candidates."

State Dinner of the Year

The state dinner honoring Iranian president Ali Khamenei on the occasion of his official visit to Zimbabwe went off as scheduled except for the lack of any speeches and—Iranians.

The Iranians refused to show up because there would be, Allah forbid, women at the head table and wine was to be served. Officials of Prime Minister Robert Mugabe's government tried to arrange a civil compromise with their guests, offering to seat the women at a table far away from the Iranians, but the offer was refused.

Earlier, Khamenei had refused to shake hands with two women government officials, and the Iranian embassy had insisted that women journalists covering the visit be made to wear veils. In the end, the government refused to give up its insistence that, in Zimbabwe at least, women and men are to be treated equally.

Smoke Screen

Cuba's Fidel Castro announced that he was giving up his trademark—puffing on Havana cigars. "I reached the conclusion long ago," he explained, "that the one last sacrifice I must make for public health is to stop smoking. I haven't really missed it that much."

The president of the Cigar Association of America, Norman Sharp, said that he "wasn't surprised. The quality of Cuban cigars is not what it used to be."

Eventually They Just Ordered Pizza and Forgot All About It

Statecraft is sometimes carried out by force. And sometimes not. Italian neo-fascists decided in 1964 to reestablish their party and to do so through the operatic gesture of recreating Mussolini's March on Rome of 1922. As it happened, most of the marchers were not residents of Rome—they were outside agitators, to use a fragrant phrase—and they soon became hopelessly lost in the Eternal City's infernal maze of back streets and twisting alleyways. Then the march simply evaporated. It was several years before the elected government even found out that it had been staged.

The humiliation took a lot of starch out of the neo-fascist movement, whose members were unable to pull themselves together for another march until 1974, and that coup was called off on account of rain.

Concentration Camps? He Thought They Were Youth Hostels!

The TV miniseries *Holocaust,* telecast on NBC, upset a lot of people for a lot of reasons. In America and Canada, various neo-Nazi groups denounced it for perpetuating the lie of the Holocaust—the phony claim that the Nazis had murdered six million Jews, and any number of other people, such as homosexuals, gypsies, etc. —who had in some way given offense. The French government television network refused to show it, fearing a renewal of questions about French anti-Semitism during World War II, and of course, the Germans would have preferred a musical comedy about young love in Old Bavaria.

Among those upset was a widow who said her late husband, a Nazi official of high rank in the SS, was made a "scapegoat" by the program. She told reporters, "I didn't recognize the character as my husband." She added that her husband had not been a murdering, anti-Semitic monster but a regular guy. As for herself, she knew nothing about murdering any Jews; it was all a big surprise to her. "Some were arrested, of course, but I don't know anything about the details," she said. "The Final Solution had nothing to do with my husband. That was something falsely attributed to him. The European Jews were all shipped to the Urals."

I'll Give You Liberty or Give You Death!

General Figueiredo, on his installation as president of Brazil, made his intentions plain. "I intend to open this country up to democracy," he said. "And anyone who is against that, I will jail, I will crush like a bug."

Then He'll Unleash
Frank Sinatra on the Democrats

Warming up before a radio broadcast, President Reagan tested the microphones by saying, "My fellow Americans . . . I've signed legislation that will outlaw Russia forever. We begin bombing in five minutes."

And a Lot of Fun at Parties Too

From Walter Scott's famous "Personality Parade" column comes this gem: *Q.* There's no mention of Khrushchev's drinking habits in his "memoirs," but wasn't he once quite a belter? *A.* "Vodka" should have been his middle name. Once, when drunk, he threatened to call the White House on the hotline "and start World War III," but passed out when he reached the phone and was put to bed by an aide.

Walter Scott gets a lot of fascinating questions, including queries about where to get in touch with the movement to have Elvis Presley made a saint by the Roman Catholic Church, and this one: "After Watergate, wasn't Richard Nixon secretly committed to a mental institution run by Quakers and replaced by the CIA with a Hollywood double? Isn't this the real reason his wife, Pat, refuses all interviews—because she is afraid reporters will ask about the look-alike she is living with, and she will have to tell?"

**Send These, Your Homeless, Tempest-tossed to me—
Complete With Valid Visas, Identification
Papers, Letters of Reference From Past Employers,
Proof That They Have Jobs Guaranteed Them Upon
Arrival,
Two Copies of a Recent Photograph
(2″ x 2″, Three-quarter-View Head Shots, Plain
Background Only),
Plus The Full, Complete and Unequivocal Permission
Of Whatever Tyrant They Are Fleeing—I Lift My Lamp
Beside the Golden Door.**

In October, Ukrainian seaman Miroslav Medvid tried to defect by jumping into the Mississippi River from the grain freighter *Marshal Konev* and swimming ashore.

After a difficult time making himself understood, he was eventually returned to his ship by the U.S. Border Patrol, locked in handcuffs they thoughtfully provided.

Medvid tried graphically—by making the international gesture of drawing an outstretched finger across his throat—to indicate that returning to his ship would mean trouble and even danger for him, but never mind, back he went. He then flung himself into the river again and swam ashore, but he was overpowered and again returned to his ship.

Throughout the days that the Medvid case dragged on—and it did drag on once the press got hold of the story—U.S. agencies consistently violated their own internal regulations, to say nothing of common sense, in a grossly insensitive refusal to help a desperate man. Congressman Fred J. Eckert (Rochester, New York) pointed out that U.S. officials failed to give Medvid time to be interviewed fully and to make application for asylum, failed to tape-record their interviews with him, failed to inform their superiors promptly of a sensitive incident, and failed to act on evidence that, in later interviews permitted by the Soviets, Medvid appeared to have been heavily drugged. (Representative Eckert said the U.S. government had intercepted a message from the Soviet embassy instructing the captain of the Russian ship to administer specific drugs.) They also failed to provide a proper interpreter (the State Department finally provided a Russian-speaking interpreter, even though they knew Medvid was an ethnic Ukrainian, and refused offers of help from Ukrainian interpreters. Not that it mattered much; the interpreter said the real problem was communicating with the American officials.

American officials and an American doctor who talked to Medvid aboard his ship and also aboard a U.S. Coast Guard vessel were never able to question him without the presence of Russian officials. It was observed that one of Medvid's wrists had been slit, but that is not mentioned in the State Department's report on the incident, nor does it mention that the American psychiatrist who examined Medvid believed that he knew what he was doing when he jumped ship, and that he believed Medvid had been threatened with reprisals against himself and his parents.

Five days later it was all over. Soviet ambassador

Anatoly Dobrynin came out of a meeting with Secretary of State George Schultz and told newsmen, "It's settled. He's coming home." A reporter asked, "If Seaman Medvid really wanted to return to the Soviet Union, why did he jump ship and why did he do so many other things that so clearly indicated he wanted to defect?"

"I am not a sailor," Dobrynin answered with a chuckle. Then he turned his back and walked out.

All of the U.S. officials involved in this disgrace still have their jobs. The case made enough noise internationally that the Russians decided that something had to be said about it in their own newspapers. The Russian public was told that the reason Medvid was twice found swimming in the Mississippi was that he had simply slipped and fallen overboard. Both times.

Darn the Torpedoes!

Libyan leader Colonel Moammar Khadafy announced he would back his claim that the U.S. was invading Libya's territorial waters by sailing out to confront the U.S. 6th Fleet. And with that he climbed aboard a missile-carrying 350-ton patrol boat for the 300-mile voyage from the harbor of Misurata to Benghazi, there to join battle.

A few hours later he was back ashore, never having gotten within earshot or eyeshot of the enemy, let alone gunshot. In Tripoli a European ambassador explained that "Khadafy probably intended his gesture . . . to be taken symbolically rather than literally. To him the symbol he exhibits to his country is more important than the reality of his action."

XLV.

GOVERNMENT IN ACTION

"That government is best which governs least" is a truism that has to be altered in these times to "tries to govern least." At the national, regional and local levels, people everywhere are plagued by officials, elected and otherwise, who attempt to govern but do not succeed at anything but deepening the quandary, widening the gap and spreading the confusion.

Brief Explanations

No. 1

This year, because of tax-return processing, we have not been able to process tax returns as quickly as in past years.—Wilmington, Delaware, district IRS office.

No. 2

An article in *FDA Consumer* magazine, published by the Food and Drug Administration, revealed that decomposing shellfish products can be "detected by organoleptic analysis." To the layman, the article continued, that means "smelling the product."

No. 3

Postal officials refused to deliver mail to a Land O' Lakes, Florida, nudist colony for a year and a half. The reason, said the postmaster of Lutz (a suburb north of Tampa), was that "the sight of naked bodies is offensive to our mail carriers."

Delivery was resumed on condition that residents wear clothes when going to the mailboxes.

* * *

No. 4

Washington, Aug. 2. (AP)—Postmaster General Benjamin F. Bailar on Wednesday defended the record of the postal service, saying it had improved productivity without reducing service.

Selected Officials

No. 1

Thank you . . . I am extremely grateful for the expression of trust and confidence shown in me on Feb. 22. I deeply appreciate your vote and will do everything in my power to betray that trust. I will be a commissioner for all the people.—Advertisement in the Panama City, Florida, *News-Herald*)

No. 2

Obviously the biggest challenge was to come into the harbor safely. I think we've met that challenge. As I've said, I think we've turned the corner and seen the light at the end of the tunnel."—New York City Mayor Abraham Beame.

No. 3

In Dayton, Ohio, fire department brass had questions for the doctors who examined two recruits and declared them fit for duty. Both recruits were discovered to be legally blind.

No. 4

The head of a New Jersey board of education apologized for referring to one of the board members as "our Spanish friend." That wasn't enough for some people, apparently, but it was for him. He added, "What more can I do? I have apologized publicly. What do you want—a trip to Puerto Rico?"

No. 5

The Office of Public Policy's Robert Carleson stated, "There shouldn't be hunger, at least, hunger unnecessarily of the people who would otherwise want to be fed."

No. 6

In Santa Barbara, California, the city airport commission "agreed generally that all land use at the airport should relate to aviation, except that which does not."

No. 7

Mayor Theodore M. Berry proclaimed Wednesday Riverfront Coliseum Day and called the building "an asset of infinitesimal value to the vitality and growth of our city."—Cincinnati *Enquirer*.

No. 8

At the lectern yesterday in the Parklawn Building in Rockville stood the general—U.S. Surgeon General C. Everett Koop—resplendent in black uniform with gold buttons and bars, exhorting the corps to fight the good fight against the enemies of disease and illness. —*Washington Post*.

No. 9

According to flight regulations promulgated by the government of Canada, any and all persons are forbidden from "entering an aircraft in flight."

No. 10

Canada's Juvenile Delinquents Act has been renamed. It is now called "Young Persons in Conflict with the Law."

No. 11

Dancers and waitresses who perform topless in Toronto must apply for a license to work; the license costs $55. Their employers must apply for a license for each topless performer, at a cost of $3,300 each. On the licenses, topless performers are labeled "adult entertainment parlor attendants."

Municipal Doings

No. 1

Seattle officials are considering giving drunks, winos and derelicts their own public park. City officials say it would be a last resort, to be used only if there's no other way to keep derelicts out of other city parks. But an advocate of the homeless says the idea is to give derelicts an environment in which they "can feel safe and meet their social needs."

No. 2

After a rash of UFO sightings in Lubbock, Texas, roads leading into the city were posted with signs reading, CAUTION: FLYING SAUCERS LANDING ON HIGHWAYS.

No. 3

To attract tourists, St. Helens, Oregon, has decided to sponsor an annual Toilet Paper Festival. Activities planned include a toilet-paper art contest, toilet-seat and toilet-paper throws and a nose-blowing competition.

According to the town's Chamber of Commerce, "It is the 'different' festival that creates interest and press coverage. One of the more unique aspects of St. Helens is that we have one of the largest toilet-paper-producing machines in the nation."

Yeah? Well, It Could Be He's Taking Joan Collins, Don Johnson and Gary Coleman Just a Little Too Lightly

Sylvester Stallone says he expects to become America's "second actor president."

Other tiresome performers aiming at public office include Fess Parker (the former Davy Crockett), the Senate; talk-show prattler Phil Donahue, the Senate; and Fred Grandy (who plays an oaf named Gopher on the situation comedy *The Love Boat*), House of Representatives. Grandy won—and watch your step in Carmel, California, where Clint Eastwood is the mayor.

Does It Say Anything About Accidental Burial?

Wanting always to be prepared, a Cincinnati man wrote to Washington for a copy of U.S. Government publication #15.700, "Handbook for Emergencies." Shortly thereafter he had his first emergency: he received 15,700 copies of the handbook.

(Lots of wonderful things are available from the U.S.

Government Printing Office, such as "Military Art Note Cards from the U.S. Army Art Collection. Stunning military poster art reduced to enhance twelve foldout note cards." One of the cards is decorated with a scene of Sherman tanks rolling through the smoking rubble of a German city while discouraged Wehrmacht soldiers are being taken prisoner in the lower right-hand corner. The catalogue copy adds, "Perfect for any occasions," including, we suppose, declarations of war and announcements of forthcoming air raids. Twelve cards, with envelopes, $3.50.)

Phone for Reservations—Phone!

Richard Branson, the owner of Virgin Atlantic Airlines and Virgin Records, is also the owner of 74-acre Necker Island in the British Virgin Islands. After spending some $8 million to build a posh corporate conference facility on the island, he got around to registering for a mailbox. So he headed for the island of Tortola, a half-hour away by boat, where such things are arranged. His application was accepted and put on the waiting list.

The waiting list is eight years long.

Undercover Notes

No. 1

Morbid fears about President Reagan's hearing aid have been voiced by a former aide at the National Security Agency. He believes the KGB could use the hearing aid for electronic espionage, and others in the field worry that the commies might transmit ultrasonic subversions, such as "Total disarmament now!" or "Give El Salvador a break already!" directly into the presidential brainpan. Or they could simply jam his hearing. According to another electronics authority, "A 14-year-old computer-radio whiz from New Jersey could, with a little benchwork, tap into the president's hearing."

No. 2

It has been known for some time now that the American Communist Party owes its financial life to the scores of Secret Servicemen who have infiltrated it—they're almost the only ones who pay their dues. Secret agents apparently support restaurants, too.

According to a retired CIA man and unofficial CIA historian, the following occurred in Washington in the late 1940s, when a restaurant called Les Trois Mousquetaires was in business.

Two Russian airmen, Pyotr Pirogov and Anatoly Barsov, had defected to the U.S. in 1948. After a spell, Barsov got homesick and set out to find out whether he would be allowed back. Well, yes, said the Russians. He could come back on a forgive-and-forget basis if he could get Pirogov to come with him. If he didn't, he could expect an all-expenses-paid vacation in Gulag City. Barsov said he'd give it a try.

Pirogov showed little interest in the idea, but he agreed to meet Barsov at the restaurant to talk it over at lunch. They talked and talked, with Barsov making little headway—so little, actually, that he became frustrated and attempted to hit Pirogov.

Barsov was still in mid-swing when, says the ex-CIA agent, "everyone in the restaurant suddenly rose and started pushing and shoving to get to the man he was trying to protect." Because, except for Barsov and Pirogov, every customer in the joint was either CIA or KGB.

Important Studies of American Life

According to a study funded by the Department of Agriculture, mothers prefer children's clothing that doesn't have to be ironed. The study cost $113,417.

A report by the Health Resources and Services Administration cost rather more, $180,000, but it was on a more complicated subject—health. The study reported that "Individuals in poor health were almost seven times as frequent users of physician services as those in excellent health, and spent an average of twenty-one times as many days in the hospital."

Follow These Simple Directions

No. 1

From the Federal Personnel Manual, Manual Supplement 990-3, Civil Service Commission. Part M-771. Employee Grievances and Appeals:

"If the United States is attacked, file this page in book III of FPM Supplement 990-1, in front of part 771.

Effective upon an attack on the United States and until further notice: a. Part 771 is suspended."

No. 2

Federal Communications Commission instructions for changing an incorrect zip code:

1. The U.S. Department of Commerce, Environmental Research Laboratories, has notified the commission that the zip code for its facilities at Boulder, Colorado, is not correctly printed in sections 73.711, 73.1030 and 74.12 of the commission's rules.

2. The city address zip code in sections 73.711 (c) (2) 73.1030 (b) (2) and 74.12 (c) (2) is corrected to read as follows: Boulder Colorado 80303.

3. We conclude that the adoption of the editorial amendment shown in this order will serve the public interest. Prior notice of rule making, effective date provisions and public procedure thereon are unnecessary, pursuant to the administrative procedure and judicial review provisions of 5 U.S.C. 533 (b) (3) (B), inasmuch as this amendment imposes no additional burdens and raises no issue upon which comments would serve any useful purpose.

4. Therefore, it is ordered that, pursuant to sections of 4 (1), 303 (4) and 5 (a) (1) of the Communications Act of 1934, as amended, and section 0.281 of the commission's rules and regulations, is amended as set forth in paragraph 2 above, effective Nov. 10, 1978.

No. 3

Veterans Administration instructions to vocational schools on how to conduct a job survey:

DVB Circular 20-74-113 Appendix B Exhibit C (Con.)

(1) Establish the total number of graduates from which the selection is to be made. In this example, assume that the number on line 5 of VA Form 22-8723 is 1276.

(2) Establish the number of digits involved in this number. In this example the number is 1276, so the number of digits involved is four.

(3) Pick any arbitrary place on any pages of the "book" of random numbers as a starting point. For example, the tenth row of the eleventh column of the sample page of

random numbers might be picked as the random starting point (85).

(4) From this starting point, select consecutive groups of numbers equal to the number of digits in the total number of graduates (see subparagraph (2)). For example, the random starting point shows the number 8513. A sequential pick of other four-digit numbers results in the following picks: 7417, 3223, 0257, 3527, 3372, 2453, 0941, 1076, 4791, 4404, 9549, 6639, 6004, 5981, 4850, 8654, 4822, 0634, etc. The numbers underlined are to be used for selecting the sample: all other numbers cited do not fall within the total number (1276) from which the sample is to be drawn, so they will be discarded.

(5) From the random numbers which will be picked to select a sample of 300, exclude "0000," any duplicate numbers, and any number higher than the total number of graduates reported on line 5 of VA Form 22-8723. Thus, from the random numbers cited in subparagraph (4) above, only four would be used (257, 941, 1076 and 634).

(6) The process illustrated in subparagraph (4) above would be continued until 300 usable numbers are selected, all of which must be different.

(7) The example cited in paragraph 4 above is illustrative only and the schools will not use the attached page of random numbers as a basis for their sample selection. However, the method illustrated is to be used.

XLVI.
PIZZA AND YOU

Pizza, which figures significantly in other sections of this work, now comes to the forefront on a stage of its own.

After all, when a newspaper runs a medical story with a headline that reads,

SPECIAL PIZZA
INDUCES LABOR,

the importance of pizza becomes inescapable.

Pie in the Sky

In 1982, American students at Harlaxton College, about a hundred miles north of London, were seized by a hunger for real food. Who could blame them, English food being what it is?— dishes called Toad in the Hole, for example, and Bubble and Squeak, and the dread Eels and Mash. (The British Empire came about through the wanderings of generations of desperate men who roamed the globe in search of a decent meal.) And so they hit upon the idea of ordering out for pizza.

They ordered out from Ray's Pizza at West Eleventh Street and Sixth Avenue in New York.

The mission took about six weeks to complete, as numerous arrangements had to be made. The Pizza Committee raised $728 from 140 students who paid $5.20 for two slices each. Ray's gave them a break on the price, and eventually two members of the committee were flown to New York to pick up 40 pizzas (19 pepperoni, 10 sausage, 8 mushroom, 3 plain) and to shepherd them back to England. Dinner was set for 9:30 P.M. on the day of arrival, and the pizzas, once reheated, disappeared in short order.

One of the committee members said that although

Italy was several thousand miles closer, the thought never occurred to them. "We wanted the best pizza," he said, "and we love New York." The idea of English pizza did occur to them, but it was rejected outright. One of the organizers of the "pizzalift" said, "English pizza just doesn't compare. It's watery, and you can never get pepperoni."

Another student said it was worth the effort, which might be repeated. "Maybe we'll get hamburgers next time," he said. If they do, the source will undoubtedly be America again. The English hamburger (or Wimpy, after the burger-gorging character in the Popeye comic strip), is a wet, gray lump of meat on an awful bun, and it would gag a dog.

Baked and Fried

Before he was sent to the electric chair at the state prison in Columbia, South Carolina, former altar boy and ex-military policeman Joseph Carl Shaw was given his choice for the traditional last meal. Shaw, convicted of the murder of two teenagers, ordered a salad, a Coke and a pizza with everything on it but anchovies.

Although the pizza came from a local, family-owned restaurant, the Pizza Hut chain and its advertising experts soon threw themselves into action, quickly producing a TV commercial to capitalize on the dead convict's last choice. Their commercial also shows a condemned prisoner ordering pizza for his last meal; then, shortly after its delivery, the convict receives a pardon—but refuses to give up his pizza. After numerous complaints, Pizza Hut pulled the ad, a company spokesman admitting that it had been a "mistake."

Acidic Tide of Pizza
Sludge Threatens
South Ohio Town

That was how *The New York Times* announced the perils of life in Southern Ohio, where 400,000 gallons of waste flour, tomato paste, cheese, vegetables and pepperoni had been poured by a Jeno's frozen pizza factory into the river, where it threatened to clog drains and contaminate drinking water. The mess was cleaned up before any environmental damage was done. So far as we know.

Northern Ohio faces its own environmental dangers, notably those caused by the Cuyahoga River, which, unlike the human body, is not 96% water. So high is the chemical-waste content of the Cuyahoga that it has in the past periodically burst into flames and had to be put out by the fire department.

One Jumbo, to Go

Claimants to the title of World's Largest Pizza have been baked, since 1970, in Chicago; Cliftonville, Ohio; and Victoria, British Columbia. The title currently resides in Glens Falls, New York, courtesy of Lorenzo Amato, owner of the Oma Pizzeria in that fair hamlet.

Amato took the gonfalon in 1977 with a pizza forty feet in diameter, but he soon fell prey to nagging fears that someone would top his effort. So he decided to top himself.

On October 8, 1978, he baked his second world's largest pizza, which he christened Lorenzo's Colossal. Nearly four times as large as the 1977 model, and baked on an outdoor griddle (sheet steel on concrete blocks) in nearby Wilton, New York (Glens Falls being apparently unable to contain it), the Colossal, a conservative pepperoni job, was certified by Saratoga County Sealer of Weights and Measures David Sexton as being eighty feet in diameter and tipping the scales, so to speak, at more than nine tons.

It was made of 5 tons of flour, 664 gallons of water, 316 gallons of sauce, 1320 pounds of cheese, 1200 pounds of pepperoni, and a rather large pinch of oregano. Once baked, it was cut into 60,318 slices and handed out free to an admiring crowd (donations to the Muscular Dystrophy Foundation were encouraged).

Pizza as an Endangered Species

Pizza itself is in jeopardy from Big Business's synthetic food cabal.

The American Dairy Association has been waging its Real Pizzamaker campaign in the hope of alerting consumers to the revolting fact that pizzas are increasingly being made with artificial cheese.

A national manufacturer makes a line of artificial cheeses. The line includes mozzarella, cream cheese, provolone, and a processed-cheese substitute whose attributes include "good machineability," which suggests that it can be turned on a lathe.

Another national manufacturer, also in the business of providing nearly endless shelf life and low cost without resorting to real cheese, sells substitutes for mozzarella, cheddar (both available preshredded) and American cheese. It claims its product lines will "give your customers a breakthrough that tastes more like the real thing than other substitutes." Still another offers a "unique" mozzarella substitute "made from vegetable oil" (presumably real). One brand of imitation mozzarella is billed as being "compatible" with such devices as "extrusion machines" (possibly it can be used to make aluminum storm windows).

For the record, an ad for "low-moisture, part-skim" artificial mozzarella states that it has an "excellent cheeselike taste" and contains water, calcium caseinate, partially saturated soybean oil, salt, sodium aluminum phosphate, tricalcium phosphate, artificial flavors, adipic acid, sorbic acid as a preservative, magnesium oxide, dicalcium phosphate, zinc oxide, Vitamin A palmitate, artificial color, riboflavin, pyridoxine HCI, niacinamide, thiamine mononitrate, and cyanocobalamin (B-12).

Th-th-th-th-that's all, folks!

XLVII.
WAY TO GO!

Death is God's way of saying, "Enough is enough." It comes as it must to all of us, and its euphemisms are many: left us, departed this vale of tears, shuffled off this mortal coil, gone home, gone home (in case of any doubts) to God, called home to God, gathered to his fathers, and many more that make death seem rather a good thing, almost to be sought and certainly not to be avoided.

In any case, there's no choice in the matter, though there is some opportunity to affect the manner of death. Who would wish to linger on ludicrously like the late dictator of Spain, from whom the verb "to Franco" was coined in commemoration of a dying so dragged out that it became a joke? At one point doctors argued over whether to amputate a leg to keep "alive" a little longer a body that exhibited almost no vital signs.

Still other deaths have been surrounded in their own web of surreality.

Poles Apart

It was a shattering moment for the Warsaw housewife: Her husband had just come home from work, and soon after entering their apartment, he delivered shocking news. It was all over between them, he said; their marriage was ended; he loved someone else; he was leaving his wife immediately to join his new love. Then he turned on his heel and walked out the door, leaving her standing there.

In despair, the betrayed wife decided to end it all and threw herself from the balcony of their tenth-floor flat. Amazingly, she was not killed. Her husband, who had just left the building, and on whom she landed, was.

Sunday in the Park With Dad

Bowing to the conventional wisdom that a man should be a pal to his son, a Queens, New York, man took his boy to Flushing Meadow Park to spend an afternoon flying a model airplane. The outing ended abruptly when the plane looped back in mid-flight and struck the man in the head, killing him.

Man vs. Machine

The bout was in the rec room of a Safety Harbor, Florida, apartment complex. Daniel Erickson, 5' 10", 190 pounds, having been cheated of his money when he tried to buy a soft drink earlier in the day, decided to go one-on-one with a soft-drink machine, 7', 1000 pounds, when the machine cheated him a second time.

He pounded on it and shook it violently, but lost when the huge machine toppled over and fell on top of him. Erickson was discovered under the machine some time later, his body outlined in the machine's broken plastic front.

Dig He Must

Walter Murphy, 27, of Los Angeles, was under the influence of a hallucinogenic drug when he died in a burrow he was digging under a concrete slab, in the apparent belief that he was a gopher.

Murphy's mother said he had started digging burrows several months previously, sometimes staying underground for up to two weeks at a time. "Last July," she said, "they dug him out of the same hole. I know he was depressed. He couldn't get a job."

Target of Opportunity

Eighty-year-old Frances Farthing was killed while sitting on a bench at a bus stop in Poulton-Le-Flyde, England. A stuck car was being hauled past her by a tow truck when a wheel came loose and clobbered her.

Nothing for Him, Thanks

Two men in Illinois were trying to tow a stuck tractor-trailer with their pickup truck when they accidentally ran over and killed their buddy.

The two men had had a few beers at the time of the accident, and, rather at a loss for what to do next, put the dead man on the seat between them and drove off.

They headed for a nearby restaurant, leaving the body in the truck while they had burgers and coffee. Lunch done with, they drove to a hospital, where their friend was pronounced dead on arrival.

Big Sleep

A Pennsylvania man liked his outdoor naps, preferably in a hammock. His last nap ended when one of the trees the hammock was fastened to toppled over and flattened him.

Clean Right Down to the Shine

Carolyn Matsumoto, 25, of Berkeley, California, locked herself in her home and then committed suicide by climbing into her dishwasher and washing herself to death.

Police spokesman Michael Holland said the dishwasher's internal racks were found neatly stacked, along with some personal effects, alongside the machine, which started automatically when the lid was closed.

Nostalgia Isn't What It Used to Be

On Long Island, 70-year-old former actress Eleanor Barry died of her own passion for memorabilia. Police in Huntington Station pulled her out from under an enormous collection of scrapbooks, newspapers and press clippings, that had toppled over and buried her.

Going Up, Please!

An elevator mechanic killed himself in a New York hotel by entering an elevator shaft and tying one end of a rope around his neck, the other to the bottom of an elevator car, and then waiting patiently until someone decided to go upstairs.

When the elevator started, it jerked the man upward. As it happened, the rope broke, and the man fell into the bottom of the shaft. Police said an autopsy would be necessary to determine whether he was killed by the noose or the fall.

Play It Again, Sam

The hydraulically raised elevator piano at the Condor nightclub in San Francisco became famous in the sixties and seventies as the stage for the gyrations of one queen of silicone-expanded mammaries in the heyday of topless dancing.

More recently it caused the death of the club's assistant manager, James Ferrozzo. Ferrozzo was making love to his girlfriend on top of the piano after hours; when the piano's elevator mechanism was accidentally activated, the lovers were too distracted to notice.

The coroner's office concluded that Ferrozzo was asphyxiated when he was trapped between his girlfriend and the ceiling. Ferrozzo and his girlfriend—she suffered only bruises—were discovered fifteen feet off the floor by the janitor the next morning. The fire department's rescue team took nearly three hours to pry her loose. She told police she had been drinking heavily and could not remember anything that had happened.

Variety, the bible of show business, ran its report under the headline EXEC OF TOPLESS CLUB DIES IN FREAK MISHAP WITH PIANO, WOMAN; the story was continued on page 99 under the jump head, HE DIED HAPPY.

THE ONLY GUIDE OF ITS KIND!

Students who have been there and are now undergraduates at Harvard give the lowdown on 200 prep schools and selective-admission public high schools.

THE HARVARD INDEPENDENT INSIDER'S GUIDE TO PREP SCHOOLS

Edited by Christopher J. Georges and James A. Messina
with members of the staff of the
Harvard Independent

This unique, indispensable reference goes beyond the academic to bring students and their parents the whole up-to-date picture for each of 200 prep schools and selective-admission public high schools across the nation. Packed with "insider" anecdotes, quotes, things to anticipate, and things to beware, it gives the inside scoop on:

**Academic courses • Extracurricular activities • Social life
• Athletics • Dorm life • College-related data
• Size and enrollment • Admissions requirements
• Tuition and financial aid • The environment • The layout
• The kids • The food • And everything else that really counts!**

---

27 million Americans can't read a bedtime story to a child.

It's because 27 million adults in this country simply can't read.

Functional illiteracy has reached one out of five Americans. It robs them of even the simplest of human pleasures, like reading a fairy tale to a child.

You can change all this by joining the fight against illiteracy.

Call the Coalition for Literacy at toll-free **1-800-228-8813** and volunteer.

Volunteer Against Illiteracy. The only degree you need is a degree of caring.